Magical
Mischief

Anna Dale

BLOOMSBURY

LONDON BERLIN NEW YORK

To my niece, Lily,
with love

Bloomsbury Publishing, London, Berlin and New York

First published in Great Britain in June 2010 by Bloomsbury Publishing Plc
36 Soho Square, London, W1D 3QY

Text copyright © Anna Dale 2010
The moral right of the author has been asserted

A CIP catalogue record of this book is available from the British Library

ISBN 978 1 4088 0043 0

FSC
Mixed Sources
Product group from well-managed
forests and other controlled sources
Cert no. SGS - COC - 2061
www.fsc.org
© 1996 Forest Stewardship Council

Typeset by Dorchester Typesetting Group Ltd
Printed in Great Britain by Clays Ltd, St Ives plc, Bungay, Suffolk

1 3 5 7 9 10 8 6 4 2

www.bloomsbury.com/childrens

Chapter One

A Whiff of Magic

'My shop stinks!' said Mr Hardbattle.

He had first noticed The Smell a few months before, but had been too busy to do anything about it. Running a bookshop single-handedly meant that his time was at a premium. Finding the source of a strange new smell had been put on the bottom of his list of 'things to do' along with dusting and tidying up.

It would not have been a problem if The Smell had been a nice one. If it had smelt of candyfloss or eau de cologne it would have been delightful, but Mr Hardbattle's smell was of the noxious variety. The Smell had been mild to start off with, but over the months it had grown more powerful until Mr Hardbattle had felt compelled to express his disgust out loud.

To Mr Hardbattle's nose, The Smell resembled the stench of dung – the sort that you might find in a big heap in a farmyard – and it baffled him how such a smell could get inside his shop, which was miles from the country, in the middle of a town. Equally as puzzling was the fact that none of his customers seemed to be able to detect it. They could, however, smell other unpleasant odours of which he was unaware.

'Pooh! Hyacinths!' exclaimed one customer.

'It reeks of vinegar in 'ere,' said another. 'I'd lay odds that somebody 'ad fish and chips for their supper last night.'

'Might I suggest,' said a well-spoken lady, pink-cheeked with embarrassment, 'that you get someone in to look at your drains?'

Conscious of the need to please his customers, Mr Hardbattle tried to find the source of all the offensive smells. He looked in vain for horse manure; he poured a newly purchased bottle of vinegar down the sink; he examined all his pot plants, but failed to find a hyacinth; he even called out a plumber to inspect his drains, but none of these actions had any effect at all. Thinking that the smells must be seeping into his shop from outside, Mr Hardbattle closed all his windows.

Over the ensuing months, The Smell grew even stronger, forcing Mr Hardbattle to wear a clothes peg on his nose. Realising that bad smells were not good for business he introduced other odours into the shop to smother the nasty pongs. He bought a gallon of lavender water and sprayed it in every corner, and when it failed to make any difference he tried perfumed candles and potpourri. However, despite his best efforts, The Smell remained.

Customers wrinkled their noses and frowned the instant that they came through the front door and the stream of people, who had always frequented Mr Hardbattle's shop, dwindled to a rivulet.

After The Smell came the hallucinations. They started on a small scale and progressed to the spectacular.

At first, Mr Hardbattle thought he had had too much sherry when he saw one of the black cat bookends, which sat on a shelf above his desk, twitch its whiskers and yawn, and he rubbed his eyes in astonishment at the sight of a glass marble chasing a spider across *The Times* newspaper that he had left open on his desk. When his wastepaper basket uncoiled itself and went for a slither around the floor, Mr Hardbattle made an urgent appointment with an optometrist. The optometrist did lots of tests and shone a bright light into his eyes. She could not put her finger on the problem, but advised him that it might be worth replacing his old spectacles. Mr Hardbattle chose a new pair with horn rims and hoped that they would do the trick.

Then books began to rearrange themselves. One morning, he came downstairs at nine o'clock to open up and found all the books shelved upside down and, on another day, he discovered that the books with similar-coloured jackets had grouped themselves together. The rainbow effect of the blue books sitting next to the green books, the yellow books, the red books and so on might have appealed to Mr Hardbattle if the whole thing were not so deeply disconcerting. Thinking that he must have sleepwalked in the night and done the rearranging himself, Mr Hardbattle went to see a doctor. The doctor listened to Mr Hardbattle's troubles, nodded innumerable times and asked if he was suffering from stress. When Mr Hardbattle said that yes, he thought so, the doctor prescribed a hot, milky drink before bed.

'And a biscuit?' Mr Hardbattle asked.

'I don't see why not,' said the doctor. 'I'd recommend a fig roll or an Abbey Crunch.'

Despite enlisting the help of medical professionals, buying a new pair of spectacles and drinking a cup of cocoa every night before he turned in, strange things continued to happen.

It all got too much for Mr Hardbattle so he telephoned his Auntie Pearl. His aunt was a spirited lady who had made a lot of acquaintances in her ninety-seven years. Mr Hardbattle was surer than sure that if anyone knew the right person to ask what he should do about his predicament, it was his Auntie Pearl.

'Queer goings-on, you say? How immensely thrilling!' said the gung-ho, upper-class voice of Auntie Pearl all the way down the telephone line from her cottage in the Quantocks. 'If I were you, dear boy, I'd give Bertie Braithwaite a bell. Hold on a tick while I find his number . . .'

Bertie Braithwaite's field of interest was the supernatural, and when he heard Mr Hardbattle's accounts of marbles with minds of their own, restless wastepaper baskets and yawning bookends, he was able to assure him that his bookshop was not haunted. Anxious to be of help, Bertie put Mr Hardbattle on to a market stallholder in Crewe who advised him to try a retired brigadier in Nempnett Thrubwell who suggested that he should pay a call on Mrs Elizabeth Trinket of Two, Bolton Gardens, Brightlingsea.

Mrs Trinket was not on the telephone, and the strange goings-on in the bookshop seemed too fantastic to put in a letter so, the following day, Mr Hardbattle picked out his smartest bow tie, closed his shop and started up the van, which he used for his deliveries. The van was bottle green and, on both sides and the rear doors, the name of his bookshop, Hardbattle Books, had been painted slantwise in cream. Mr Hardbattle took with him a map, a beef and horseradish sandwich and coffee in a Thermos flask, and drove his van the hundred-and-twenty-one miles to Brightlingsea. He knocked on the door of Two, Bolton Gardens. Fortunately, Mrs Trinket was in.

'Magic. That's what's behind it,' Mrs Trinket said, waiting until her guest had lowered himself into one of her armchairs. She had learned from experience that momentous news was best delivered after its recipient had sat down. 'It's a classic case,' she continued, setting down a tray and pouring out two cups of tea. 'You've been in the same premises for years, you said. I'll bet it's dark and dingy and has never seen a duster.'

Amazed by her powers of deduction, Mr Hardbattle nodded.

Mrs Trinket slid a teaspoon into the sugar bowl. 'They're just the sorts of conditions that magic would thrive in . . .'

'Magic? Fairies and so on? Loose in my shop?' blurted out Mr Hardbattle, gripping the cushiony arms of the chair. 'It's incredible! Why, I had no inkling that magic even existed. Good heavens, madam. You've taken my breath away.'

Stunned and bewildered, Mr Hardbattle took the cup and saucer that were offered to him. His first sip of tea made him splutter. It was as if he had just dipped his tongue in seawater.

'*How* many sugars are in here, dear lady?'

'Six,' answered Mrs Trinket, stirring her own cup of

tea and smiling at him in a motherly way. 'Sweet tea is good for shock. Most folk find it hard to swallow.'

Mr Hardbattle murmured, 'I'm not surprised', and placed his cup back on the tray.

'Closed minds, that's what most people have,' observed Mrs Trinket, gesturing to her guest that he should try one of her coconut buns. 'Can't entertain the thought that magic might be real and not something that you just find in storybooks.'

'Could you tell me some more about magic?' Mr Hardbattle asked. He was a well-read, intelligent fellow and a few months ago before the arrival of The Smell, he might have regarded talk of magic as whimsical tosh. However, Mrs Trinket's theory was the only one that he had been presented with and, besides, he did not want her to think that he had a closed mind. 'How did it come to be in my shop, do you suppose?' he asked. 'Could some prankster have put it there?'

Mrs Trinket set her cup of tea to one side and leaned forward in her chair, lacing her fingers together. 'Magic is its own master, Mr Hardbattle,' she explained. 'It chooses where it goes and it gets there by any one of a hundred different ways. It can ride on the wind or attach itself to the sole of a shoe. It's even been known to burrow through the earth . . .'

Mr Hardbattle's horn-rimmed spectacles slid down his nose as a sequence of images flashed through his mind. First, he pictured magic as a host of downy dandelion seeds; then as globs of chewing gum; and finally his mind conjured up a clump of glistening toadstools, gradually spreading and festering under the floorboards of his shop.

'Magic's very fussy about where it takes up residence,' Mrs Trinket carried on. 'Everything has to be just so. It arrives in dribs and drabs: a smidgen here, a trace there. But if enough magic turns up, it will form a cluster. You can't see these clusters and you can't feel them either, but the smell that they give off is unsavoury to say the least.'

'There's been an outbreak of awful smells in my shop!' Mr Hardbattle said, spitting out coconut cake crumbs in his excitement. 'My customers have inundated me with complaints, but, curiously, none of the odours they've smelt has been the same.'

'That'll be magic, right enough,' said Mrs Trinket. 'It doesn't like to be disturbed, you see, so it gives off a pong to keep people away, but humans are a contrary lot. A shockingly awful stink to one is a balmy bouquet to another. Magic gets round that by evoking the smell that each of us hates the most.'

'In my case that's horse manure,' Mr Hardbattle told her. Just the mention of it made his insides squirm.

'With me, it's cooked cabbage,' Mrs Trinket said. 'My grandmother couldn't abide fresh fish. In her day, of course, the smells weren't so ripe. Magic was found all over, and the more thinly it's spread, the fainter the aroma. Everybody's attic had a sprinkle, but mostly it liked out-of-the-way places: barns, old churches, rambling farmhouses, water towers and poky museums. Places like that are rare these days. They've either been knocked down or done up. Half of them have been made into homes for the ridiculously rich. Dark, dry, secluded places are hard to come by in this day and age. Your bookshop's like a raft in a time of flood. No wonder magic's taken such a shine to it.'

'I should feel privileged, I know,' said Mr Hardbattle worriedly, 'but the truth is it's quite inconvenient.' He explained about his recent loss of customers and consequent plummet in sales.

'You could buy a vacuum cleaner. That would do the job. Magic's worst enemy, they are.' Mrs Trinket shot him a piercing look, challenging Mr Hardbattle to take her advice if he dared.

'Er . . . well, hmm . . .' he said, unable to look her in the eye. 'It seems a little *insensitive*.'

Mrs Trinket relaxed her stare and took a slurp of tea.

'Perhaps I should parcel it up and send it abroad. It would be sensible to relocate my magic somewhere wild and unfrequented . . . like Borneo . . . or Antarctica.' Mr Hardbattle beamed, mildly amazed by his own resourcefulness.

'Lord, no, that would never do!' said Mrs Trinket, so

appalled that she spilled spots of tea down the front of her blouse. 'You can't go mixing up magic! There are different strains and they've all got requirements. English magic is like a house spider. Remember I told you it hankers to hide in old buildings that are dimly lit? Well, in Holland, magic likes to be on the move. It clings to the roofs of trains and sneaks inside the saddle-bags of bicycles; and Scottish magic's only content when it's somewhere dank and marshy. There's an old Scottish saying: "Where'er there are midges, there's magic." Surely, Mr Hardbattle, you've heard of it?'

'No, I can't say that I have,' he replied before heaving a weighty sigh. 'What do you suggest that I do, Mrs Trinket? Put up with the smell? Try to ignore the peculiar happenings?'

'If you really want rid of it, flick a duster around . . . redecorate,' said Mrs Trinket, her tone a trifle crisp. 'It will move on if you goad it enough, but *where*? That's the question.'

'It seems to me,' Mr Hardbattle said after a few minutes' thought, 'that magic has had a raw deal. It can't be nice for it, pushed from pillar to post . . . its old stamping ground taken over . . . people like me viewing it as a nuisance.' He shook his balding head despairingly. 'I'm at a loss to know what to do for the best.'

'Poor dear,' said Mrs Trinket tenderly. 'Have another bun.'

Chapter Two

Birthday Surprises

Tea at Mrs Trinket's had proved to be most illuminating. When Mr Hardbattle returned to the town of Plumford that same evening, he was clued up on every aspect of magic and was only slightly unnerved to find his metre rule and poker engaged in swordplay on the hearth.

'Careful you fellows don't hurt yourselves' was all that he said.

Mrs Trinket's assertion that magic had recently had a tough time of it had won Mr Hardbattle round. He began to see himself as the protector of a hard-done-by species (a smelly, invisible, odd one, though it was), and he vowed to let the magic settle wherever it pleased and not to interfere with it or threaten it with dust-removing apparatus. This meant that he was unable to do any housework, which secretly he was pleased about.

Living alongside magic was, at first, a pleasurable thing. Mr Hardbattle would come down in the morning, armed with a can of air freshener, to find staples playing a skipping game with a piece of string or books reading themselves or ducks, escaped from a painting of Lake Tahoe, flying round the room. Sometimes the magic would leave him a gift, which it had fashioned itself. On more than one occasion, he discovered an item of head-gear made from cobwebs hanging on the hatstand (the ten-gallon hat was his favourite); in his briefcase he chanced upon a rubber band band, pinging *The Blue Danube* by Strauss and underneath his desk, in a corral of coloured pencils, he came across a flock of bleating, origami sheep.

Naturally, his takings took a nosedive. The rivulet of customers drained to a drip. Of the small number of people who dared to brave The Smell, most left soon after they had entered the bookshop, spooked by some-thing strange that they had seen or heard. The only customers with any staying power were the loners who liked to stop by for a chat or the devoted bibliophiles who were so absorbed by the books in the shop that they failed to notice anything odd.

Mr Hardbattle helped to make ends meet by concen-trating on the delivery side of his business. He could often be seen behind the wheel of his bottle green van or humping boxes in and out of its rear doors. With his modest profits, he treated himself to a moleskin waist-coat (a crimson one) and a spotty mongrel dog with black frilly ears and a plume-like tail, whom he chose to call Scallywag. He also acquired an elephant, but unlike the waistcoat and the dog it arrived quite by accident. It was left behind by a small girl, who carried it into the shop in a pink beaded bag, read it a story and departed without it. The elephant was a He, and Mr Hardbattle named him Trunk. Trunk was soft, grey and made in China, and every time the bell over the door jingle-jangled, he got to his bean-filled feet and looked to see if the person who had come into the shop was his little owner who had, at last, remembered him.

As more and more magic descended on the tall Victorian building which housed Hardbattle Books, the situation inside became hard to bear. In the ten years since Mr Hardbattle's visit to Mrs Trinket's, the magic had evolved from manageable clusters into wayward, roguish clumps. It had wriggled into every crack and crevice and The Smell had grown so powerful that fainting fits were commonplace among the bookshop's customers.

Far worse than The Smell, in Mr Hardbattle's opinion, was the magic's erratic behaviour, which could vary from mischievous to uncontrollable. Most of the time, the magic was content to play with the curtains, switch things on and off and bring inanimate objects to life, but every so often it went berserk and the mess that it made on these occasions took hours and sometimes days to clear up. These instances of unruliness were happening more and more frequently, and Mr Hardbattle soon learned to watch out for the warning signs, which signalled that a chaotic episode was about to begin. If the potted palm on the landing began to shake its leaves or the second to last stair turned to custard, Mr Hardbattle whistled to Scallywag, snatched up a copy of *The Times* and took himself off to his tool shed where he stayed until all of the magical hoo-ha had died down.

On the morning of his seventieth birthday, Mr Hardbattle woke to find that he had spent the entire night in his shed. He had slept in a deckchair with a picnic rug tucked round him and was dressed in his shirt, trousers and waistcoat from the day before, all of which were now as creased and crumpled as a tramp's. 'Fine place to wake up on your birthday!' he grumbled, and felt inclined to go back to sleep again. However, when he remembered why he had taken refuge in his shed, he sat bolt upright and threw off the rug.

'Stir your stumps, Scallywag!' Mr Hardbattle shouted, making a determined effort to get out of the low-slung chair. 'If we're to open by nine o'clock, we'll have to work like Trojans!'

Scallywag had made a cosy nest for herself in a pile of wood shavings. She pricked her ears, but did not budge.

'There's bacon and eggs for breakfast,' Mr Hardbattle said. 'Do you want me to give your share to the cat next door?'

His lively tone and the word 'cat' had the desired effect. Scallywag sprang out of her bed, scattering wood shavings everywhere, and sat by her master's ankles while he fumbled with the latch. Once outside, Scallywag made sure that the backyard was cat-free before rejoining her master at the back door of the shop.

Mr Hardbattle drew the key from his waistcoat pocket and inserted it in the lock.

'Brace yourself, Scally!' Mr Hardbattle warned, pausing on the doorstep before he opened the door. 'Remember the terrible muddle the last time the magic went wild? I nearly wore out the bristles on my broom sweeping up the mess!'

Steeling himself to expect the worst, Mr Hardbattle turned the door handle and went in. The sight that met his eyes made his jaw drop.

'Well, I'm blowed!' he declared.

The shop was festooned with decorations. Strung from each corner of the ceiling and from bookshelf to bookshelf all around the shop were long, quivering paper chains. As Mr Hardbattle walked past each bookshelf, dozens of streamers uncoiled themselves and threw out their ribbons of paper so that his shoulders were covered in a cloak of multicolour. When the final streamer had unravelled itself, a team of spiders wriggled into action and lowered a crown made from cobwebs on to Mr Hardbattle's head.

'What's this?' he asked, patting the fragile crown with his fingertips. 'My, how kingly!' he said.

The magic had gone to extraordinary lengths to mark Mr Hardbattle's birthday. Most impressive of all was the banner that the magic had suspended from the ceiling. It was made from the pages of the largest world atlas in the shop and a greeting had been cut into it, which read: *MANY HAPPY RETURNS*.

His uncomfortable night in the tool shed forgotten, Mr Hardbattle tried to express how grateful he was to the magic for all the trouble it had taken, but he was hampered in his efforts by a sudden attack of awkwardness and a sizeable lump in his throat, which made his speech shorter and less fluent than he would have wished. '*Never* expected . . . I'm a lucky chap . . . can't thank you enough . . . very touched,' murmured Mr Hardbattle, dabbing both eyes with his handkerchief.

Scallywag had been unfazed by the dangling paper chains and the drifting ribbons of paper. She was used to the magic's theatrical ways, having lived in the shop for most of her life. Trotting over the streamer-strewn floor to the doormat, she gathered the morning's post in her mouth and delivered it into her master's hands. Of the four envelopes, three contained birthday cards, which Mr Hardbattle stood on the mantelpiece. The fourth envelope had a letter inside. The letter had been typed, and began: *Dear tenant* . . .

Mr Hardbattle's face clouded over immediately. He stopped reading the letter and removed his birthday crown. It was not the sort of letter that he felt should be read whilst wearing frivolous attire. Crownless and solemn-faced, Mr Hardbattle sank into a chair by the fireplace. Sensing that her master needed comforting, Scallywag sat down beside him and rested her chin on his knee. For the next few minutes, all was quiet in the bookshop apart from the loud, insistent ticking of the mantel clock.

When he had finished reading the letter, Mr Hardbattle sat stock-still and stared ahead with unseeing eyes. It took a nudge from Scallywag's nose to bring the old man to his senses.

'Woeful news, Scallywag!' he said to her gloomily. 'Our dear landlord, Henry Honeycomb, has died! You remember him, don't you, girl? He was the kind old gentleman who visited from time to time and always made a fuss of you. I've paid rent to Henry Honeycomb for thirty years!'

Feeling choked, Mr Hardbattle slipped his handkerchief from his sleeve and blew his nose ferociously before carrying on. 'This letter is from his son, Piers. It's Piers who owns the property now – and he's *not* a chip off the old block, it pains me to learn. Piers is putting up the rent by five hundred pounds each month! He says that I've been paying a pittance and that his father was a mug.' Mr Hardbattle sighed and clasped his forehead. 'I can't see how we're going to manage. We're living like paupers as it is!'

The arrival of magic in the bookshop had wrecked Mr Hardbattle's chances of running a highly profitable business. It had become a struggle to find the money to pay the rent each month and a hike in the payment was nothing short of disastrous. Mr Hardbattle sat in his chair for several minutes longer, trying to think of a way in which he could raise the extra funds. When he realised that it would soon be time to open the shop, Mr Hardbattle put Piers Honeycomb's letter in his desk drawer and went upstairs to prepare his birthday breakfast.

By the time that he had eaten his fill of bacon and eggs, changed his clothes and opened his shop, it had started to rain. It carried on raining all morning and Mr Hardbattle's waning celebratory mood was further eroded. (There is nothing more depressing than rain on your birthday.) Detecting his glum demeanour, the magic attempted to cheer Mr Hardbattle up. The black cat bookends jumped down from their shelf and wound themselves around his legs and some leather bookmarks ran about on their fringed ends doing somersaults, but their efforts only succeeded in bringing a tired smile to his face, which faded almost as soon as it had appeared.

It turned cold. Mr Hardbattle put some logs in the

grate and lit a fire. Magic turned the flames green, then purple, then green again.

Outside in the street, umbrellas vied for space and puddles were stepped over by grown-ups and sploshed through by children too young to be at school. Damp pigeons huddled in the eaves of buildings. The sky was dark and overcast.

In the morning the bookshop had no customers and Mr Hardbattle's frame of mind grew more and more despairing. Then, in the afternoon, the bell jingle-jangled. Trunk got up to see who it was and sat down again, disappointed. The customer was a thin student with spectacles and a beaky nose who bought a collection of Edward Thomas's poetry and left.

Then, at a quarter to four, when Mr Hardbattle's thoughts had once again turned to his financial problems, something of interest happened in the street.

The collision occurred on the stretch of pavement right outside the shop. It was a drama worthy of an audience. Magic breathed on the window of the bookshop so that Mr Hardbattle could see out. Putting her paws on the window sill, Scallywag joined her master, and the rumpus proved enough of a lure for Trunk to shuffle along his shelf and peer out too.

A boy wearing a cagoule, his hood tied tightly around his face, and a woman with an umbrella, were sprawled on the ground. The spokes of the woman's umbrella were protruding at strange angles and her white, woollen cap had slipped off her head. In a matter of seconds, passers-by had rushed to her aid and pulled the woman to her feet, but the boy jumped up by himself, preferring not to be helped.

On the ground, close by, were two bags in a puddle. The largest of these, a shopping bag, had spilled its contents over the pavement and, one by one, oranges were rolling into the gutter. Next to this bag was a school bag with a broken strap, which had leaked some books, a lunch box and a pencil case. Before the boy and the woman could make a move to recover their gear, the passers-by had collected the pair's scattered goods like chickens pecking up grain. Once the Good Samaritans had dispersed, the boy stooped to rescue the last of the oranges from the gutter while the woman tried in vain to close her mangled umbrella. She gave up and looked across at the bookshop, and it was then that Mr Hardbattle realised who she was.

Her name was Beatrice Quint. She was a spinster, in her forties, and had once occupied the bookshop's comfiest wing chair by the fire for a whole afternoon, during which time she had drunk three cups of tea and told Mr Hardbattle her life story. So intent had she been on talking that Miss Quint had not noticed any magical shenanigans. Before she left she had bought a paperback romance for ninety-five pence.

'I do believe they're coming in,' said Mr Hardbattle, perking up when he saw Miss Quint and the boy approaching his shop doorway. 'Three customers in the same afternoon!' he said brightly to Scallywag. 'How about that, eh? Things are looking up!'

Chapter Three

flaming Peculiar

The cagoule-wearing boy was called Arthur. His full name was Arthur William Goodenough, but his siblings – of which he had five – called him Artie; his friends shortened this to Art; and his form teacher chose to refer to him simply as Goodenough or more usually *Not* Goodenough, accompanied by a smirk.

On the rainy Wednesday in April which was Mr Hardbattle's birthday, Arthur had been in a hurry to get to the library.

Plumford Library was where he did his homework every day between the end of school and teatime. With five brothers and sisters at home, a father and mother, two guinea pigs, an axolotl and a cockatiel, it was almost always noisy and crowded and an impossible environment in which to get to grips with schoolwork. Arthur found studying hard, and without plenty of peace and quiet he could not manage to concentrate. His older brother was brainy and his older sister was too and Arthur did not like being described as 'an average student' and he absolutely detested being called Not Goodenough by Mr Beaglehole, his bully of a form teacher. Doing well was important to Arthur and that was why he always tried to do his best, even if it meant forsaking games of football with his mates and hanging out in the library instead of the amusement arcade.

On Wednesdays, the library closed early at five so Arthur tended to make an effort to hurry on this day of the week. On this particular Wednesday, with the rain pelting down, Arthur had hurried all the more. He had lowered his head against the driving rain, droplets running off his hood into his eyes. Miss Quint's approach had not registered with him until it was too late.

Neither had blamed the other for the collision. Both had been swift to admit that they had not been looking where they were going. When Miss Quint had mentioned that she knew of a place close by where they could dry off and enjoy a hot drink, Arthur had been only too willing to go with her.

The bell above the door jingle-jangled as the two dishevelled, dripping wet people lugged their sodden bags into Mr Hardbattle's shop. Trunk glanced at them with his black felt eyes.

'Good afternoon,' said Miss Quint shakily. Her eye make-up was blotched, her tights laddered, and there were streaks of dirt on her mackintosh. 'Do you mind if we sit by your fire for a moment? We've taken a tumble and as you can see, we're soaked from head to toe. I expect you saw the whole thing. It was my fault as much as this boy's. His name's Arthur.'

At which point she turned to Arthur and whispered, 'Say "Hello", dear.'

'Er . . . hi,' said Arthur bashfully, pulling down his hood to reveal a thatch of wavy brown hair which grew almost to his shoulders. His ears poked out either side like mushrooms pushing through undergrowth.

Miss Quint ventured further into the shop, leaving a trail of dark spots on a Turkish rug. 'I thought I'd have a chance of catching the ten to four bus if I put on a spurt,' she explained to Mr Hardbattle, 'but the oranges weighed me down.' Frowning disappointedly, she poked around in her shopping bag. 'All split or bruised,' she declared. 'I shan't be making prize-winning marmalade with these!'

'You make marmalade,' said Arthur, astonished, 'that wins *prizes*?'

'If everything goes to plan, I do,' Miss Quint told him with a wink. 'I'm a member of the Women's Institute. They're holding a cookery contest on Friday. There are prizes for marmalade, jam, fruit pies, cakes . . . all sorts of things.'

'Couldn't you cut out the damaged bits?' Arthur asked

Miss Quint, taking an orange out of her bag and trying to squeeze it into shape. It seemed very wasteful to write off all the oranges, especially as he and the people in the street had gone to the effort of gathering them up.

'I'll never win a red rosette with substandard oranges,' Miss Quint told him with a shake of her head. '*I* know what I'll do. I'll make a batch of scones instead. Scones don't have the prestige of marmalade, of course, but such is life. It can't be helped. Scones are quick to make, which is just as well. Mirabel gets moody if I hog the kitchen for too long and I can see her point, as it is *her* kitchen after all.'

Arthur opened his mouth to ask who Mirabel was, but Miss Quint was too fast for him.

'I'm living with a friend just at the moment,' she said. 'I did have my own flat, but there was this explosion. All my belongings were blown sky-high. A faulty gas pipe, they said it was. Luckily, nobody was in that night. Mr and Mrs Jones, below, had gone on holiday to Spain, and Mr Clark, above, had popped out for a take-away. It took three fire crews to get the flames under control!'

Arthur gaped at Miss Quint with a mixture of horror and awe. He thought of his own house and his axolotl and cockatiel and everything in his bedroom, which he would be broken-hearted to lose. The only comforting thought was that if *his* house exploded, his guinea pigs would be all right because their hutch was at the bottom of the garden.

Arthur thought that Miss Quint was extremely brave to talk about the destruction of her home so matter-of-factly. It appeared that Mr Hardbattle had formed the same opinion because he moved closer to where Miss Quint was standing and held out his hand.

'You told me of your unfortunate mishap the last time you were here,' he said, seizing her cold hand in his warm, dry grip. 'In January, I think it was. It's Miss Quint, isn't it?'

'That's right!' said Miss Quint, delighted to be remembered. She beamed at Mr Hardbattle and began to unbutton her mackintosh.

'Yes, do get out of those wet things!' Mr Hardbattle urged, relieving them of their coats, Arthur's school scarf and Miss Quint's woollen cap. He hung them on coat hooks by the door. 'Why don't you make yourselves comfortable while I put the kettle on?' he said.

'May I use your bathroom first, if you don't object?' asked Miss Quint, patting her hair, which was collar-length, auburn and not looking its best. She plonked her shopping bag in the middle of the floor and, clutching her handbag, disappeared upstairs. Miss Quint had been to the toilet on her previous visit and knew where it was to be found. (You cannot drink three cups of tea and not need to use your host's facilities.)

Arthur dragged his school bag over to a wing chair. Rather than being concerned with warming himself up, he unzipped his bag and began to line up his books on the hearth, resting them on their spines and opening each one.

The young boy's regard for his books gladdened Mr Hardbattle's heart. The magic, too, was impressed. It stoked the fire and made the flames leap higher. Arthur had his head bowed and did not see the poker lurch sideways and plunge its tip three or four times into the heap of ash and blackened logs. The tapering flames burned indigo blue.

'It's Arthur, isn't it?' Mr Hardbattle said, stooping to look at the boy's collection of literature. 'You're keen on reading, I can see that. Well, you've come to the right place.'

'I'm not hooked on books, exactly,' said Arthur. He glanced up at the old man before delving into his bag once more. The book that he lifted out was a small dictionary. With the utmost care he separated its soggy pages. 'These are for homework. I've got a test tomorrow and an essay to finish as well. I was hoping to get some work done in the library. That's why I was rushing and didn't see the lady till she nearly knocked me out with her umbrella.'

'Nasty things, brollies,' Mr Hardbattle said. He pushed his horn-rimmed glasses up his nose and knitted his greying brows together. 'So, Arthur, what's your essay about? My bookshop isn't as well stocked as a library, but I dare say I can find a book or two on your chosen topic, which might help.'

'Thanks,' said Arthur. He sat back on his heels and looked around him. 'I've never been in here before. Mum always takes us to that bookshop in the centre of town: the big one with a coffee shop. She likes their comfy sofas and their offers. Mum won't buy a book unless it's got money off.' Arthur bit his lip, aware that what he had said might have sounded rude.

'Shops like that are two-a-penny,' Mr Hardbattle said, smiling at the boy's stricken expression. 'There are hundreds of bookshops like that the length and breadth of England – whereas *my* little shop is one of a kind. It's got something that no other bookshop has.'

'What's that?' said Arthur, casting about him. 'Paper chains? Huge great cobwebs? I know . . . a dog!'

Mr Hardbattle shook his head at Arthur and grinned. 'Let's have a look at that essay first, young man. Then I'll make us a pot of tea and *then*, if you haven't worked it out for yourself, I'll tell you.'

Miss Quint had spent an inordinately long time in the toilet. When she emerged from the stairwell, she had neatened her appearance, her face was powdered and she was wearing a pair of unscathed tights.

'There's a cup of tea for you on the mantelpiece,' Mr

Hardbattle said to her, peering out from behind a sheaf of papers. He was busy reading through Arthur's essay, the conclusion of which had been a joint effort. 'This is good stuff, Arthur,' he murmured, 'though I think your spelling is . . . how shall I put it? *Unconventional.*'

Arthur grunted in response. He was sitting on the rug in front of the fire with Scallywag's head in his lap. The heat from the flames, the dog's steady breathing and a stomach full of hot tea were sending him to sleep. The only thing that spoilt the ambience was the aroma of nit shampoo. 'So, are you going to tell me what's special about your bookshop now?' asked Arthur, his eyelids beginning to droop.

'It's a magic bookshop,' Mr Hardbattle said in an off-hand way.

'Magic?' said Arthur drowsily. 'What d'you mean by that?'

'How pretty!' said Miss Quint, taking her cup of tea from the mantelpiece. 'The flames keep changing colour! An up-to-the-minute, hi-tech gas fire, I suppose. Was it very expensive? I wonder if I could manage to talk my friend Mirabel into buying one. A fire like that would look breathtaking in her front room.'

Miss Quint lifted her cup off its saucer, but did not lower her chin to drink. The desire to continue talking was too great.

'I must say, Mr Hardbattle,' she chattered, 'I wouldn't

have thought you'd be the type to embrace new technology. Upstairs, Arthur, there's a mirror that writes messages. It tells you if your parting is crooked or if you've got lipstick on your teeth. That fire takes the biscuit, though. The logs seem almost real, don't they? It's really clever the way the flames switch colour like that.'

Arthur's eyes, which had been closed, suddenly opened wide. 'Gosh, they're pink and now they've gone back to orange!' he exclaimed. 'But it doesn't look modern to me. It's a real fire, I'm sure.' He breathed in through his nose. 'I can smell the woodsmoke!'

'Well, I can't,' said Miss Quint, sniffing the air and recoiling. 'The only thing that I can smell is curdled milk.'

Mr Hardbattle crouched down stiffly by the fireplace. He lifted the lid off the log basket and dropped another log in the grate. Turquoise sparks shot up the chimney, making Arthur gasp.

'It's a log fire all right,' Mr Hardbattle said, 'but every so often the flames act unusually. It's the magic that's behind it. It likes to interfere.' Mr Hardbattle gave Arthur's elbow a nudge. 'I told you that my bookshop was magic, didn't I, Arthur?'

Tearing his eyes away from the flames, which had turned a dark resplendent red, Arthur stared at Mr Hardbattle, overwhelmed and respectful. 'Are you some kind of wizard, sir?' he asked with a gulp.

'Good heavens, no!' Mr Hardbattle chuckled. 'I'm just an old man who created the perfect place for magic to thrive, quite by accident.'

Miss Quint tittered to herself. 'That's codswallop, of course. Don't believe a word he says, Arthur!' she warned. 'He's teasing you.' She sat down in a chair and heaved her shopping bag on to her knee, but not before she had glared at Mr Hardbattle reproachfully.

'It's the honest truth!' insisted Mr Hardbattle, making a sweeping gesture with his arm. 'There's magic in every corner of my shop, Miss Quint. All you need to do is take a good look!'

Holding up her hands in mock surrender, Miss Quint gave a weary sigh. 'It's up to you if you want to indulge in a little make-believe,' she said, 'but please don't involve me. I shan't be joining in.' Having said her piece, Miss Quint ferreted in her bag. She pulled out a women's magazine, which had orange pips stuck to its cover, and started to leaf through its pages.

While Miss Quint was occupied with reading about women's matters, Mr Hardbattle treated Arthur to a tour of his shop. They walked in and out of every alcove, with Arthur admiring the books and the quantity of dust. When they had finished surveying the bookshelves, Mr Hardbattle told Arthur all about The Smell and introduced him to Trunk the elephant, the black cat bookends and the flock of origami sheep. Raindrops continued to slip down the windowpane as Arthur and Mr Hardbattle talked and talked.

'So this Mrs Trinket knew all about magic, did she?' asked Arthur.

'Oh, yes,' Mr Hardbattle said. 'She's an authority on it. I was advised to let the magic be, and over the years more and more kept arriving. I dare say there's more magic here in my shop than in every county south of the Thames!'

'Cool!' breathed Arthur.

'It is rather marvellous, yes,' Mr Hardbattle agreed. He was thrilled to have found a customer, after so many years, who shared his opinion that the magic was top-hole.

'This is the best shop I've ever been in!' blurted out Arthur excitedly. 'I'll come in here every day after school. Could I do that, Mr Hardbattle? Would you mind?'

Mr Hardbattle paled. He produced a smile although he felt like groaning. The conversation with Arthur had been so pleasurable that Mr Hardbattle had not wanted to spoil things by admitting that the magic was a curse as well as a blessing; and that in the next few weeks, without the advent of a miracle, he would have to turf the magic out or become homeless himself.

Mr Hardbattle took off his horn-rimmed glasses and

wiped them carefully on a clean corner of handkerchief. When he replaced his glasses, his eyes met Arthur's eager gaze.

'I haven't been totally honest with you, Arthur,' he said humbly. 'There's something I need to explain . . .'

Chapter four

The Search Begins

Miss Quint heard whispering. She closed her magazine. In her experience, people tended to whisper when they wanted to pass on a secret or a tasty morsel of gossip, and Miss Quint was partial to both these things. Without wasting another second, she got up from her chair and followed the irresistible sound of hushed voices. Emerging from in between two rows of bookshelves, she glimpsed Mr Hardbattle and Arthur standing close together by the cash register, talking nineteen to the dozen.

As she approached them, Miss Quint managed to hear a snatch of their conversation.

'Problem? What problem?' she asked, forging her way into their midst.

Arthur and Mr Hardbattle stopped talking and stared at her. The interruption had caught them unawares. Neither of them knew how to answer Miss Quint's question. It would be difficult to explain about the new landlord's ultimatum without mentioning the magic in which Miss Quint did not believe.

'I'm pleased to see you've abandoned your game of Let's Pretend,' Miss Quint said, undaunted by their mute response. 'So, what were you discussing, hmm?'

Arthur opened his mouth and closed it again and Mr Hardbattle hooked his thumbs in the pockets of his waistcoat. He wetted his lips, but did not say anything.

Their silence only succeeded in making Miss Quint even more curious. She studied their troubled faces for a moment, then her sharp eyes slid downwards to a letter lying on the desk. 'What's this?' she asked and reached out her hand. Before she could pick up the letter, however, the magic intervened.

On the desk was a carton full of drawing pins and the moment that Miss Quint's fingers touched the letter, they leaped out of their carton, rose high into the air and drummed into the letter with bullet-like speed. Miss Quint barely managed to snatch her hand away in time. Once she had recovered from the shock of almost having had her hand impaled on the desk, she noticed that the drawing pins had landed in formation, spelling out a four-lettered word.

'MYOB?' Miss Quint said, puzzled. 'What's that supposed to mean? MYOB? That's not a word. That's a load of nonsense –'

'Actually, it's an abbreviation,' Arthur cut in helpfully.

'The letters M Y O B stand for Mind Your Own Business.'

Miss Quint was speechless for a moment, then she said, 'Of all the nerve!' and flushed with embarrassment. 'Mr Hardbattle, are you going to let those . . . those drawing pins speak to me like that?'

'I'm dreadfully sorry, Miss Quint,' Mr Hardbattle said. He leaned over the desk and reprimanded the drawing pins. 'Back to your box, you little scamps!' he said, shaking his finger sternly, which was as close to bawling them out as he was going to get. 'Miss Quint is a friend. She may read my letter if she wants.'

The drawing pins sprang out of the letter and regrouped in mid-air, then they rained into the carton, falling like pennies down a chute.

'I suppose you're going to tell me that those drawing pins got from here to there and back again . . . by magic,' said Miss Quint uneasily.

Mr Hardbattle nodded. 'That's the long and short of it.'

'I . . . I know I saw them with my own eyes,' Miss Quint said in a halting voice, 'but I can't bring myself to believe in magic. I can't! The idea's . . . well . . . *preposterous*.' Miss Quint was so involved in her thoughts that she did not cast more than a fleeting glance at the cat, which had jumped on to the desk and was strolling towards her along its length. Being fond of cats, Miss

Quint extended her hand to stroke it and got a horrible shock when she discovered that it was made of wood.

'Where's its fur?' she asked, knocking her knuckles against its coat.

Her disrespectful conduct failed to charm the book-end, which hissed at Miss Quint and returned to its shelf. She watched the black cat rise on to its hind legs and press its paws against a book, mirroring the stance of its pair.

Miss Quint turned to Mr Hardbattle. A tight smile flickered on to her face.

'First, magic drawing pins . . . and now, a magic book-end! All right, I believe you. It is magic, it must be. You were telling me the truth.'

For the briefest of moments, Miss Quint thought about leaving the shop right there and then. It was not that the magic unsettled her so much as the realisation that in scorning its existence she had made an idiot of herself. However, Miss Quint was not in the habit of running away from rum situations and, besides, her skirt was still damp and she wanted to know what the letter contained.

A gentleman to the core, Mr Hardbattle did not say, '*I told you so.*' He merely patted Miss Quint's arm and offered to make a fresh pot of tea. Remembering how Mrs Trinket had catered for his bewilderment when he had found out about magic, he resolved to put several teaspoons of sugar in Miss Quint's cup.

In the next quarter of an hour, in between gulps of tea, Arthur and Mr Hardbattle told Miss Quint everything. She was most upset to learn that Mr Hardbattle might have to close his shop.

'Money is the root of all evil,' she said, and winced as she sipped her over-sweet tea.

'I couldn't agree more. Money's a nuisance,' said Mr Hardbattle, 'but the cold, hard truth is that I need to make more of it!'

Arthur was in favour of encouraging customers into the shop by making a big to-do about the magic. 'It's sort of like the Ferris wheel at a fairground,' Arthur explained. 'Magic would be your big attraction. It would draw people in.'

'A crowd-puller? Ah, I see,' said Mr Hardbattle, nodding. 'I prefer the dodgems myself, but I see your point. You think that magic would invite more custom.'

'Yes, that's what I reckon,' said Arthur. He got up from his chair and began to pace the floor, enlivened by the idea that was taking shape in his mind. 'I bet if we told everyone that you had magic in your shop, they'd be fighting each other to get through the door. I could make posters to put in the window and Miss Quint could hand out leaflets. Loads of people would come and you'd be rich,' he finished confidently.

'Problem solved, eh?' said Mr Hardbattle.

'Yeah!' said Arthur, beaming.

Miss Quint glanced up at them both. 'It wouldn't work,' she said, 'if we're being realistic.'

'What do you mean? Why wouldn't it work?' Arthur was crestfallen. He looked to Mr Hardbattle for support and his stomach turned over when he saw the pained expression on the old man's face.

'It's an unfortunate fact,' said Mr Hardbattle tenderly, 'that most people aren't as open-minded as you are, Arthur. They're scared of things they don't understand and they shy away at the drop of a hat. The Smell would put most people off, and finicky people would hate the dust, and nervous types would scream and run at the first hint of anything magical.'

Arthur slumped into his chair and folded his arms. 'Human beings are quite disappointing, aren't they?' he said.

At half past five, they were forced to admit that none of them could think of a scheme to make more money while the magic was still in the shop.

'It looks as though I'll have to get rid of it,' Mr Hardbattle said.

Arthur nodded dismally. 'It looks that way to me too.'

'And me,' said Miss Quint. 'I wondered when you'd both see sense. Do you two have any idea what it's like to be made homeless?'

Arthur shook his head and Mr Hardbattle looked

shamefaced. They had both forgotten that Miss Quint's flat had been destroyed by fire.

'I felt bereaved at first and I took some time off work,' she said, 'but when my spell of leave was up, I found I couldn't go back; not to the way things were, to the life I'd had before the explosion. For the past three months I've been trying to think what I should do next and every day Mirabel says she wishes I'd hurry up and decide, but it isn't easy to know which way to turn when you've had your roots pulled up.'

Almost moved to tears by Miss Quint's emotional speech, Mr Hardbattle said that he had come to a decision and that he did not want to risk losing his home or his livelihood. He agreed to discuss the practicalities of evicting the magic, but only if Miss Quint would consent to lower her voice.

'I wouldn't want the magic to get wind of what we're up to. It mightn't take the news very well,' he explained.

In deference to Mr Hardbattle's wishes, the remainder of their conversation was conveyed in whispers. They discussed the sorts of places where they thought the magic would feel most at home and then tried to think of buildings in Plumford which might fit the bill.

Together they came up with a handful of suggestions, which included a boarded-up pub, an allotment shed and a cricket pavilion. Arthur was keen to go and look at them that instant, but Mr Hardbattle said that it was getting far too late. Reminding Arthur that his family must be expecting him home for tea, Mr Hardbattle promised to visit each place on their list the very next day.

'And I'll come too!' said Miss Quint. 'I've nothing else to do!'

When Arthur turned up at Hardbattle Books on Thursday after school to find out how the two of them had fared, he was disappointed to learn that none of the places had passed muster.

'The pub wasn't derelict,' Miss Quint explained, warming her cold fingers on a mug of steaming tea. 'It was being given a facelift by the brewery that'd just bought it . . . and the allotment shed was far too small and constantly in use.'

'As was the cricket pavilion,' Mr Hardbattle said as he glanced at the list in his notebook. 'The house by the river was the best of the bunch. It was old and run-down and seemed ideal, but unfortunately we were wrong about it being empty. An old fellow lives there with a German shepherd dog. I asked him how he'd feel about sharing his home with some magic and he charged me with being a madman and threatened to call the police!'

Having ruled out Plumford, it was clear that they

would have to look further afield. They each thought of all the places they had ever visited and tried to come up with a new list of buildings with potential for storing magic.

Mr Hardbattle rooted out some large-scale maps, which he thought might help to jog their memories, but despite poring over them, no one could come up with any ideas.

'I can only think of an old slate mine,' said Arthur, who had been to Wales on holiday the year before. 'But *Wales* is no good for *English* magic, is it?'

'There's nothing else for it!' Mr Hardbattle said. 'I'll have to go on trips to the nearby towns and villages, until I strike lucky and find a suitable place.'

'That's a bit random!' said Miss Quint. 'It could take you ages! How long have we got?'

They read through the letter from Piers Honeycomb again. (Despite being punched with holes, it was still legible.)

'It says we've got six weeks,' said Arthur. 'The rent must be found by the tenth of June.'

'That'll zoom by in a flash!' said Mr Hardbattle. He groaned. 'We need a better plan. Can either of you two think of one?'

They all thought immensely hard, but their effort was not rewarded. Eventually, Arthur announced that he was due home for tea.

'We need some more thinking time,' he said, as he wound his scarf around his neck and pulled on his cagoule. 'I've got football practice tomorrow after school, but on Saturday morning I'm not doing anything. I bet one of us will have thought of a good idea by then!' He picked up his school bag and opened the door of the shop. 'Let's meet here at half past ten, OK?'

Chapter five

A Trip to the Paper Shop

On Saturday morning, straight after breakfast, Arthur wandered down to the bottom of the garden, which is where he always went when he needed space to think. Time was running out. He was meeting his new friends at the bookshop at half past ten and he had not thought up a single idea which would help them to rehome the magic. Despite concentrating hard, Arthur's brain came up with zilch, so he got up from the grass and went back indoors, intending to ask his family's advice.

In the kitchen, his mother and his older sister, Penny, were clearing away the breakfast things.

'Say you're tired of something, right,' said Arthur, 'and you want to find it a new home – a good home – but you haven't got much time. What's the quickest way of doing it?'

Arthur had been so caught up with this quandary that

he had forgotten to wipe his shoes on the doormat. It had also slipped his mind that he was holding a guinea pig.

Neither of these things escaped Arthur's keen-eyed mother. The dirt on the floor worsened her mood and the presence of the guinea pig caused her to jump to entirely the wrong conclusion.

'A guinea pig isn't a plaything that you can cast aside when you feel like it,' she told her son sharply.

Arthur gaped while his mother hammered her point home.

'Cuddles and games in the garden are only one part of keeping a pet. I warned you that you'd have to clean out the hutch twice a week and you children assured me that you didn't mind. If you agree to do a thing you should stick to it. Your guinea pigs are staying right here.'

'But –' began Arthur.

'End of story!' said his mother, and turned away from him to open the door of the fridge.

Arthur's feelings were hurt. He was astounded that his mother could think that he would want to rehome his two beloved guinea pigs. He stroked the dainty ear of the guinea pig in his arms, which was nibbling a neat hole in his jumper.

'You've got the wrong end of the stick, Mum!' he said in injured tones. 'I wasn't talking about Quasimodo or Peanut. It's my friend. He's got something he wants to get rid of. The thing that he wants to find a new home for isn't alive, well . . . not exactly.'

His mother made an exasperated noise and complained that he had not made himself clear. Then she busied herself rearranging the food in the fridge to make room for the milk jug. '*I* don't know what your friend should do,' she muttered. 'Why doesn't he ask his *own* parents?'

Arthur's sister, Penny, was loading the dishwasher and reading a library book at the same time. She was a person of many talents, and being able to concentrate on several things at once was one of her most enviable skills.

'When I wanted to sell my CD collection,' Penny said, turning a page of her book with one finger and slotting a dirty dish in the rack, 'I put an advert in the *Plumford Gazette*.'

Arthur felt a rush of adrenalin flood through his veins. 'Advertising! What a fantastic idea! Thanks, Pen! That's the answer!'

He rushed outside and ran to the end of the garden, where he dropped Quasimodo into a run with his hutch mate, Peanut. In the shed next to the guinea pigs' living quarters were bundles of newspapers, tied with string, which were waiting to be recycled. He found a copy of the *Plumford Gazette* and turned to the narrow-columned section near the back. This part of the newspaper was called 'The Classifieds'. Items that people wanted to sell were grouped under headings such as *Cars for Sale*, *Domestic Pets*, and *Furniture and Furnishings*.

Arthur's bicycle was leaning against five others. He stuffed the *Gazette* into his saddlebag and wheeled his bicycle up the garden path.

'I'm off out!' he yelled as he passed the back door. 'I'll be back by lunchtime! See you later!'

Mr Hardbattle almost jumped out of his skin when Arthur burst into his bookshop a full hour earlier than had been arranged. Neglecting to ask Mr Hardbattle if *he* had had any brainwaves, Arthur recounted his own idea enthusiastically.

'You want to advertise . . . in the nationals?' Mr Hardbattle was not convinced. 'I don't think that *The Times* would print that sort of advertisement, Arthur.'

'Oh,' said Arthur, trying not to feel discouraged. 'What about some other paper . . . or a magazine, perhaps? Let's go and do some research.'

'Now?' Mr Hardbattle said. 'What about my customers?'

'What customers?' said Arthur. There was no one in the shop.

Feeling a little browbeaten, Mr Hardbattle walked to the door and flipped over the sign so that it said *Closed*. Then he put on his hat and coat and allowed Arthur to lead him to the paper shop in the next street. It was a small shop, but despite being the size of a beach hut, it stocked hundreds of newspapers, comics and magazines. These were crammed on to shelves, which spread from ceiling to floor. In order to find the publication of your choice a lot of rummaging was usually involved.

'We need to think carefully about the type of person that we'd be appealing to,' Mr Hardbattle said. Despite initial doubts, Arthur's idea was beginning to grow on him.

'What about *Homes & Gardens*?' asked Arthur. He held up a magazine.

'The people who buy *Homes & Gardens* like their houses to be spick and span,' pointed out Mr Hardbattle. 'We need someone with lower standards who doesn't mind if their furniture's shabby or if their garden goes to seed.'

'But they have to be *kind*,' insisted Arthur, keen for the magic to have a considerate minder. 'Old ladies are kind,' he said, pointing to the cover of a magazine which featured a grey-haired lady in a cashmere cardigan, holding a Persian cat.

'Something more unorthodox, that's what we should

be looking for,' Mr Hardbattle said, burrowing under a pile of sticker albums. 'A magazine for oddballs who believe in the weird and wonderful, like witches and crop circles . . .'

They decided that they would take out adverts in *Kindred Spirit*, *The Lady* and *Farmers Weekly*. Mr Hardbattle purchased a copy of each magazine and a bag of peppermint-flavoured sweets, which he felt would aid them in their task of putting together their advert.

'Have a bullseye,' he said in the doorway of the shop.

'Cheers,' said Arthur, taking a huge, round sweet out of the bag and popping it in his mouth.

Cheeks bulging, they marched back to the bookshop and once they had put their hands on pencils and paper, they got down to business straight away. It took longer than they had imagined to write the advertisement. Arthur was not that bothered about the wording, but Mr Hardbattle was a perfectionist when it came to composing even the briefest piece of writing. The task was made even harder by the arrival of Miss Quint, who insisted on putting her twopenn'orth in. It took until midday to come up with an advert that all three of them were satisfied with.

FREE TO GOOD HOME!
MAGIC REQUIRES TRANQUIL, RUN-DOWN
RESIDENCE TO LIVE IN FOR THE

LONG-TERM. HOMEOWNER MUST BE KIND AND RESILIENT. THOSE OF A HOUSE-PROUD NATURE NEED NOT APPLY.

PLEASE CONTACT: MR M. G. HARDBATTLE OF HARDBATTLE BOOKS, MEADOW STREET, PLUMFORD, EAST SUSSEX.

They had to wait weeks rather than days for their advert to be printed in the three magazines. By the middle of May, readers were starting to reply and soon post was pelting Mr Hardbattle's doormat daily. After sifting through the letters, Mr Hardbattle put aside twelve identified as having potential. Of the remaining replies, eight were from time-wasters, three were from family or friends enquiring about his health and the last – on per-fumed notepaper – was from Mrs Elizabeth Trinket, who expressed the hope that Mr Hardbattle knew what he was doing.

Late on a Friday afternoon, towards the end of May, Mr Hardbattle, Arthur and Miss Quint had a conference.

'Twelve possibles,' Mr Hardbattle murmured, moving towards a map of Great Britain, which he had tacked on to the wall. 'They all sound promising, but, of course, they'll have to be checked out. What's the name of the first place, Arthur?'

'Somersham,' said Arthur, taking the letter from the top of the pile. It was from a Mrs Jean Passworthy who lived in a labourer's cottage in the countryside.

'That's in Suffolk,' said Mr Hardbattle, taking the lid off a marker pen. He found Somersham on the map and drew a thick red circle round it. 'Read out the next place, Arthur, please.'

By the time that they had finished, the map looked as if it had contracted chickenpox.

'One of the places is quite nearby,' said Arthur, smearing the red ink with his finger as he pointed it out on the map. Several miles north-east of Plumford was a village called Thornwick.

Miss Quint looked up from a letter that she had been perusing. 'Arthur and I could tackle that one for you, if you like.'

'Good idea!' said Mr Hardbattle, staring at the map. His eyes moved rapidly behind his horn-rimmed spectacles. 'Common sense dictates that I should hop from one place to the next, but that would mean I'd have to take at least a week off work,' he said, 'and I daren't leave the shop for any length of time. There's no telling what mischief the magic might get up to.'

'You need someone to shop-sit!' concluded Arthur.

'I'd do it if I didn't have to go to school!'

Mr Hardbattle's hazel eyes widened and after smiling at Arthur he shifted his gaze to Miss Quint. 'I wonder, dear lady, if *you'd* consider stepping into the breach?' he said. 'Your duties wouldn't be too burdensome. You'd merely need to keep an eye on the shop, feed Scallywag and see that Trunk's spirits don't sink too low.'

Miss Quint considered his proposal for a moment or two, then with a determined nod of her head she said, 'I'll do it!'

The prospect of looking after the shop prompted Miss Quint to take a walk around it. 'This place could do with a woman's touch,' she said, running her finger along a dust-caked shelf. 'I assume you'd be offering me bed and board. I'll break the news to Mirabel right away. I could move in as soon as you like.'

'Great!' Arthur said and glanced at Mr Hardbattle, who, to his surprise, looked less than pleased.

It had not occurred to Mr Hardbattle that Miss Quint might want to move into his shop. He had lived on his own for more years than he could remember and it filled him with horror to think of someone else hanging their clothes in his wardrobe and having a soak in his bath. He felt that it was only right that he should warn Miss Quint about the inconveniences that she would have to put up with.

'The mattresses are lumpy and the cistern makes a

gurgling noise. And there are spiders – huge fellows – and no television set. Oh, and the windows mustn't be opened more than a crack for fear of disturbing the dust.'

Miss Quint did not turn a hair at the mention of these aggravations. 'It sounds like a palace compared to Mirabel's!' she joked. Then she unzipped her handbag and drew out a pen. 'So, that's settled. Good. Where's your notebook, Mr Hardbattle? I think it's high time we discussed your trip.'

The spiral-bound notebook was produced and Miss Quint began to compile a list. 'You'll need to work out your route beforehand and plan where you're going to stay each night,' she said, scribbling down each thought as soon as it occurred to her.

Mr Hardbattle was rather put out to have his expedition organised for him. However, he was too polite to say so, and had to be satisfied with contributing the odd remark: 'My camera could do with a new film . . . I'll need to shine my shoes before I go . . . Travel sickness pills – they're a must . . . I'd better take a torch. Oh, and a pair of overalls.'

Arthur thought of five or six suggestions of his own, the best of them being an evaluation sheet, which he offered to draw up.

'This way every building gets a score,' Arthur explained as he started to rule lines on a sheet of A4 paper. 'I'll put in lots of categories and each of them can be marked out of ten. We'll also need columns for total percentage and rank.' In minutes, an impressive-looking table had taken shape. After writing *The Best Place for Magic to Live In?* in large, untidy letters at the top of the page, Arthur glanced up at Mr Hardbattle and grinned.

'If only my homework was this interesting!' he said.

Chapter Six

Company for Miss Quint

Having been persuaded to travel by bus (which was free to all holders of a senior citizen's pass), Mr Hardbattle dangled the keys of the van above Miss Quint's outstretched palm. He did not seem to want to let go of them. As he stood in the doorway of the bookshop, suitcase at his feet, he gave her the low-down on getting the best from his much-cherished vehicle.

'Let her engine tick over before you put her in gear, and go easy round corners. Try not to yank the steering wheel if you can help it. Keep an eye on the temperature gauge. Don't let her overheat. Oh, and remember to check her oil. She gobbles it up, the greedy girl.'

'What is it about men and cars?' said Miss Quint to no one in particular. She snatched the keys from Mr Hardbattle's grasp and shooed him away. 'Go on, you old fusspot! You'll miss your bus!'

'My instructions!' he fretted. 'You haven't mislaid

them? Oh, and say goodbye to Arthur from me.'

'No,' said Miss Quint patiently. 'And yes, I will.'

'Poor chap!' said Mr Hardbattle. 'He'll be in double Geography now with that buffoon, Mr Beaglehole. I do hope our map of South America was up to scratch. You'll take an interest in his homework, won't you, Miss Quint?'

'Yes . . . yes,' Miss Quint muttered. 'Off with you, now! Not a word more. Go and find a new home for the You Know What – and don't lose any sleep in the meantime. Your shop is in safe hands.'

Mr Hardbattle had not walked more than half a dozen steps when he heard a mournful whine coming from an upstairs window. Scallywag's spotted muzzle was poking through a Venetian blind. That morning, sensing that something was up, she had followed her master all over the house, then lain down by his suitcase, her head on her paws. When the time had come for Mr Hardbattle to leave, it had been necessary to shut her in an upstairs room or she would undoubtedly have bolted after him.

There had been no need to go to such lengths with Trunk. Fond of Mr Hardbattle though the elephant was, he had never been known to stray from his shelf, haunted by the fear that his forgetful little mistress might return without him noticing.

'Cheerio, Scally, old girl! I'll be back in a week or so!' shouted Mr Hardbattle, wiping a tear from his eye. He walked to the corner of the road and stopped to wave before vanishing round it.

'Right!' said Miss Quint, shutting the door of the bookshop. The bell jingle-jangled with a note of melancholy. 'That's got rid of *him*. Now, I'm sure I saw some fruit cake in a cupboard in the kitchen. Time for elevenses, I think.'

Miss Quint soon stamped her personality on the shop. Though she had promised not to polish or vacuum, she made changes. In the shop, she tidied as much as she dared, putting books in order on the shelves and filing paperwork. She cleared out the till drawer, finding a shilling amongst the change, which had long since ceased to be legal tender.

Upstairs in the living quarters she was just as thorough. Beds were aired and floors were swept lightly with a dustpan and brush. Everything out of date in the kitchen cupboards was thrown away. Miss Quint baked bread. She made marmalade and jam. The mop was encouraged to slosh water a little more tidily over the floor, and the salt and pepper shakers were asked not to empty themselves over every dish (they had always had a tendency to be overly keen). She used up leftovers and fed vegetable peelings to the dog. On the third day, when the magic ran amok, she made trifle topped with custard from the second to last stair. Her arrival brought order and thriftiness and the magic did not know quite what to make of her.

For the first few days she kept herself busy and then boredom set in.

A people person, Miss Quint's whole purpose of being was to chat and there was not much of that in a book-shop whose average clientele was three customers per day. Scallywag could be relied upon to wag her tail, sigh, yawn, bark and scratch at the door, but that was the limit of her communicative powers. The origami sheep could only bleat repeatedly, and Trunk did not say anything, having a trunk and a pair of tusks, but sadly no mouth. Miss Quint yearned to be asked to hand deliver books and when she received a request she made the most of it, keeping the customer talking on their doorstep for as long as she could. However, these opportunities were few and far between.

For the most part, Miss Quint had to content herself with listening to Mr Hardbattle's old transistor radio, but after a while, the magic started to change the station at vital moments in news bulletins and afternoon plays, and it also developed the habit of turning the volume up and down. Eventually Miss Quint grew so annoyed with the magic that she returned the radio to the bathroom cabinet where she had found it.

Without fail, Arthur dropped by every day after school. Trunk barely acknowledged him, but both Scallywag and Miss Quint viewed Arthur's arrival as the highlight of their day. Scallywag greeted Arthur by tugging at his trouser legs (the only bad habit that she had retained, following on from a naughty puppy-hood). There was a brief interlude while Scallywag fetched her lead, then copious tail wagging until he took her for a walk. Miss Quint's form of welcome was more demure, but no less enthusiastic. Watching for Arthur from the window, she was always ready at the door to let him in. She took his bag, hung up his coat and asked about his day, before telling him in great detail about her own.

While Scallywag and Arthur were taking their walk to the park, Miss Quint occupied herself with pouring him an orange squash, putting biscuits on a plate, plumping the cushion on the wing chair that was Arthur's usual seat and setting out his exercise books and pencil case on a small oak table. On his return, she babbled to Arthur until he asked her to stop so that he could make a start on his homework. Miss Quint was no scholar. She had only three O levels to her name, but she did her best to assist him as well as she could. She found books on relevant subjects on the shelves and made what she thought were helpful suggestions, but otherwise respected his wishes and tried to leave him alone (never fully succeeding).

It was a Thursday afternoon, almost four days after

Mr Hardbattle's departure, when the solitary lifestyle of a bookseller finally defeated Miss Quint.

On that Thursday in May, Arthur's school bag was bulkier than normal. With half-term coming up, he wanted to get most of his homework out of the way so that he could help Miss Quint in the shop, and, more importantly, travel with her to Thornwick. In Thornwick there lived a lady called Mrs Carruthers, who had offered to make room for the magic on her farm.

Arthur had two tests to revise for, a page of sums to plough through, and he needed to finish a project which required drawing diagrams (not his forte at all). Scallywag's walk was short that afternoon: to the top of the road and back, and Miss Quint was disappointed to find that Arthur was most unwilling to take part in even the briefest conversation.

'You haven't touched your squash!' she said to Arthur, who was hunched over the little oak table, colouring something in.

'Sorry, Miss Quint,' mumbled Arthur. He picked up the glass and drained it without taking his eyes or his pen off the half-filled-in page in his exercise book.

'What's that you're drawing?' Miss Quint asked, attempting to peer over his shoulder.

'A subduction zone,' said Arthur, his scribbling getting more feverish.

'Biology?'

'Geography,' he said, and tensed. Tactfully, Miss Quint withdrew.

Not having been a conscientious student, Miss Quint found it hard to understand Arthur's devotion to work. She had been more than happy to scrape through exams, get mediocre marks and take home less than glowing reports. Her schooldays had been one long period of chatting too much and regularly losing house points.

Miss Quint began to wonder if it was her that was the problem. Arthur had seemed to get on famously with Mr Hardbattle. Perhaps Arthur had buried himself in schoolwork so that he did not have to talk to a gossipy, middle-aged female (charming and youthful-looking though she thought she was). Miss Quint was perfectly aware that she did not know the sorts of things that boys liked to talk about, not having any children or nephews of her own. She found herself wishing that Arthur were a girl. It was obvious that she and a girl would have so much more in common. There would be endless opportunities for long, intimate chats, and they could play cat's cradle, make pastry together and sing songs.

Arthur pushed aside his diagram of a subduction zone and opened a book with squared pages, which was dotted with sums.

Bored and deflated, Miss Quint wandered around the bookshop, picking up books and reading random paragraphs. In one book, she found a passage about some children playing, and decided to read it aloud, but quietly so as not to interrupt Arthur.

It was an old book called *High Jinks*, which had been written in the 1950s. In the part that she read out, the central characters (a boy called Reginald and his best friend, Keith) were leaping in a daredevil manner from one playground device to the next. Also in the snippet was an unnamed girl who, in contrast to the energetic boys, was not moving at all. She was standing by herself beside some railings, waiting for a go on the swings.

'If that little girl was here now,' Miss Quint said, pressing her finger on the place in the book where the girl was mentioned, 'we'd have a super time, I'm sure. I bet she wouldn't want to waste her time doing *homework*.' Miss Quint looked dejectedly over her shoulder at Arthur. 'If only that little girl was here right now. Oh, how I wish she was!'

Making wishes out loud was a risky business in a building that was filled to the brim with magic, but Miss Quint, who had barely glanced at Mr Hardbattle's instructions, was not to know. Ever so slowly and faintly, a light-coloured apparition started to glow in a corner of the shop. Miss Quint did not see it. She had closed the book containing the playground scene and moved on to another one. The hazy, fog-like blur morphed into a figure, which grew bolder in colour with every minute that passed.

Trunk was the first to see the girl. The sight of her made his black felt eyes try to pull away from their blobs of glue. When he realised that she was not *his* little girl, his surge of joy turned to bafflement. He had not heard the bell and could not understand how the girl could have entered the shop. Trunk examined his ears with his soft plump feet to check that the stuffing had not fallen out of them.

'Oh! H-hello,' said a startled Miss Quint, when, after several minutes, she peered through a gap in a bookshelf and saw a person standing in the furthest corner of the shop. Being less observant and not as alert as Trunk, she could not be sure if the bell had rung or not, but, in any case, it was clear that her afternoon had improved vastly. A customer had come in.

Miss Quint walked briskly around the blocks of teetering shelves. She felt that she should speak to the customer face to face rather than hold a conversation through a tiny space with the chance that she might breathe in a shelf's worth of dust.

'Good afternoon!' said Miss Quint, nearing the corner where the person stood. 'How nice of you to visit our establishment.'

'Hello,' said the customer, sucking the end of her plait.

Miss Quint's heart leaped. What a stroke of luck! She had wished that a little girl would join her in the book-shop and here one was!

The girl stared at Miss Quint solemnly. Under thickly powdered, pastel-blue lids, Miss Quint's eyes took in the plain, chubby-cheeked, listless girl in front of her. The little girl was not quite the pretty, charismatic child that she had had in mind but, as Miss Quint had come to learn, you could not always have everything. She gave the girl her brightest smile.

'How can I help you, cherub?' she said.

Chapter Seven

A full Shop

When asked what kind of assistance she needed, the girl was not forthcoming. She only seemed able to shrug her shoulders and say 'Don't know'. Eventually, Miss Quint was forced to resort to guessing games.

'You've come to buy a storybook on ponies. Am I right?' she asked.

'Don't know,' said the girl. Her eyes were big and expressionless.

Miss Quint tried a different tack. 'Perhaps you're lost. Did you find yourself on your own and come in here to ask for help?'

'No,' said the girl dully. 'I'm not lost – I'm waiting.'

'Waiting for what, pet?' Miss Quint was flummoxed. 'For someone to find you? Your mummy, perhaps?'

'I'm waiting . . . for a go,' said the girl.

'A go?' said Miss Quint.

'On the swings.'

Miss Quint was taken aback. 'But the park's a fair distance away. I don't understand. It won't do much good you waiting here.' She had an idea that the girl must be simple. Miss Quint touched her gently on the arm. 'This isn't a *play* area. This is a bookshop, dear.'

The girl stared.

'What's . . . your . . . name?' asked Miss Quint, speaking each word slowly.

'Don't know,' said the girl.

Miss Quint's patience deserted her. 'Don't be ridiculous! You must know what your name is! Everyone knows that. Now, think!'

The girl's front teeth bit nervously into her bottom lip. 'I don't know what my name is,' she said. 'It doesn't say.'

Miss Quint was close to having a fit of hysterics. 'What do you mean, "it doesn't say"?'

'In the story,' said the girl, biting her lip harder.

'The story? What story is that?' Miss Quint fell silent. Suddenly, everything the girl had said slipped into place and made perfect sense.

'Good gracious!' she said and seized the girl by her shoulders. 'It can't be possible! I'm crazy to believe it! You're the girl I wished for. The girl in the book!'

The girl would have shrugged if she could have

managed it, but Miss Quint's hands were like clamps.

'I'll get you an orange squash and a chocolate biscuit. Would you like that?' Miss Quint asked sweetly. She fussed over the girl, retying her hair ribbons and making flattering comments about the colour of her eyes (which were an unattractive, murky blue). 'I'm sorry that I was curt just now,' Miss Quint said, pressing her cheek against the girl's. 'I didn't realise who you were. I know this bookshop is magic, but I never thought that it could make wishes come true!'

With an arm around the girl's shoulders, Miss Quint led the nameless child across the shop floor and up the stairs to the kitchen, where she laid on a feast. When they came down again, Arthur was closing his books and zipping up his pencil case, having made a satisfactory start on his homework.

'I'm off now, Miss Quint,' he said breezily. 'It's almost teatime. Thanks for the squash and stuff.' His gaze landed on the po-faced girl holding Miss Quint's hand. She could only be a year or two younger than he was, but she was kitted out like a kindergarten child. She had on a gingham dress, white ankle socks and sandals. Her hair was tied with ribbons and dangled down in thin brown plaits.

'Who's this?' he asked.

Miss Quint gave a tinkling laugh and squeezed the

girl's hand. 'That's what I've been trying to find out!' she said. 'I've decided to call her Susan.'

Arthur frowned. His head was still congested with algebra, but he was sure that what Miss Quint had said had not sounded right. Had she just announced, gleefully, that she had renamed someone's child? He was half inclined to get to the bottom of things, but his brain felt too overloaded to do any more working out. Besides, it was a Thursday, which meant that there were chips, eggs and beans for tea. Thinking that the girl must be a customer and that he must have been too absorbed in his homework to hear the bell jingling when she had arrived, Arthur made his excuses.

'Mum freaks if I'm late for tea,' he said, stuffing all his books and school gear into his bag. 'Can't come in tomorrow. Got to take Bubbles to the vet's straight after school. He's our cockatiel. I'm the only one he hasn't tried to bite. We're going to my granny's on Saturday morning, but I'll come round in the afternoon. You'll keep it free, won't you, Miss Quint, so we can check out that farmhouse. Bye then.'

'Goodbye, dear!' said Miss Quint gaily, untroubled by Arthur's news that he would not be able to come to the bookshop until after lunch in two days' time. What did it matter now? She had magicked up the perfect companion for herself!

Miss Quint tired of Susan long before Saturday afternoon came.

It was not that Susan was badly behaved. In fact, Miss Quint had never met a more compliant child. Susan did not lark about, throw strops or sulk. She accepted the name 'Susan' without a word of argument. She made no demands, did as she was told and never left Miss Quint's side, trailing after her like a loose thread.

Conversations were one-sided. Miss Quint would think up an interesting topic upon which Susan would have nothing to say. She had no opinions of her own and no amusing anecdotes to share. It quickly became apparent that Susan was lacking any kind of personality, but when Miss Quint had another flick through *High Jinks*, the book from which Susan had been spirited, she realised that the girl's blandness was not her fault. It was the author who was to blame. Susan was mentioned only once in the whole book; standing by the railings in the park in the extract that Miss Quint had read out. She was a girl waiting for a go on the swings and nothing more. There was no fuller description. She was a blank slate.

For an outspoken chatterbox like Miss Quint, having the constant company of a dreary, soulless person was the worst sort of torture imaginable.

When the telephone rang on Friday morning, Miss Quint rushed across the shop to answer it, muttering 'Hallelujah!' under her breath. The caller was an awkward old gent called Mr Wax who had caused offence to every other bookseller in the county. He spoke to Miss Quint in a rude and demeaning way, but she did not care one jot. In fact, she almost broke down with relief to finally talk to someone with opinions.

Mr Wax wanted three books to be delivered: 'Not this afternoon. Not next week. Right this minute, thank you, Miss.' If the books were in a damaged state when they arrived, he would, apparently, see to it that Miss Quint was fired from her job.

Glad to have the chance to escape from the bookshop for an hour or two, Miss Quint locked up Hardbattle Books and herded her two helpers into the bottle green van. Scallywag rode in the back with the books and in the passenger seat sat Dreary Susan (as Miss Quint had got into the habit of calling her).

Mr Wax lived in an isolated cottage twenty miles outside Plumford. It had once been surrounded by a large, thriving community until Mr Wax had moved to the area and upset everyone.

The excursion did them all good. Scallywag had a long sniff of a gatepost while Miss Quint stood on Mr Wax's doorstep and refused to let him bully her. On the way back, Susan almost displayed excitement when she saw a herd of cows in a field.

The afternoon crawled by with sloth-like ponderousness, enlivened only by the antics of magic. One of the ducks from the painting of Lake Tahoe flew into the windowpane and had to be revived with a drop of pea-pod wine (nothing else seemed to do the trick); the paperclips linked themselves together and went on a march; and the black cat bookends spent several hours stalking a pincushion mouse. Wherever Miss Quint went, her new friend, Susan, followed. No customers came and the telephone did not ring. After unsuccessfully attempting to unwish Susan, Miss Quint had an attack of guilt. Vowing to be nicer to the girl, she asked her what she would like for tea, but, predictably, Susan did not know.

They went to bed early, when it was still light. Miss Quint had cleared out a box room for Susan to sleep in. Her bed was an old canvas put-me-up, but Miss Quint had found a feather quilt and a thick Aran jumper, which made a fine pillow.

By Saturday lunchtime, Miss Quint had nearly been driven round the twist by the absence of stimulating company. She had watched in vain for customers since nine o'clock, but none had arrived. It was a sunny day in May and the people of Plumford evidently had better things to do than poke around in dark dingy bookshops that smelt unpleasant. It reached the point when Miss Quint could no longer bear the poor companionship of Dreary Susan. If she could not unwish the girl then she would have to wish for some different people to join them both; adults, this time, with fully rounded characters and plenty of life experience. She took down books from the shelves and started to leaf through them, looking for anyone who sounded vaguely interesting.

Going through exactly the same motions as she had done before, Miss Quint pressed her finger on the character's name that she had selected and wished out loud that they could be with her. The magic in the bookshop did not disappoint. People began to appear gradually, just as Susan had done. An eminent politician materialised in one of the wing chairs, wearing a top hat and a monocle; a parlour maid bobbed a curtsy by the fireplace; a boot-black took shape in a kneeling position, a tin of boot polish and a cloth in his hands. Thrilled by the emergence of each character, Miss Quint wished for more and more companions and, dutifully, the magic obliged.

Scallywag was ecstatic. Her tail wagged itself into a blur as she ran up to each new arrival, then she sat at their feet and leaned against their legs, inviting them to stroke her. Susan loitered shyly by the cash register, not possessing Scallywag's talent for mingling. Trunk, meanwhile, was in a stew. He paced up and down his shelf, his grey ears flapping as he shook his head unhappily. There had not been a single jingle-jangle of the bell and yet the bookshop was filled with customers. He did not know how it had happened, not having a proper brain (even magic stuffing has its limitations), but he felt uneasy and was convinced that something was terribly wrong.

The bookshop had never been so full. By the time that Miss Quint had summoned her final guest, the floor was almost impossible to glimpse under the multitude of feet. There was a mixed assortment of footwear on show, every pair of which was buffed by the bootblack over the course of the afternoon. Unlikely characters chatted together (who would have thought that an actress, a bellhop and a mountaineer would have anything in common?), and Miss Quint swanned and sashayed amongst them all, her face frozen in rapturous delight.

When Arthur turned up at ten past three, he could barely get through the door. He was amazed to find the bookshop heaving with customers, and by the look of the headwear on the hatstand they were a diverse bunch.

Miss Quint accosted Arthur before he had crossed the doormat. She thrust a shopping bag and a list into his hands. 'And here's my purse!' she said, having to shout to make herself heard over the tumultuous din. 'I haven't got nearly enough in my cupboards to provide these good people with tea.'

'Since when have we started feeding customers? Mr Hardbattle didn't put *that* in his instructions,' Arthur protested worriedly, 'and where did all these people come from? You haven't decided to have a sale, have you, Miss Quint? What would Mr Hardbattle say?'

'Shush about Mr Hardbattle!' ordered Miss Quint, growing more irritated with Arthur by the second. 'He left the bookshop in my charge, didn't he?'

'Well, yes,' admitted Arthur, 'but he wanted me to look after it too.' Arthur peered past Miss Quint and frowned. 'Are these the sort of people he'd want in his shop? No one seems to be looking at the books or buying anything, and that bloke over there's wearing armour AND he's got a great big sword. You were meant to have closed the shop by three. Tell them you're shutting and throw them out. Mr Hardbattle's counting on us to take a look at that farmhouse. You promised that we'd go there *today*.'

'Something more pressing's come up,' said Miss Quint. 'Our trip will have to be postponed. Do stop scowling, Arthur. A little delay won't matter. Mrs Carruthers said in her letter that we could pop round any day we liked. We'll go tomorrow instead.'

'Don't suppose I've got much choice, have I?' Arthur said.

'No, so perk up, do! You're being a party pooper!' Miss Quint dropped her purse into the bag and gave Arthur a firm push. 'I've put bread and butter on the list and fillings for sandwiches, and some fairy cakes and pastries as well. Don't be tempted to get anything cheap or out of a jar. No peanut butter or chocolate spread or anything like that. There's a Right Honourable and a Duchess amongst this lot.'

'Can't *you* go?' complained Arthur, who did not derive much pleasure from supermarket shopping. 'There are so many aisles. I won't know where anything is.'

'Take Susan with you,' said Miss Quint, who had become aware of a familiar, irksome presence sidling up to her. 'She'll be very helpful, I'm sure.'

'Her again?' said Arthur, recognising the girl in the gingham dress as the one he had seen two days previously. 'Why has she started to hang out here? Hasn't she got a home to go to?'

Miss Quint glared at Arthur with just the right degree of displeasure to make him back out of the door.

Arthur glanced resentfully at the girl who had been foisted on him. 'Come on, then, what's-your-name,' he grumbled.

'It's Susan!' she said, and tried to hold his hand.

'Get off!' said Arthur, horrified. 'Hold this if you want to hold something!' He pushed the shopping bag into her arms and started to walk away. 'Let's go, Suze. We've got a lot of shopping to do.'

'All right,' Susan said amiably, 'but afterwards, do you think there'll be time to have a go on the swings?'

Chapter Eight

The Tea Party

Miss Quint turned out to be wrong about Susan. On the shopping trip she was not helpful at all. While Arthur dashed up and down the aisles, hunting high and low and ticking things off the list when he found what he was searching for, Susan ambled after him, clutching the shopping bag to her chest and gazing at everything in awe. When they had arrived at the supermarket, Arthur had asked her to find a few items, but it had been almost too painful to watch her floundering without a clue and in the end he had given up and taken the task upon himself.

As they traipsed back to the bookshop, each holding one handle of the bulging shopping bag, Arthur kept giving Susan curious sidelong glances. She was the oddest girl that he had ever met. Her dress sense was disturbingly nerdy, but it was her strange behaviour that gave him the most concern. Susan was not a talkative person and she tended to stare a lot. When she did speak, she often used old-fashioned words and phrases that he had heard his granny utter from time to time. Everyday sights like people talking on mobile phones would cause her to stand and gape, and the roar of a motorbike would make her jump out of her skin. She seemed to be like a tourist from a faraway place, and Arthur's heart, which had hardened towards her, slowly began to soften.

After ten minutes of stumbling along the pavement with their achingly heavy load, Arthur thought that they deserved a rest. He remembered that Susan had asked if they could stop at a playground, and despite the mile or so it added to their journey, he decided to take her to the park.

It being a warm day, the playground was busy, and they had to wait in line to have a turn on the swings. Susan did not seem to mind. In fact, she looked completely content and at ease standing in a queue with the other more fidgety children. It was as if she had finally returned to the environment in which she felt most at home.

When her turn came, she spent the first minute kicking her legs out in front of her, then quickly folding her knees. Gradually, she gathered momentum, soaring higher and higher; the chains that held the swing squeaking and clanking under the strain.

'Thank you, Arthur,' said Susan, when she had finished

her go and left the swing wobbling enticingly, awaiting the bottom of the next eager child. Susan's face, which was usually blank or conveying puzzlement, had lit up like a sunbeam.

'That's all right,' said Arthur, smiling. 'It beats making tons and tons of sandwiches, which I reckon is how we'll be spending the rest of our afternoon.'

The tea party was a resounding success. Arthur and Susan were recruited to hand things round and the guests happily tucked into the inviting range of sandwiches, which the children had indeed been roped into making. It had not escaped Arthur's notice that the customers were a motley crew. He had already spotted the guest who was wearing a breastplate and gauntlets (which the man had had to remove in order to eat a cream puff). It appeared that several others had opted to come in fancy dress as well.

Returning to the kitchen to refill a plate of sandwiches, he found himself wondering yet again where Miss Quint had chanced upon these people and how she had attracted them into the shop. He had meant to confront Miss Quint with these questions, but she had proved difficult to pin down. As soon as he had spied her and pushed through the crowd to talk to her, she had slipped away to the opposite side of the room, almost as if she were avoiding him.

Arthur and Susan were reunited at the kitchen sink after all the food had either been eaten or dropped on the floor. Susan turned on the taps.

'The cucumber sandwiches were popular,' commented Arthur.

'Everything was,' observed Susan, sheathing her hands in yellow rubber and dipping them into the bowl. And it was true; in double quick time, their entire supermarket shop had been polished off.

'Mrs Doasyouwouldbedoneby said she liked the eclairs the most.' Susan selected a dish mop and began to clean a plate.

'Mrs who?' asked Arthur, a tea towel clutched in his hand. 'Was that really her name?'

Susan nodded.

'I've heard that name before,' said Arthur, picking up the plate that Susan had stacked in the drainer. 'Mrs Doasyouwouldbedoneby. Yes, I've seen it written down. Was she the lady in black?' he asked.

'Oh, no!' said Susan. She tossed her head twice, flicking her plaits behind her so that their ends did not dangle in the soapy water. 'The lady in the black frock was Nurse Matilda.'

'Nurse Matilda?' exclaimed Arthur. 'Are you sure?'

'Yes,' Susan said. 'I heard her say so.' Since her go on

the swing, Susan had acquired a new decisiveness. She lifted a pile of china from the worktop and let it sink gently into the bowl.

'But Nurse Matilda's not real,' said Arthur, confused. 'She's a made-up person. My sister, Beth, drew a picture of her at junior story club. The picture's stuck to our fridge. I'm certain Nurse Matilda is a character from a book.'

Susan shrugged and busied herself with her dish mop.

'Oh, good, you've made a start.' Miss Quint popped her head round the kitchen door to check that the washing-up was under way. 'Hasn't it been a wonderful afternoon?' she said.

'Not especially,' Arthur replied. He wiped a plate with exaggerated care and placed it on some others on the worktop.

'You're a plucky pair,' said Miss Quint with admiration. 'As a reward for all your hard work, how would you like a trip to the seaside? We could take the van to Plentiful Sands!'

'Sounds nice,' snapped Arthur. Normally, he would have been thrilled at the prospect of a day at the beach, but the eager-to-please note in Miss Quint's voice merely added to his worries about the gathering of peculiar customers downstairs. He eyed Miss Quint with growing unease as he dried a handful of teaspoons. 'When are your guests going to leave?' he asked.

Miss Quint's face turned azalea pink.

'Yes,' joined in Susan. 'When *are* they going home? I'm jolly tired, Miss Quint. I think I'd like it if they went.'

'Soon, I hope,' said Miss Quint, her smile beginning to lose its radiance. 'I'm feeling a bit done in myself. This hostessing lark takes it out of you. I'll put it about that it's time they took themselves off. All right?'

From the kitchen on the first floor, Arthur and Susan heard the bell jingle-jangling time and time again. When they had finished the washing-up and were confident that all the customers must have left the shop, Susan peeled off her gloves and Arthur threw down his tea towel. Together they raced downstairs.

When they reached the bottom step, Arthur and Susan saw that the bookshop had emptied itself of everyone that did not belong there. They flung themselves into the chairs by the fireplace, greatly relieved.

Relaxing after a busy afternoon was not something that Scallywag, Trunk and Miss Quint seemed to be able to manage. Rather than flopping into the chair behind Mr Hardbattle's desk, Miss Quint stood fretfully beside it, staring out of the window at some unseen spectacle in the street. Scallywag was similarly ill at ease, but she was seated on the doormat with her head tilted and her ears pricked. The only part of Trunk that was visible was the knot in the end of his tail. Unlike the other two, he was not preoccupied with whatever was outside. He had travelled the length of his shelf and hidden behind a flowerpot, which was a sure sign that everything had got too much.

'What's up with everyone?' asked Arthur.

Susan shook her head. 'Don't know.'

Arthur got up from his chair. He trod past Scallywag, who was now lying down, making snuffling noises at the bottom of the door, and walked to the window to see what had secured Miss Quint's interest. She flinched when Arthur edged up beside her, but did not avert her gaze. Arthur squinted through the layers of age-old grime on the windowpane and was shocked to see a large group of people assembled on the pavement outside. He might have supposed that they were holding a demonstration, but as far as he could tell they were not wielding placards. He rubbed his sleeve on the glass so that he could see more clearly.

'Miss Quint,' he said after a minute of peering intently, 'why are all your guests standing around outside the shop? Why haven't they gone home?'

Miss Quint gave a feeble moan. 'I've wished and wished that they'd go,' she said, more to herself than to Arthur.

'Perhaps we should call them a taxi,' Arthur suggested practically, 'or rather a whole rank of them.'

Miss Quint sighed and patted her nostrils with a

handkerchief. 'I'm not sure they'd be able to pay the fares,' she said, 'and I haven't any money to lend them. I've only got coppers left in my purse. Everything else went on food for the party.' Miss Quint turned to face Arthur. Her cheeks had lost their healthy pink tinge. She looked drained and tearful, and, unusually for Miss Quint, she appeared to be lost for words.

'Who are those people?' asked Arthur suspiciously. 'Magic wasn't involved in their coming here, was it? You haven't done anything stupid?'

Miss Quint blanched. 'Susan, dear!' she called in a high, quavering voice. 'Would you be a poppet and run upstairs to fetch the keys from the saucer in my bedroom so I can lock the shop?'

Susan jumped to her feet. 'Yes, of course I will, Miss Quint,' she said and trotted up the steps.

Arthur's suspicions deepened when he saw the bunch of keys that Miss Quint had requested, hanging from her belt.

'But, Miss Quint –' he began.

'I know,' she said, following Arthur's befuddled gaze. 'I wanted Susan out of the way. I think it's time I owned up.'

Guilt-ridden and contrite, but not so humbled that she left out the part about how lonely and miserable she had been, Miss Quint confessed that the guests at her party had been characters from books. She explained to

Arthur that she had only needed to wish for them to be real and the magic in the bookshop had done the rest.

Arthur was tongue-tied with fury, but after a moment, he found his voice. 'Miss Quint!' he raged. 'Mr Hardbattle *said* you mustn't! What's the good of instructions if you won't read them? I can't *believe* this! What were you thinking of?' When he had calmed down, Arthur ran his fingers through his hair. 'So, what are we going to do?'

Miss Quint took a hopeful peek outside. 'They might move off in a minute,' she said.

'Move off? Where to?' said Arthur, exploding with anger again. 'You can't just put them out on the street and expect them to fend for themselves! They'll end up living in cardboard boxes. They might be mugged or kidnapped, and that guy with the sword is bound to take someone's head off if he swings it about like he's doing now. You'll have to get them back in here and undo all your wishes.'

'Don't you think I've tried that?' whined Miss Quint. 'I did my utmost to unwish Susan, but as you've seen she's still flesh and blood.'

'*Susan?*' Arthur took a step back. 'You mean she's one of *them*? You're telling me that I've been out shopping with a fictional character?' His astonishment melted away as the realisation sank in. 'Does she know?' he asked quietly.

Miss Quint shrugged her shoulders. 'She seemed to when we first met, but I think she's forgotten. That's why I got rid of her just now. I thought she might be a bit upset to be reminded.'

A slight flurry of movement outside caught Arthur's attention. Somebody new had joined the throng, and that someone was wearing a helmet and a smart, black uniform.

'Oh, heck!' said Arthur. 'It's the police. We're in big trouble now.'

Chapter Nine

A Spell of Unwishing

Afterwards, Arthur was forced to admit that Miss Quint had been magnificent. He had been the resourceful one who thought up the idea, but she had acted as the linchpin, without whom the plan would not have been possible to execute.

At first, Miss Quint had doubted that she was up to the challenge of duping a policeman, but Arthur had assured her that it was worth a try. She had made an unpromising start; tottering out on to the street in her high-heeled shoes, waving weakly and shouting, 'Yoo-hoo!' However, Miss Quint had held her nerve and gone on to charm the pants off the humourless policeman. Lying through her teeth, she had managed to convince him that the milling crowd was an untidy queue of book-lovers who were waiting for a famous author to turn up to sign his latest book.

The policeman had been surly to begin with, and, perhaps to save face, he had insisted on confiscating the knight's sword with the words 'Simmer down, lad, and hand it over. Knives are for chopping up spuds, not for carrying . . . and . . . and the same goes for swords an' all.'

The knight had been unwilling to give up his shining steel blade and there might have been a scuffle (in which the policeman would surely have come off worse) if the politician in the black top hat had not stepped in. Fitting his monocle to his eye, the fictional MP for North Lonsdale had said some fine and eloquent things. No one had fully understood what these had meant, but his distinguished tone of voice had had the desired effect. The situation was diffused, the knight gave up his sword and both parties were persuaded to shake hands.

Fooling a policeman was a minor challenge when compared with unwishing a roomful of people.

'So, how exactly did you go about each wish?' enquired Arthur after they had seen off the policeman and herded all of Miss Quint's guests back into the shop. (Scallywag was best at this because she was part sheepdog.)

Miss Quint despatched Susan to put the kettle on the stove and get the cups and saucers out, before applying her mind to Arthur's question.

'Well, let's see . . . um . . . I picked out a book and turned its pages until I found a character that seemed . . . *promising*. Then I put my finger on their name and wished.'

'And when you tried to unwish Susan, what did you do?' asked Arthur.

Miss Quint was about to give her reply when a fictional fishmonger attempted to involve her in a conversation on whelks. Miss Quint excused herself politely, and pulled Arthur to a more secluded section of the shop. She chose the most cobwebby corner, which was a no-go area for all arachnophobes.

'What did you ask me, Arthur?' she said. 'How did I go about unwishing Susan?' Miss Quint struggled to remember. 'I was finding her annoying. She wouldn't leave me alone, you see. I whispered it under my breath, I think, so she wouldn't hear. I said, "I wish this darned girl would go back to her book", or something similar.'

Arthur regarded her critically. 'You didn't find the book or point at her name then?'

'She didn't *have* a name, but no, I can't say that I did,' Miss Quint admitted. 'Do you think that would have made a difference?'

'I don't know,' said Arthur, fishing a spider out of his hair, 'but Mr Hardbattle said that magic won't be bossed about. If you'd asked a bit more nicely, or been clearer about what you'd wanted it to do . . .'

'I think it's worth another stab,' Miss Quint said, and Arthur was quick to agree. 'Although there's one slight snag,' she added, glancing around them at the dusty shelves.

If Miss Quint had been thinking straight and had not been in such a desperate hurry to people the bookshop with suitable companions for herself, she might have set aside the books that she had used, piled them all together and put them somewhere safe, but Miss Quint had been swept up in the excitement of the moment and had thrust the books back, willy-nilly, on the shelves. If she and Arthur were to match each tea party guest to the book from which they had been summoned, it was going to take a very long time.

'Let's start with Nurse Matilda,' said Arthur, dropping to his knees and scanning the shelves in front of him. 'She comes from a book with the same name. The author's somebody Brand.'

It took them twenty minutes of scrutinising spines to find it.

'Right,' said Arthur, handing Miss Quint a yellow jacketless book. 'Here you are. You take that and I'll watch Nurse Thingamy to see if she disappears.' He sought out the ugliest old lady in the room, who was dressed from head to toe in black.

'Poor Susan!' he said, distracted by the sight of his fellow washer-up passing behind the old woman, her arms supporting a heavy tray. 'She's *still* handing out cups of tea.'

'I hereby solemnly declare,' Miss Quint asserted in a sing-song voice, keeping to one constant note as if she were chanting a canticle in church, 'that I really do ever so regret wishing that this lady, Nurse Matilda, would pop out of this book and be a real human and I'd be for ever in your debt, not to mention eternally grateful –'

'That's grovelling,' Arthur interrupted. 'I shouldn't think the magic would be too impressed by that.'

'All right, then,' said Miss Quint tetchily, reverting to her normal way of speaking. 'I'd be *obliged* if your good self . . . selves . . . whatever you are . . . could grant me another wish and put this Nurse Matilda person back where she came from.'

Miss Quint removed her finger from the page she had chosen with a triumphant gesture. 'How was that?' she asked.

'A bit long-winded,' said Arthur bluntly. 'We've got thirty-eight more to go.'

'Thirty-nine,' said Miss Quint, correcting him. 'You've forgotten Susan.'

Arthur grunted. 'Does she seem a bit paler to you?'

'Who, Susan?' asked Miss Quint. 'I wouldn't have said so. She seems to have caught the sun today. Her nose has gone all freckly.'

'Miss Quint, I wasn't referring to Susan,' said Arthur, suddenly feeling weary. 'I meant the nurse.'

Stretching her neck, Miss Quint looked over to where Nurse Matilda was lecturing an elderly bearded clergyman who had laid claim to one of the wing chairs. Every now and then the nurse dug the old man in the ribs with her stick to ensure that he stayed awake. 'Well, bless me!' exclaimed Miss Quint. 'I do believe she's gone grey around the edges!'

Miss Quint and Arthur grinned at each other and watched to see what would happen next.

Her jaw continuing to exercise itself, Nurse Matilda slowly ebbed away, fading into nothingness like a dawn mist. The clergyman's head fell forward on to his chest and remained there. No stick jabbed him between his ribs to interrupt his nap because Nurse Matilda had dematerialised.

'Job done!' said Arthur. 'Well, nearly.' He gazed around the shop, his eyes flitting from person to person. They would all have to be dealt with in the same laborious way. The enormity of the task ahead was daunting, but Arthur felt upbeat. 'What's the next book we've got to look for, Miss Quint?' he asked.

It went quite well to begin with. Fifteen guests were removed from the shop without any hitches. All of them took their leave gradually, like aspirins dissolving in water. The other guests were untroubled by their departure and assumed that their acquaintances had gone outside for a breath of air or upstairs to use the lavatory.

At half past six, Arthur made a phone call home and asked his mother if he might be allowed to sleep over at his friend's house that evening. With six children to look after, a cockatiel, two guinea pigs and an axolotl, not to mention a scatterbrained husband, Arthur's mum could not be expected to remember the names of all of her children's friends. She expressed no surprise when Arthur told her that his playmate was called Susan.

'Susan? Fine, but you'll have to pop home for your pyjamas and your toothbrush,' she told him.

Things started to go awry when Arthur left to collect his night things. He had brought his bicycle and was not away for long, but winds can change in an instant and large clusters of magic are just as fickle. With Scallywag asleep on a rug by the fireplace, Susan dozing on the bottom stair (worn out from her tea-making duties) and Trunk still refusing to come out from behind his flower-pot, Miss Quint was left to cope alone.

She had her first inkling that the magic was starting to misbehave when a ballet dancer vanished with a bang. Up until that moment, every character had evanesced gently, over a period of minutes, but the instant that Miss Quint wished for the dancer to disappear, there was an ear-splitting crack, the ballet dancer was engulfed by smoke and when it had cleared there was nothing left of her. The other guests did not react well to this event. Everyone threw up their hands in surprise, most of the ladies screamed and the gentlemen – depending on their upbringing – said 'Yikes!' or 'Cor blimey!' or 'What the dickens was that?' All over the shop there was the sound of breaking china as dropped teacups and saucers shattered on the floor. Susan ran to fetch a brush and dustpan, Scallywag dashed upstairs after her, and Miss Quint hid and dithered, not knowing what to do.

After about a minute and a half an idea came to her. 'Marvellous!' declared Miss Quint, striding into the frightened crowd. 'Excellent! Superb! What an amazing stunt!' Expecting the others to believe that the ballet dancer's sudden disappearance had been some kind of spectacular trick was wildly optimistic and, at first, they stared at her as if she were mad. Refusing to abandon her plan, Miss Quint kept up the pretence, and slowly the crowd began to relax and smile and join her in remarking upon the wondrous nature of the ballet dancer's feat. Soon they had separated into little groups and resumed their former conversations.

A little while later, when Miss Quint had picked the next person to unwish and had the right book open in her hands, she paused, afraid that the same alarming exit would befall this person too. She weighed this fear against the knowledge that she could not afford to dilly-dally. There were still around twenty guests to evict from the bookshop and if she did not get on with the job she would find herself unwishing people into the early hours.

Taking a deep breath, she put her finger on the char-acter's name and pleaded with the magic to do as she asked. 'And I'd rather you did it without all that razzmatazz this time.'

The magic outdid itself, but not in the way that Miss Quint had hoped.

Instead of getting fainter, the character that she had unwished (a cook with an apron tied round her waist) grew fatter. The unfortunate woman swelled to three times her normal size, and the squeals and exclamations of those watching her were matched in volume by the zinging sounds as the buttons on the woman's dress detached themselves and shot across the room. A lone drawing pin emerged from its carton and began to encircle her like a fly. She flapped at it with her podgy hands, but it zigzagged out of reach. It hovered in mid-air, then with a rapid dive it struck, puncturing the cook and making her pop like a balloon. The drawing pin dropped to the floor. Nothing of the cook remained.

Pandemonium followed. A group of ladies cowered in a corner and there was screaming and shouting and lots of running to and fro. Miss Quint's attempts to calm everyone merely made things worse and, grouping themselves together, the bulk of the guests made a rush for the door.

Fortunately, Arthur arrived back just at that crucial moment.

'Stop them, Arthur!' cried Miss Quint. 'Bar their way! Pull the bolts across!' She steamed towards him in a frightful panic. 'Whatever you do, don't let them escape!'

Chapter Ten

Meddling and Muddling

In an agitated state, Miss Quint lobbed the door key at Arthur. It sailed over the heads of the stampeding guests and, timing his jump to perfection, Arthur snatched it out of the air. He turned round quickly and locked the door, then slipped the key into his pocket before the others could do anything about it.

'Boy, give up that key and stand aside!' the MP for North Lonsdale bellowed pompously. 'A policeman must be summoned at once. Betsy the cook has been murdered!'

'Right in front of our eyes!' said the parlour maid, clutching the MP's arm and trembling. 'It were *'orrible*.'

''Twas not an honourable death,' said the knight, sounding aggrieved. He curled his gauntleted fist and placed it over his heart. 'Betsy deserved a bloodthirstier end. I myself desire to have my gizzards slashed open and my eyes gouged from my head.'

'*Gross!*' muttered Arthur.

Everyone thought that the knight's comments were in poor taste and it was agreed that in future he should keep his ideas about noble ways to die to himself.

'The key, you insolent upstart!' roared the MP impatiently. 'I demand that you hand it to me this instant. If you refuse, I shall have no choice but to search your person.'

'Alas! If only I had my sword,' bemoaned the knight, slapping his empty scabbard and cursing in Old English. 'I would smite this young churl's head from his shoulders with one blow –'

'That's enough of that sort of talk!' interrupted Miss Quint, appalled by the threats, which were being levelled at Arthur, who was only a schoolboy after all. She elbowed her way through the unfriendly mob. 'Leave the boy alone!' she yelled. 'There'll be no smiting of heads or searching of persons or running to the cops for that matter. You've all got your facts wrong. There hasn't been any murder! Your friend Betsy the cook is as right as rain.' Miss Quint waved the dog-eared paperback book in her hand. 'Betsy isn't dead. She's just been returned to her story!'

Miss Quint's explanation did not seem to convince the outraged crowd, who were growing more restless by the minute. None of them seemed to recall that they were characters, borne out of the imaginations of authors. They refused to believe that any of their number belonged between the pages of books, and stuck stead-fastly to their theory that the cook had been done in.

'Betsy blew up and exploded. We all saw her,' piped up the bootblack.

'She did *what*?' said Arthur. 'What's been going on, Miss Quint?'

'It's the magic,' whispered Miss Quint, squeezing past the final few guests and reaching Arthur's side at last. 'It hasn't been toeing the line. Things have been getting out of hand.' She told him what had happened to the ballet dancer and then described the sequence of events, which had led to the bursting of Betsy.

'Crikey!' Arthur said. 'We're in a bit of a fix.'

Miss Quint chewed her lip worriedly. 'I daren't unwish another one. This lot will go berserk.'

With his back pressed against the door and a small army of angry, fearful people advancing towards him, Arthur decided that he needed to take action.

'They're really ticked off,' he said to Miss Quint. 'I'd better do something or this could get nasty.' In an appeasing gesture, he raised his hands above his head and asked them to listen to what he had to say.

'OK, I believe you,' Arthur told them. 'Something upsetting has happened to Betsy. You're right. We should get the police involved. I'll phone them now. Everyone stay calm.' Arthur edged past the hostile crowd and hurried over to where the telephone rested on the desk. He picked up the handset and, holding down the button switch, he cut off the dialling tone and spoke to a dead line.

'Is that the police station?' Arthur said to nobody. 'Hello, this is Arthur Goodenough here. I'd like to report a murder, please. I'm calling from the bookshop on Meadow Street. You'll come immediately, won't you? Thank you very much.' Pretending to look relieved, he put down the receiver and smiled at the crowd, who were on tenterhooks. 'The Plumford Police Force are on their way,' he said.

Ignoring the clapping and cheering that greeted his announcement, Arthur dashed to join Miss Quint by the door. He got to her in the nick of time. Her face had been paralysed by shock and she was swaying unstably as if she were about to faint. 'Miss Quint!' whispered Arthur, putting an arm out to steady her. 'Don't panic! The police aren't really coming. It was all a bluff.'

By now, Arthur and Miss Quint were getting used to dealing with sticky situations. They stood in a conspiratorial huddle beside a display of cricketing books and talked in hushed voices.

'It's a shame we can't unwish them all in one go,' lamented Miss Quint, anxiously shifting her weight from one high heel to the other.

'Hey! I think you've got something there,' said Arthur. 'Why don't we split them into groups? We could put the groups in different rooms and call them in here when we're ready for them. I reckon we could manage to unwish three or four people at once. That way, no one would see any funny disappearances and get worked up.'

Miss Quint gave an awestruck gasp and patted Arthur's shoulder. 'First-class idea,' she said. 'That would certainly speed things along.'

Arthur nodded. 'They're expecting the police to arrive, don't forget. It's important that we get rid of these people quickly. If we take too long they might get suspicious. The only problem is I can't think how to persuade them to split up.'

'Parlour games!' Miss Quint cried out exultantly.

'Huh?' said Arthur.

Reaching behind his head, Miss Quint plucked a book from the shelf and grinned at him. The book was called *Popular Parlour Games*. She turned to its index, and ran down it with her finger. 'Blind man's buff, charades, postman's knock, hunt the thimble . . . This should keep them busy. We could put Susan in charge.'

Arthur was doubtful. 'Do you think they're in the right sort of mood to want to play games?' he asked.

'Oh, yes!' Miss Quint waved a dismissive hand. 'We could tell them that it'll keep their minds off Betsy until the police get here. They'll go for it. I know they will. We could even have a beetle drive. Who can resist one of those?'

'Er . . . I'm not even sure what one is,' said Arthur, scratching his head. He peered warily over his shoulder. Miss Quint's voice was getting very loud and squeaky. In his opinion, she was becoming overexcited.

'Don't worry, Arthur. Leave it to me,' said Miss Quint. She tweaked his nose. Then, clutching the book, she bustled off, calling out Susan's name. 'Where are you, cherub?' she cried. 'I've got a little project that I want you to help me with!'

Much to Arthur's astonishment, the guests did not object when Miss Quint asked for their attention and explained to them why she thought it might be a good idea if everyone joined in some games. Perched on a pile of old musical scores, Susan had her nose in *Popular Parlour Games* while Miss Quint delivered her spiel. There was a slight interval while the guests decided which groups they wanted to be in. When they had made up their minds, Miss Quint stepped behind Susan and gripped her shoulders.

'This is Susan, everyone,' said Miss Quint. 'She'll be supervising your games while my young friend, Arthur, and I will be preparing a special treat for you.'

Having been briefed on her task, and with the copy of *Popular Parlour Games* wedged under her arm, Susan took each of the six groups to their allotted rooms and explained the rules of the games that Miss Quint had selected from the book. It had been decided that Susan should flit from room to room to check that everyone had enough paper and pens and that they were all obeying the rules. From the ripples of laughter, which could be heard throughout the house, the games seemed to be providing light relief.

The first four groups were summoned, one by one, to the shop floor and, working as an effective team, Miss Quint and Arthur sent them back to their books with a minimum of fuss.

The fifth group to be unwished contained the knight. Miss Quint was glad to be seeing the back of him, as he had shown himself to be hot-headed and reckless. Having watched the knight participate in a game of beetle, Susan had reported that he was a terrible cheat as well.

The knight and his two companions lined up in front of Arthur and Miss Quint, expecting to be rewarded with a treat. Arthur had two books opened in front of him and Miss Quint held *A Tale of Derring-do*: the book in which the knight's story was told. Placing their forefingers on each of the character's names, Arthur and Miss Quint wished them back into their stories. Magic achieved this by spinning them like tops while they faded into nothingness.

Feeling a strange tingling in her palms, Miss Quint glanced down and saw *A Tale of Derring-do* reducing in size until it was only a few pages thick. 'Oh, dear!' she said as the reason for this new compact version dawned on her. 'We sent the knight back without his sword.' She turned to the last page and her face crumpled in revulsion.

'Let's see!' said Arthur, pawing at the final page.

'No!' Miss Quint told him sharply. She slapped his hand and slammed the book shut. 'It's not the sort of thing your mother would want you to read. Let's just say the knight got what he wanted.'

'Ohhh,' said Arthur in a drawn-out breath. 'You mean his gizzards and – eugh! – his eyeballs . . .'

'I don't wish to discuss it,' said Miss Quint. 'Call the last group, please.'

When it came to the sixth and final group a problem arose. Miss Quint and Arthur could not find the books that they needed, even though they hunted on every shelf and in every corner of the shop.

'Oh, never mind,' said Miss Quint tiredly, sending the people away again. 'We'll move on to Susan, shall we? Well, that's a funny thing,' she said, her hand hovering above a column of books. 'I'm sure I put Susan's book on top of these others.' Arthur and Miss Quint searched and searched, but finally they were forced to admit that they could not find Susan's book, *High Jinks*, either.

By nine o'clock the three remaining guests had played so many games of Consequences that they were heartily sick of it. Susan brought them downstairs, where they confronted Miss Quint and asked her where the police force had got to.

'Oh, the police have been and gone,' Miss Quint told them casually. 'They dusted for fingerprints and cordoned off the crime scene . . . and . . . and then they un-cordoned it, because they'd solved the murder and they've gone now, so everything's done with. Nothing to worry about at all.'

'Who did it?' asked one of the men.

'And where, pray, is everyone else?' asked the well-dressed woman.

Miss Quint's stockpile of lies was all used up and it was left to Arthur to spin a story. '*They* did it,' he said. 'All the others did. They're not here any more because they've been taken away for questioning!'

Miss Quint gawped at Arthur admiringly while the two men and their female companion expressed their shock. Susan was so traumatised that she started to cry and, hearing a little girl's sobs, Trunk peered around his flowerpot.

'There, there, sweetheart!' Miss Quint said soothingly. She pulled Susan towards her and embraced the distraught child. 'It's been a long day, hasn't it? I think it would be sensible if we all retired for the night.'

'Where are we all going to sleep?' asked Arthur.

Miss Quint relinquished Susan and looked thoughtfully at the assembled group.

'Mrs Voysey-Brown can have my bed,' she said, 'and Susan won't mind snuggling down in the box room.

She's slept there for the last two nights. I'll put Mr Blenko and Mr Claggitt in the spare room. You can take the couch on the landing, Arthur, and I'll sleep down here in one of the chairs. I know it's not ideal, but it's only for one night.'

Arthur raised his eyebrows at her questioningly.

'We'll have them all back in their books in the morning,' she whispered. 'You'll see.'

Chapter Eleven

Blenko and Co.

On Sunday morning, Arthur rolled off the couch where he had spent the night, and wandered into the kitchen in search of breakfast. The females of the household were already there. Miss Quint was pouring coffee, Susan was taking an age over laying the table and, mesmerised by the smell of frying sausages, Scallywag was getting under everyone's feet. A motionless figure languished in a chair in the midst of all the activity. She had curled, black eyelashes and unbrushed hair and seemed to be asleep.

'Er . . . hi,' murmured Arthur.

Susan looked up and gave him a smile. 'Hello, Arthur! Did you sleep well? I did, like a log.'

'How ghastly for you. *I* shouldn't care to resemble a log, even in repose,' sneered the woman in the chair, speaking in a lazy drawl.

Susan's cheeks reddened. She turned to fetch more knives and forks.

'Arthur, could I trouble you to hand this cup of coffee to our guest?' asked Miss Quint, putting on a refined accent. 'Mrs Voysey-Brown is in *films*,' she added, breathless with admiration.

Arthur was not surprised to hear it. Mrs Voysey-Brown was a strikingly handsome woman and she looked every inch an actress despite being clothed in Miss Quint's raggedy old dressing gown.

'Thank you, darling,' purred Mrs Voysey-Brown, revealing her eyes, which were violet blue. She raised the cup of coffee to her painted lips and took a delicate sip.

'Morning, Claggitt!' she said as a bearded colossus strode into the room. He reached the kitchen table in two strides and sat down.

'Slept in,' said Mr Claggitt, shaking his bobble-hatted head. Unlike his friend, he had bothered to get dressed. He was wearing a jumper, a parka with a fur-lined hood, trousers made from a waterproof fabric and hiking boots. 'Wanted to check out the terrain before breakfast,' he said. 'Thought I'd do some exploring later.'

'You like walking, do you?' asked Arthur, who had come to enjoy exercising Scallywag every afternoon.

'Walking?' Mr Claggitt poured scorn on Arthur's remark. 'Do I look like a cissy to you? I'm a mountaineer, boy! I've scaled all the greats: Everest, K2, Kanchenjunga. Wanted to see what Plumford had to offer. Was hoping to glimpse a peak or two from my window.'

'There's a hill in Victoria Park,' said Arthur.

'Really?' Mr Claggitt said, showing a keen interest. 'What gradient are we talking about?'

'Oh, I don't know,' said Arthur, 'but it's quite steep. My mad friend, Ollie, skateboarded down it once and did a lot of damage to his kneecaps.'

'Breakfast is served!' announced Miss Quint. She forged a path through the crowded kitchen with two plates of appetising food in her hands. 'Give Mr Blenko a call, would you, Arthur?'

Arthur went to the door and was on the verge of shouting up the staircase when he saw a young man in a reddish-purple uniform strolling down the steps, sniffing the air.

'A fry-up, eh?' said the man, skipping down the last few steps and patting the newel post as he passed it. 'This ain't such a dive after all!' The young man winked at Arthur and proceeded to introduce himself. 'Me mates call me Jimmy,' he said, shaking Arthur's hand.

'Mine call me Art,' said Arthur, preoccupied with Jimmy's attire. Jimmy was dressed like a drummer boy in plum-coloured trousers edged with gold piping, a close-fitting jacket and a round, brimless cap.

'Want to know 'bout me uniform, do you, Art? I'm a bellhop, ain't I? London's finest.' Jimmy brushed his jacket sleeves and grinned at Arthur's bemused face. 'A bellhop's a feller who works in a hotel. When the bell's rung we 'op to it sharpish, carrying cases and opening doors.'

'Like a sort of servant,' muttered Arthur.

'Ain't they bangers I can smell?' said Jimmy, pushing past Arthur. 'Out the way, chum! Let me at that nosh!'

Breakfast was a riot. The three more senior members of the group gathered at one end of the table and Jimmy the bellhop seated himself at the other, flanked by Arthur and Susan. Mr Claggitt talked the most. In a voice that never dipped below the volume of a foghorn, he regaled the two ladies with stories of his hair-raising adventures in the world's most hazardous mountain ranges. He hardly ever paused for breath, but when he did, Mrs Voysey-Brown was ready with a dry, sarcastic comment. Miss Quint barely said a word. She was far too busy frying more food and refilling the mountaineer's plate to make any contribution to the conversation, although she did find time to shoot scathing looks at Jimmy, whose table manners were dreadful.

Everyone ate at different speeds. Mr Claggitt tucked into his helpings of sausages, eggs and tomatoes with gusto, more than making up for Mrs Voysey-Brown's poor appetite. A thin, willowy person, she picked at her plateful of food like a finicky cat, and spent the duration of the meal dabbing at the corners of her mouth with a napkin. Miss Quint snatched the odd mouthful of titbits on the hoof.

At the other end of the table, the children finished their meals long before Jimmy Blenko had gobbled down his. Jimmy was a born entertainer. He knew a raft of jokes and rattled them off, one after the other, keeping Arthur in stitches. Susan giggled too on the rare occasion that she managed to understand one. An excellent mimic, Jimmy progressed to doing impressions of all the staff and clientele, from toffs to riff-raff, who had passed through his hotel.

When breakfast was over and Susan and Miss Quint were bent over the kitchen sink doing the washing-up, Arthur changed out of his pyjamas and went downstairs, intent on having a root around the shop in search of the missing books, *Tinseltown Ticket*, *Rockfall!* and *Champagne for Geraldine*. Miss Quint had mentioned to him that she had had a probe at daybreak when everyone else was still in bed. Her search had proved to be fruitless, but Arthur was hopeful of doing better.

The bookshop was quiet and undisturbed. Everything was in its proper place. The books were filed correctly, the black cat bookends stood symmetrically either side of Ibsen's plays, and the ducks in the painting of Lake Tahoe were asleep with their heads tucked under their wings. The only lively presence was Trunk. He was frolicking back and forth on his shelf, curling up his trunk and shooting it straight out again, like a party blowout. His behaviour was very out of character. Arthur asked the elephant if something was the matter, but, of course, having no mouth, Trunk was unable to answer him.

After half an hour, Arthur abandoned his hunt for the books, which were still nowhere to be found, and made his way towards the stairwell. Before he could reach it, however, Arthur heard the sound of feet tramping down the stairs and was joined on the shop floor by Miss Quint (closely followed by Susan), the three new house guests and Scallywag.

Miss Quint was carrying a shopping bag and Mr Claggitt had a tartan rug tucked under his arm. Mrs Voysey-Brown was wearing a pair of borrowed sunglasses.

'The weather forecast is tip-top!' declared Miss Quint. 'It's a shame I never got round to buying a new swimsuit. Still, there's more to being beside the sea than bathing. All set, Arthur? Plentiful Sands, here we come!'

Arthur gaped at Miss Quint in disbelief. 'We're not going to the seaside *today*!'

Susan's face fell immediately. 'Aren't we?' she said. 'Why don't you want to go, Arthur? Miss Quint says there are castles built out of sand and fish made from jelly and watery things called waves.'

Feeling like a heel, Arthur struggled to explain. 'It doesn't mean we can't go another day,' he said. 'It's just that today Miss Quint and I had made plans. We need to have a look around a farmhouse. It's urgent. We've already put it off once.'

Susan started to sniff. Within seconds, Arthur found himself accused of making her cry.

'What did you expect me to do with them?' Miss Quint whispered fiercely in Arthur's ear. 'I've got to entertain these people *somehow*. They've been promised a day on the beach. I can't suddenly change my mind!'

'Face facts,' said Mr Claggitt, slamming his hand on to Arthur's shoulder. 'You're outvoted, sonny boy!'

Miss Quint drove and Mr Claggitt blotted out half the windscreen with a map and made a hash of doing the navigating. For a seasoned explorer, he did not seem to understand the basics of map reading. He urged Miss Quint to take short cuts through barbed-wire fences, in between trees and over railway tracks, until Miss Quint was able to get the message across that in England, when journeying in a car, one was required to travel on roads.

'Up and over,' Mr Claggitt advised whenever they came to a roundabout. 'Go, go, go!' he shouted when the traffic lights were red.

The odds were against them arriving in one piece with Mr Claggitt in the passenger seat, but they did eventually reach their destination without so much as a scratch, mostly thanks to Miss Quint's cool head and the regular smattering of signposts.

Plentiful Sands was well named. The cove arched in a golden crescent for miles and miles. It was not quite summer, but the sun was out and the weather was pleasant enough to entice the usual horde of day-trippers, who were prepared to don their bathing costumes at the first sighting of a patch of blue sky.

There was a place that hired out deckchairs, and an ice cream kiosk, but Miss Quint told the others, regretfully, that she could not afford any extra treats. She spread the tartan picnic blanket over the sand and gave them each a paper bag, which contained their lunch, explaining that they would have to make do.

Jimmy had other ideas, it seemed. Kicking off his shoes, he sauntered down the beach and returned with a beach ball, a deckchair, and two straw sun hats for the ladies. Later on in the afternoon, on another jaunt, he came back with a bucket and spade and six ice creams. Arthur and Jimmy leaped about with the beach ball, spraying sand everywhere, getting hot, pausing for a dip in the sea and then starting their ball game all over again.

They were not the only members of their group to find ways to enjoy themselves.

Never one to let the chance of a paddle pass her by, Miss Quint took off her tights and ventured down to the water's edge. While she was swishing about in the water, Scallywag thundered across the sand and launched herself into the waves, barking with insane delight. Susan was more reserved than the other two and would only allow the foam to tickle her toes.

Mr Claggitt hung around for a short while, moaning that the beach was far too flat. As soon as he had sighted some cliffs in the distance he was off. He weaved a route through the sandcastles and windbreaks in his parka, weatherproof trousers and hiking boots.

Mrs Voysey-Brown confided to the others that she was more of a St Tropez type of person. She hogged the only deckchair and hid underneath her wide-brimmed hat for the entire afternoon. To amuse herself, she criticised people's swimwear, and she flatly refused to help Susan look for seashells along the shore.

'Really, darling, have some sense,' she told the disappointed child. 'Famous actresses don't get their ankles wet in public!'

All in all, it was a thoroughly enjoyable day and they were loath for it to end. They waited until the setting sun was poised to touch the horizon before they plodded from the beach and piled into the van. They were sticky and sunburnt and had sand between their toes, but no one could remember having had a lovelier time.

When they pulled up outside Hardbattle Books, Arthur yelled a hasty goodbye and scooted off home on his bicycle. It was left to Susan and Miss Quint to organise supper. The sea air seemed to have sapped everyone's strength and most of them were too tired to lift their forks to their mouths. Once the meal was out of the way and the others had trooped off to bed, Miss Quint tidied up the kitchen.

Crouching down to pick up a napkin, which had fallen on to the floor, Miss Quint spied a small pile of letters under the kitchen table. It was Scallywag's job to collect the mail from the doormat every day, and while she was fairly successful at this, she was not so adept at delivering it to Miss Quint. Consequently, it was not unusual to find letters scattered all over the house.

Miss Quint retrieved the pile of post. There were three brown envelopes and a postcard.

She laid out the post on the table in front of her, then opened the three brown envelopes first. Two were bills and one was an order. Finally she looked at the postcard. On its front was a picture of a pier, which was described as being in Great Yarmouth. She turned the postcard over and saw that Mr Hardbattle had sent it. The weather in East Anglia he described as 'good' and the food as 'rather chewy'. He mentioned that Arthur's method of rating the buildings had been working well, and listed the marks that he had dolled out thus far. Miss Quint noted, with a sharp intake of breath, that only one of the eight places he had visited had racked up a score of more than forty per cent.

Contained in the final few sentences were the words

that Miss Quint had been dreading: *Will be returning Tuesday eve. I assume all is well. Kind regards, Mr H.*

Miss Quint was not the sort of person who went in for swearing. 'Oh, knickers!' she said, and reached for a chocolate biscuit.

Chapter Twelve

Arthur Manages

The next morning, Arthur skidded to a stop outside the bookshop. He flung his bike on the pavement and knocked insistently on the door until his knuckles hurt. The reason for his urgency was the call from Miss Quint. She had telephoned his house very early that morning, before any of the Goodenoughs were up, and had left a rambling, incoherent message on the answerphone. He had recognised her voice, high and hysterical though it had been, and he had heard her say his name and also the phrase 'We're in the soup'. As it was half-term week, Arthur was able to head straight over to Hardbattle Books without the worry that it would make him late for school.

He gave up knocking, and pushed the letter box open instead.

'Hello!' he yelled through the slender gap. 'Is anyone there? Miss Quint, can you hear me? Are you all right?'

Arthur heard a muffled exclamation and saw a familiar

floral pattern pass across his vision. He recognised it as the print of the dress that Miss Quint had been wearing the day before. There was the sound of a key turning in a lock. Arthur let go of the letter box flap and waited for the door to open.

'Miss Quint, you look strange,' he said. For a person who took pride in always dressing neatly, she had let her standards slip. She stood in the doorway, bleary-eyed. Her dress was creased, her hair was wild and on one side of her face there were tell-tale weals, which indicated that she had been resting it on something uncomfortable. Her appearance suggested to Arthur that she had not been to bed.

'Oh, Arthur!' said Miss Quint dramatically. She beckoned him inside. 'We're in bother.'

'What have you done now?' asked Arthur, lingering warily in the doorway. 'You haven't been making any more wishes –'

'No. Perish the thought!' Miss Quint said, shuddering. 'It's Mr Hardbattle. He's been in touch. He's coming home tomorrow, and from what he said in his postcard, I don't think the places he's seen have been much good.'

'What a bummer!' said Arthur.

'He's pinning his hopes on us,' yammered a panic-stricken Miss Quint, 'and we haven't got our act together and looked around that farm yet!'

Like Miss Quint, Arthur felt at fault. He had had no

choice but to go to school in the week, and on Saturday his schedule had been full (what with the visit to his granny's and the tea party), but Arthur knew, just as Miss Quint did, that Sunday had been free, and that they should have spent it checking out the farm at Thornwick instead of at the seaside having fun.

'We've been a bit stupid to leave it so late,' he said. 'But I don't really get why you phoned up in such a tizz. We've still got time to go to the farm.'

'You've forgotten about our other problem,' said Miss Quint. 'Our four other problems to be precise.'

'Oh, you mean the book characters.'

Miss Quint nodded and wrung her hands. 'Can you imagine what Mr Hardbattle will say when he finds out about Susan and the rest of them? I've been thinking that we might try to conceal them in the attic, but I can't see Mr Claggitt being cooperative. He's too outdoorsy to agree to being penned in.'

'Ah! It's all making sense now,' said Arthur. '*They're* the reason why you got in such a state and phoned my house mega-early this morning! You're scared of Mr Hardbattle finding out that you broke his rules.' Arthur heaved a sigh of relief, which turned into an enormous yawn. 'I don't understand why you're making such a fuss. All we've got to do is find their books and do some unwishing.'

'That's easy to say, young man, but not so easy to do,'

said Miss Quint. She pulled her fingers through her unkempt hair, giving herself a wiggly parting.

'Yeah, all right,' accepted Arthur, finally condescending to step inside the shop. 'It might take some doing to find those books, but it wasn't worth dragging me out of bed. I rode really fast to get here, and I haven't even had my breakfast yet. Mum was going to make pancakes. We hardly ever have those . . .'

Arthur stopped grumbling and gazed around the shop in amazement. It was in total disarray. Books had been tossed on the floor and wedged into places that they did not fit. They were no longer arranged in any logical order. It looked as if a whirlwind had swept through the shop, leaving a scene of devastation in its wake.

'Oh, Miss Quint!' said Arthur, turning on the spot with his mouth hanging open. His eyes rested on Trunk who seemed to be just as shocked as he was. The elephant stood at the nearest end of his shelf, immobile and blank-faced, with his trunk outstretched.

'This is *bad*,' said Arthur. 'Why didn't you say? The magic's really flipped out this time. It must have made one heck of a racket in the night. No wonder you look as if you haven't slept.'

'I haven't!' said Miss Quint. 'I've been awake for hours. You see, the magic didn't make this mess. I did.'

'You!' blustered Arthur, glaring at her angrily. 'What on earth for? Have you gone loony? It's lucky Mr

Hardbattle's not back yet. He'd have a fit if he knew what you'd done.'

'Don't tell him! You mustn't tell him!' pleaded Miss Quint. She sank on to the floor and started to snivel, groping up her sleeve for a handkerchief. 'I panicked!' she wailed. 'I've been looking for those blessed books all night long. They're not here, Arthur. I'm certain of it. I've searched *everywhere*. There isn't a nook or a cranny that I haven't poked around in. *Tinseltown Ticket*, *Champagne for Geraldine*, *Rockfall!* and *High Jinks* must all have been sold.'

'If we'd sold them we would have written their sales in the ledger,' pointed out Arthur.

'They must have been stolen, then,' Miss Quint said miserably.

'Stolen? No!' said Arthur, aghast. 'Borrowed, maybe.'

'Whatever's become of them, they've gone!' Miss Quint lamented. She screwed up her face and dissolved into tears. The sight of Miss Quint falling apart was far more alarming to Arthur than seeing the bookshop in a terrible mess.

'Don't cry!' he said, patting her shoulder awkwardly. He began to collect up some books from the floor. 'We'll have this place tidied up in no time, and things will sort themselves out. You'll see.'

Miss Quint sobbed a little louder. She did not show that she appreciated Arthur's attempts to comfort her.

Nor did she raise a finger to help him pick up the books. She seemed determined to sink into a mire of woe.

Trunk was still in a cataplectic state, standing as rigidly as a pointer dog that had just scented a pheasant.

'Why don't you have a word with poor old Trunk?' said Arthur. 'He's not looking well. He could do with some cheering up.'

Miss Quint shook her head and did not change her position. Fearing that she might stay slumped on the floor in a wretched heap for the remainder of the morning, Arthur made further suggestions to try to encourage her to get to her feet. 'Perhaps you'd feel better if you took a bath or changed your clothes or had something to eat,' he proffered brightly.

'I'm not hungry,' mumbled Miss Quint. 'After supper I ate a whole packet of chocolate biscuits.'

'Suit yourself!' said Arthur, his patience exhausted. He turned his back on her and stooped to retrieve some books from under a chair. There was only an hour and a half until the shop was due to open and he could not afford to waste any more time attempting to perk up Miss Quint.

Arthur tried to ignore his growling stomach and immersed himself in his back-breaking task. The magic did not assist him. In fact it made his job harder by changing the weight of the books so that they were either so heavy that he could barely lift them or so light that they kept floating out of his reach. If he lost his temper, the magic reacted by irritating him even more. He was dive-bombed by the ducks, assailed by the rubber bands and at one point, Arthur was rooted to the spot while two dozen drawing pins played tag around his feet. Gradually he learned that if he ignored the magic's tomfoolery, it was far more likely to leave him alone.

By a quarter to nine the shop was remarkably shipshape, and Arthur felt that he deserved a medal as well as a sit down and a cup of tea. As he looked about him, reflecting upon his achievement, he noticed that Miss Quint had gone. Avoiding the drawing pins, which had formed a circle and were whizzing anticlockwise at a mesmerising speed, he trod wearily up the staircase in search of some breakfast.

There was a smell of burnt toast coming from the kitchen. When Arthur went in, he found Jimmy, Mr Claggitt and Mrs Voysey-Brown seated at the table. They were grasping cutlery impatiently and Susan was scurrying between them with a plate of charred bread in her hand.

'Lightly toasted, I said, not singed!' grumbled Mr Claggitt, smearing his toast with great lumps of marmalade.

Jimmy laughed, took a slice and scraped off the worst of the burnt bits with a knife. 'Just like me ma used to make!' he said.

'I won't,' said Mrs Voysey-Brown when Susan held out the plate to her. 'Darling, I feel I should point out that catering is not your thing. Be an angel and open a window, would you? Before we all expire from the fumes.'

They were all delighted to see Arthur.

'Any good with a frying pan?' Mr Claggitt asked him. 'The Quint woman's deserted us, and Susie's efforts aren't up to much.'

Having spent the best part of an hour tidying the bookshop on his own, the last thing that Arthur wanted to do was to cook breakfast for everyone.

'How about some cereal?' he said, producing a box from a cupboard and filling a jug with milk from the fridge. He noticed Susan's downcast face and gave her a friendly nudge.

'Don't let them get to you, Suze,' Arthur whispered. 'You just need some practice, that's all.'

When breakfast was almost over and the remnants of the toast had been crunched up by Scallywag, Miss Quint appeared at the kitchen door. She had changed into her nightdress, and looked jaded and grey. 'You'll amuse yourselves, won't you?' she mumbled tiredly. 'I'm off to bed. I'm bushed.'

Leaving the others to mutter discontentedly, Arthur followed Miss Quint on to the landing and grabbed her arm. 'Who's going to open up the shop?' he asked.

Miss Quint focused her red-rimmed eyes on Arthur. 'Shan't be fit for anything till I've had some sleep,' she said. 'Shop'll have to stay closed. Can't be helped.'

Arthur groaned. Miss Quint's ill-timed nap meant that the shop would be unmanned *and* that their trip to the farmhouse would have to be postponed *again*. The excursion to Thornwick could be put off until the next morning, but losing a day's takings seemed a rash thing to do when every penny was so important.

'Where are the keys, Miss Quint?' Arthur asked suddenly. 'Me and Suze and Jimmy, maybe . . . we can look after the shop.'

Miss Quint led Arthur along the landing to the broom cupboard. Not wishing to sleep in the chair downstairs during daylight hours, she had transformed the cupboard into her bedroom. Three sofa cushions from the couch served as her mattress, and draped over these was a sleeping bag.

After a quick rummage in the pockets of her dress (which dangled from a hanger on the doorknob), Miss Quint found the shop keys and pressed them into Arthur's hands. 'Do whaddever you want,' she said thickly, and gestured that he should go.

Arthur unlocked the door at nine o'clock sharp and sat down at the desk, awaiting the first customer. The cash register occupied the left-hand side of the desk and next to it was the ledger in which every sale was recor-

124

ded. Lined up by an inkwell were the drawing pins, staples and assorted writing implements. Arthur picked up a pencil, intending to play noughts and crosses with himself, but the pencil would only write Latin words and phrases, so he swapped it for a crayon which was less intractable.

Susan felt purposeless without Miss Quint to follow around and when Arthur asked her if she would give him a hand in the shop, Susan said yes straight away. Showing gumption that she had not displayed before, she started to put some maps in numerical order. Arthur had hoped that the other three would help out too, but they revealed soon after breakfast that they had other plans.

Jimmy, Mr Claggitt and Mrs Voysey-Brown said that they were going to spend the day touring the sights of Plumford. Arthur considered this to be a bad idea. He hated the thought of the three book characters roaming the town unchaperoned, but there was very little that he could do to stop them. He argued that apart from a Saxon church and a bungalow, which had been the birthplace of a famous comedienne, there was nothing else of interest to visit. However, the three grown-ups would not be persuaded to change their minds.

Mr Claggitt wrenched open the door with a powerful tug, causing the bell to reverberate like an alarm. 'Best foot forward!' he said determinedly as if he were setting out on an expedition rather than a walk around a small English town.

'Goodbye!' called Arthur. 'Be careful, won't you? Don't get lost!'

Business was not brisk in the bookshop. By midday, Arthur had served one person, who had asked if the shop stocked washing machines. After lunch, Arthur was inspired to give the windows a wipe so that people passing by would be more likely to come in. This proved to be a successful ploy. Four customers entered the shop in the afternoon. One returned a book for a refund, one opted to purchase a book on trains, and the other two (a husband and wife) were scared away by a rug, which kept altering its pattern while they were looking for a book on stamps.

By closing time, Arthur had decided that a career in retail was not for him. He glared enviously when the three sightseers returned in buoyant mood. Mrs Voysey-Brown's neck was swathed in a new silk scarf and the two men were sporting gold-coloured wristwatches. It seemed that fictional money was accepted in Plumford's stores just as readily as the regular kind.

Miss Quint surfaced after nightfall, by which time Arthur had gone home and Susan had put herself to bed.

The next day, Arthur detected a change in Miss Quint. She was waiting at the door of the shop to let him in when he turned up at a quarter to nine. She welcomed him with her arms outstretched and Arthur retreated swiftly, not wishing to receive a hug. Only when the threat of an embrace had subsided did he feel that it was safe to draw closer.

'I'm sorry, Arthur!' Miss Quint said. 'I was a nitwit yesterday, wasn't I?'

'Not a nitwit, exactly,' said Arthur.

'I let you and Susan run the shop all by yourselves. A couple of youngsters!' she said. 'It wasn't right.'

With his hands stuffed in his pockets, Arthur leaned against the doorpost. 'We managed,' he said in a non-chalant way. 'We sold one book and a lady brought one back. There were holes in all the pages. Pin-sized holes.'

Miss Quint frowned. 'Those drawing pins are devils. I've half a mind to lock them away. There's an old tea caddy in the kitchen that would hold them –'

'Please don't!' said Arthur. 'They wouldn't like that. The magic was ever so well behaved yesterday, on the whole.'

'Oh, all right,' Miss Quint conceded. 'I promise I won't shut them up.' She gave his shoulder a friendly squeeze. 'I've been a prize ninny. I'll admit that. Fretting about the trouble I'll be in when Mr Hardbattle gets back from his travels! I should have remembered what a nice man he is. Not the sort to blow his top. Thank heavens I went to my meeting of the Women's Institute last night. They set me straight. Gave me a good talking to.'

'You told your friends about the shop?' asked Arthur. He stopped leaning against the doorframe and stood up straight. 'You explained about the magic? And they believed you?'

'I mentioned bits and pieces,' Miss Quint told him.

When Arthur had tried to tell his friends at school about the magic, they had laughed in his face and said that he was being daft.

'And they didn't think you were nuts?' he asked.

'Naturally not,' replied Miss Quint. 'They were very supportive, in fact.'

Precisely what had been said at the meeting was never disclosed because at that moment Susan appeared at Miss Quint's shoulder, holding a cardboard box in her arms and Scallywag on a lead.

'Ah, there you are!' Miss Quint said. She chivvied the children and dog out of the shop and on to the pavement.

'What's in the box?' asked Arthur.

'Books, of course,' replied Miss Quint. She felt in her pocket for the door key. 'They need to be delivered to a house in Rabbit's Cross. I thought it'd be nice if we all went, and on the way back we paid a visit to a friend in the countryside –'

'Mrs Carruthers at Down-the-Ages Farm!' cried Arthur.

Miss Quint winked at Arthur, and Arthur winked back.

Susan, who was standing between the pair of them, realised that something had happened which she had not understood. 'Why did you and Arthur twitch your eyes like that?' she asked.

'It's because we know a secret,' said Miss Quint as she slotted the key in the lock.

'Can't we tell her?' Arthur begged.

Miss Quint raised her eyebrows at Arthur, and turned to give Susan a long, hard look. 'As you're a good girl, and not the type to tittle-tattle, Arthur and I will tell you all about it on the way.'

Overjoyed, Susan skipped on the spot. 'Ooh! Thank you! I won't spill the beans. That's a promise, truly it is!'

Arthur chuckled to himself. He felt glad. By now, he considered Susan to be a friend, and it seemed unfair to keep the rehoming of the magic a secret from her. As long as Susan did not learn that the magic had been responsible for bringing her to life, he did not think that involving her in their project would be an ill-advised thing.

Letting his gaze wander from Susan's flushed, excited face, Arthur glanced to his left, and his smile faded rapidly.

'Miss Quint,' he asked in a puzzled voice, 'where's the van?'

'Right there in the road where I parked it,' replied Miss Quint, twisting the door key with a flourish and dropping it into her pocket.

'Um . . . I think you'll find it's *not*,' said Arthur.

Annoyed at having her word doubted, Miss Quint looked up. She gaped with shock when she saw the empty portion of road next to the kerb.

'Oh my giddy goodness!' she exclaimed. 'It's been pinched!'

Chapter Thirteen

Ups and Downs

'Mr Hardbattle worships that van!' Miss Quint said. She clapped her hand to her mouth in dismay and spoke through her fingers. 'He'll blame me. He will! He'll spread it around that I'm useless. He'll kick me out and no one else will want to employ me. If Mirabel won't have me back, I'll be destitute!'

Arthur shook her elbow. 'Miss Quint, you're getting all gloomy again. A minute ago you were saying how nice and kind Mr Hardbattle is. It's not your fault the van's been stolen.'

Susan set down the box of books on the pavement, and knelt beside Scallywag to give her a pat. 'Gosh!' she said. 'What rotten luck! We shan't be going to see your friend at Down-the-Ages Farm, now, shall we?'

Arthur smiled at her sadly. 'Not unless we all sprout wings and fly there, we won't,' he said.

'Like pigeons?' said Susan. 'Golly, wouldn't that be fun? I wish I did have wings. I wish . . .'

Almost before the words had left her mouth, Susan bent one arm behind her back and began to scratch her shoulder blades. 'Ooh! I think I've been bitten by something. I can feel lumps,' she said.

'No, it couldn't happen,' said Arthur. 'We're out of the shop. You've locked the door.' He grimaced at Miss Quint and she glared angrily back at him.

'Why did you have to put that idea in her head?' scolded Miss Quint as she peered at Susan's back. Two knob-like growths had burst through the yoke of Susan's dress.

'Me?' said Arthur. 'What about you? Why didn't you tell her she mustn't wish?'

They stared at each other obstinately and then, without saying a word, they seemed to accept that awarding blame would not achieve anything.

'How do you think it could have happened?' asked Miss Quint. 'Did the magic squirm through the keyhole?'

'Perhaps it was in the drainpipe,' said Arthur, 'or maybe you wafted a cloud of magic outside when you closed the door.'

Susan stood up. She twisted her neck as far as it would go in order to see the peculiar bony stems that were protruding from her back. They grew thicker and longer, with threads swelling along them like teeth on a comb. 'What are those horrid things?' she asked, biting her lip and blinking back tears. 'Ooh, they hurt like billy-o. Take them off!'

'They're wings, dear,' Miss Quint said as the slim, pale threads blossomed into tawny feathers. Scallywag backed away from Susan, barking huskily.

The wings grew at a staggering pace, and in no time they were beautifully curved and fully formed. Each wing was huge, easily matching Susan's height. The feathers were the same shade of brown as her hair, and not unlike an eagle's.

'You wished for them,' explained Arthur to Susan. 'Say you've changed your mind. Unwish them quickly, Suze, before they fly away with you.'

'T-take them off me!' begged Susan as the wings flexed and began to flap. They displaced so much air that Arthur was nearly knocked off his feet.

Susan was frightened. She gulped and sniffed while tears began to stream down her cheeks. Arthur and Miss Quint had to shout to make themselves heard above the rasping, rhythmic wing beats. They unwished as earnestly as they could, but it did not appear to have any effect. Nevertheless, they kept trying.

The wings flapped harder. Susan gave a high-pitched scream as both feet lifted off the pavement. Jerking her roughly with every beat, the wings took her higher. Her heel clipped the top of a postbox and she tried to catch hold of a lamp post. Moments later her toes loosened some roof tiles and then there was nothing above her but sky.

'Stop unwishing!' yelled Arthur, clutching Miss Quint's arm and gazing above him at Susan's shrinking figure. 'She's too far up. If we unwish her wings now she'll never survive the drop!'

They watched in helpless wonder as the great brown wings carried Susan in her gingham dress and sandalled feet over the rooftops of Plumford and out of sight.

'We'll have to go after her,' said Arthur, his face taut with worry. 'Do you think we should wish for wings too?'

'No,' Miss Quint said firmly. 'We'll go on the bus.'

Miss Quint unfastened her handbag and after delving deeply, she drew out a crumpled bus timetable and consulted it. 'Aha!' she said. 'The 48A stops at Thornwick. Down-the-Ages Farm is on the outskirts of the village and that's where the wings will have taken her.'

The bus was not due at the stop at the end of the road for seven minutes so Arthur judged that there would be time to run inside the shop and tell the others where he, Miss Quint and Susan would be for the rest of the morning. However, on reaching the first floor, he found the kitchen empty. Too well-mannered to wake them up, Arthur scribbled a message on the back of an envelope and propped it against the bread bin. He thought about calling the police to report the stolen van, but decided that it might cause too much of a delay. Catching the bus to Thornwick was what mattered most of all. A missing van was a trifling crime when compared with the abduction of Susan.

Miss Quint paid the bus fare (she had been to the bank and refilled her purse). They chose a seat on the top deck so that they would have a better chance of catching sight of Susan in the sky. Scallywag whined until Arthur pulled her on to his lap. The ride was a bumpy one, but neither Miss Quint nor Arthur complained. They were of the opinion that their journey must be arguably more comfortable than Susan's.

In actual fact, once Susan had recovered from the shock of her own pair of wings transporting her into the atmosphere, she stopped crying and started to enjoy herself. Having no tail feathers (for she had not wished for those) meant that the flight was not smooth, but her wings did their best to keep her the right way up and swooped to avoid wisps of cloud, which were cold and clammy, and soared when they found an amenable current of air. It was freezing cold in the sky and the wind's gusts pummelled her and filled her ears with noise, but Susan had never felt more alive, and when she summoned the courage to look below her, the view of all the fields and lakes and houses reduced to geometric shapes and bold, stark colours made her eyes swim with tears of delight. Flying, she decided, was not so very different from riding on a swing, only there were no chains and no plastic seat, and the distance from the ground was rather more awe-inspiring.

Susan's fear returned when she began to lose height. As the wings took her downwards, the minuscule features of the landscape grew larger and more recognisable, and she started to dwell upon the perilous manner in which she was hanging in the sky and the scary realisation that she would soon be landing.

With a stomach-turning dive and a flurry of wing beats, Susan's wings conveyed her to the ground. They avoided a flock of sheep, an oak tree and a roof of thatch, but it was not a textbook landing, by any means. As her toes touched down, Susan panicked, tripped and tumbled head over heels. Fortunately for her pride, there was no one nearby to witness her clumsiness. Susan lay still for a moment and caught her breath, then she patted herself all over and was relieved to find that all her limbs were intact.

When Susan got up from the patch of grass, her wings folded against her back. She looked about her curiously to see where she had arrived.

Not far away was a large, white, timber-framed building, which had a plump, thatched roof and tiny windows, and closer still was a giant tree with a sturdy trunk and tapering branches, partly obscured by clusters of frilly light green leaves.

Susan decided to head for the house. It stood to reason that where there was a building there would be people and if Susan was to find out where she had landed and how she could get home again, she would need to ask someone for help. Susan guessed that she could not rely on the wings to return her to Meadow Street. Although they were joined to her body, they moved of their own accord, and she could not be sure that they would do as she asked.

Encumbered by her huge wings, Susan made her way across the field, through a gate and into a cottage garden. She walked along a dirt path, past beds of unruly plants, until she reached a wooden door, which was ajar. Susan had to open it wide before she could squeeze herself and her wings through the narrow entranceway.

Inside she found a dark, low-ceilinged room with a flagstone floor. There was a bench, a table, a fireplace and not much else. The lack of possessions made Susan think that the people who lived in the house must be poor. She was just about to call out and ask if anyone was home, when a tall, bearded man ducked under a door-jamb and took a few paces into the room. He froze when he saw Susan and consulted his watch.

'You're early!' he said. 'Make yourself scarce, kid, and come back in half an hour, OK?'

Susan was too astonished to move. She did not understand why this man had been expecting her. Could he have mistaken her for someone else?

'Kid? What kid?' called another voice. 'Dave! Them goats got loose again, or what?' At first all that Susan saw was a linen cap. Then a woman in a brown dress bustled into view.

'Gawd!' she said when she clapped eyes on Susan. 'Where'd you spring from? It can't be ten o'clock!'

'It's not,' said Dave, sitting down on the bench, 'so, please, Lind, don't pester me to show this little girl around.' He swung his long legs up on to the table and crossed his ankles.

'But, Dave –' said the woman, shooting Susan a regretful look.

With a shrug, Dave reached inside his tawny jerkin, pulled out a newspaper and opened it up. 'Listen, just because that nutcase, Gary, decides to let someone in early, it doesn't mean we've got to start work, all right?'

Dismayed by the couple's less than friendly welcome, Susan clasped and unclasped her hands. 'I'll go, shall I?' she asked.

'No, don't be silly!' Lind took Susan's hand. With a nod of her head, she gestured towards Dave, whose face was obscured by his newspaper. 'Don't you pay any mind to that old grump! Come on, hon, I'll show you round the farm.'

'This is a farm?' cried Susan. 'Golly! Do you mean to say that this is *Down-the-Ages* Farm?'

138

Lind led Susan towards the door. 'Well, course, it is, babe!' she said. 'Don't you know where you've been brought?'

As they stepped outside, swapping the dimly lit room for bright sunshine, Lind noticed Susan's wings for the first time. 'Cor!' she said. 'They're smart. My little niece has got a pair too.'

Susan was amazed to hear that someone else had wings. 'I thought I was the only one,' she said.

'Nope, wings are popular with little girls,' Lind told her. 'Emily's are pink with sparkly glitter on. She's got a tiara to match and a wand. Wears them all the time. Even to the dentist's.'

'Really?' said Susan, suddenly feeling less self-conscious.

They walked a little way before pausing by a clump of mint where the path divided into two.

'Right,' said Lind, squeezing Susan's hand. 'What do you fancy first, hon? Being pulled on a cart by a draught horse or having a go at making some cheese?'

Chapter fourteen

A Stinging Attack

Susan's tour of Down-the-Ages Farm lasted for half an hour, and by the end of it she found that she had learned a lot. She knew, for instance, that Lind was short for Lindsey. She also knew that Dave and Lind did not live on the farm and were not husband and wife, as Susan had supposed. The farm was a museum. It was owned by a man called Dr Godfrey Webb and had been opened to demonstrate to its visitors what life on a farm had been like down the ages (hence the farm's name). Lind and Dave were employed by Dr Webb to impersonate a couple from centuries past, and they spent their working week showing members of the public around the various rooms or 'time zones' in the farmhouse. The hall was medieval, the kitchen late Tudor, and upstairs was mainly Victorian. The museum was open six days a week between the hours of ten and four, teas were served in the granary, and dogs were allowed on leads.

For the whole of Susan's tour, she was the museum's

only visitor. She walked two thirds of the site with Lind, stopping at the cattle shed which housed two oxen, the pigsty where four Tamworths rooted in their troughs, the stables where the draught horses lived and the dairy where butter and cheese were made. At ten o'clock, Gary, who sat in a shed at the museum's entrance, opened the shutters and let the visitors in. Muttering her apologies, Lind went back to the farmhouse and Susan continued the walk around the farmstead on her own.

She liked the goats, but was fonder of the sheep and spent a good long while watching the lambs wriggling their tails and leaping about in a madcap manner. It was the bees, however, that Susan liked the best.

The bee-keeper, whose name was Pam, told Susan that the bees' cone-shaped homes were called skeps and that bees knew when bad weather was coming and that bees would only sting you if you made them cross.

Pam asked Susan about her wings and when Susan told her how they had grown, she did not seem surprised. 'I thought as much,' Pam said. 'It doesn't do to make wishes in the wrong sort of places. I know that to my cost. When I was ten, I wished for chocolate fingers and I think you can guess what happened . . .'

Apart from Susan, the only visitors to Down-the-Ages Farm were two families with children and an old, white-haired couple with a rotund dog. None of the adults, apart from Lind and Pam, made any remarks about

Susan's wings, although she did get the feeling, from time to time, that alarmed looks were being cast in her direction. Without exception the children found the wings deeply fascinating, and one small boy called Jarrett thought that he had the right to tug at them and to yank out the longest, most lustrous feathers.

'You're being a pest,' Susan hissed at him. 'Go away, little boy!'

It seemed that Jarrett was not only a nuisance to Susan. All around the farmstead she heard his mother shouting, 'Jarrett, don't touch that!' and 'Jarrett, get down! You'll hurt yourself!' and 'Jarrett, I won't tell you again!' except, of course, she did because Jarrett was a boy who did exactly what he wanted and never took any notice of what his mother said.

When Susan had seen everything, she decided to seek out Lind and ask her how she might get home. On her way to the farmhouse, Susan passed the granary and wished that she had some money to spend on a cup of tea and a bun.

Then, for the second time that day, her wish came true.

'There she is!' shrieked a voice, and Susan looked across the field to see Miss Quint waving her hands and Arthur and Scallywag racing towards her along a dirt track. Scallywag reached Susan first, but Arthur was not far behind.

142

'You all right?' asked Arthur.

Beaming, Susan said, 'Yes, thanks. Golly, I'm glad to see you! How did you get here without the van?'

'We . . . took . . . a bus,' said Miss Quint, who was slightly out of breath, not being quite as fit as her companions. She kissed Susan's cheek, and glanced around impatiently. 'Where's this teashop, then? The man at the entrance told us about it. I think we all deserve a sit down and a bite to eat.'

Over three pots of tea and an equal number of Swiss buns, Susan told the others about her flight and all that she had seen and heard at Down-the-Ages Farm. When she had finished, it was the turn of Arthur and Miss Quint to speak. They described their journey by bus and admitted the reason why they had wanted to visit the farm in the first place.

It was explained to Susan what magic was and that the magic in the bookshop needed to be moved elsewhere. They managed this in the time that it took for Susan to eat her bun, and while she licked the icing off her fingers they told her of the advert, Mr Hardbattle's trip and the letter from Mrs Carruthers. Susan was a trusting, impressionable girl, and believed every word that she had been told. She liked the idea of going on a quest.

'Can we find Mrs Carruthers *now*?' asked Susan, taking one last sip from her teacup and rising out of her chair.

'Yeah, let's go!' said Arthur, following Susan's lead. 'I don't reckon it'll be too hard to track her down.'

They made the decision to split into two groups and reconvene twenty minutes later on a bench beside the hen coop. Arthur agreed to comb the fields with Scallywag and Miss Quint said that she and Susan would make enquiries in the farmhouse and the stables. When the time came to meet up on the bench, acute disappointment was etched on all their faces.

'I suppose this woman does exist,' said Miss Quint, taking off her shoes and massaging her feet.

'They only know each other's *first* names,' grumbled Arthur. 'It's going to be tougher to find her than I thought.'

They sat on the bench in dejected silence, watching the chickens, which were scratching in the earth, then a shout rang out across the farmstead.

'Help me, someone! Jarrett's gone missing!'

Arthur, Miss Quint and Susan rushed to help Jarrett's mother at once, and the other family, the couple with the dog, and Pam, Lind and Dave, who had all been within earshot, sped to offer their assistance too.

It emerged that Jarrett's mother was of the opinion that her son had been kidnapped, but this was poohpoohed by the rest of the group, who had seen enough of Jarrett to be sure that no one in their right minds would want to go anywhere near the boy.

'Let's spread out and look for him,' suggested Pam. 'We've got fifty acres to cover so we'll have to be as quick as we can. He's only five years old. He could be in danger.'

'I don't know why I'm botherin' to help out,' muttered Dave, striding towards the cattle shed. 'Ruddy little tyke put chewing gum in my beard.'

As the group scattered, Susan remained where she was. She had had an ingenious thought and, as luck would have it, her wings had come up with the exact same one. The best way to track down Jarrett in the fastest possible time was to carry out a search by air.

Susan's wings unfolded and shook themselves, and she braced herself to withstand the pull on her shoulder blades, which would come with every beat the wings made. The wings began to flap, stretching higher and wider until they had reached the required speed to lift Susan off the ground. None of the search party saw her take to the sky because they were far too busy looking in feeding troughs and behind hay bales for the missing boy.

When the wings judged that Susan had risen to a sufficient height, they started to sweep through the air in a wide circle over the farmland.

She saw Arthur moving towards the sheep pen with Scallywag at his heels and other human shapes that she could not identify, all haring from one place to the next like worker ants. She picked out the stables and the farmhouse, and then in the furthest corner of the plot she saw who she was looking for.

Jarrett was standing by the beehives, striking at the air with his fists, and as the wings swooped to carry her lower, Susan could hear his yells and squeals. She recalled Pam's advice: that bees were placid creatures unless you made them cross. Over the course of the morning, Jarrett had annoyed almost everyone at the farm and now it seemed as if he had met his match.

Before she could worry about the likelihood that she would be stung, the wings had plunged her through a cloud of buzzing dots. Susan stretched out her arms and grabbed the tormented boy and then the wings flapped hard, driving the bees away and taking Susan and Jarrett up into the clear, cold air, which was free from angry bees and their painful stings.

Holding on to Jarrett was not easy or pleasant. True to form, he was uncooperative; pinching and kicking Susan and shouting for his mum. Eventually, the horror of being high up stopped Jarrett from squirming and his roars quietened to a murmur.

Sensibly, the wings brought them to earth again within minutes. The landing was chaotic. Both children ended up lying on the ground with their limbs inelegantly splayed. Susan got to her feet first and seized Jarrett's hand so that he could not run off and get into further mischief.

They had landed behind a barn, which was used to store farm machinery. Susan walked around it, struggling to keep hold of Jarrett, who was straining to get away.

She spied Dave in the distance and waved to get his attention. Soon the others arrived, having received the message that Jarrett had been found. Jarrett's mother smothered him in kisses and cried over the smattering of red marks on her son's arms, which showed where the bees had vented their displeasure. She complained to Pam the bee-keeper and was given short shrift.

'My bees aren't bad-tempered,' insisted Pam. 'They must have been provoked.' She took hold of Jarrett's hand. 'You come along with me, young man, and I'll put ointment on those stings, and maybe this little encounter will teach you to keep your hands to yourself in future, eh?'

Not receiving the sympathy that Jarrett felt was due to him, he thrust an accusing finger at Susan.

'That girl grabbed me and hurt my arms. Then she flew me up into the sky. If she'd dropped me I would've gone splat.' Jarrett ended with a feeble attempt at a sob.

No one believed his claim (except Arthur, Miss Quint and Pam, who stayed silent). The old couple shook their heads and muttered a rhyme about telltales and dicky birds, and Dave lifted his lip in a sort of snarl. Lind glared and pushed up her sleeves, and a couple of children sniggered.

'That's naughty!' said Jarrett's mother, turning on her son. 'Well . . . all the other things you did today were naughty, but lying about this lovely girl who saved you from those bees is really, extremely naughty, Jarrett, and Mummy isn't pleased with you.'

Jarrett scowled and kicked a tuft of grass with the toe of his trainer. As he was led away between Pam and his mum, he turned his head and put out his tongue at Susan.

'Do it back to him!' urged Arthur; so Susan did.

Later, when Pam sought them out to thank Susan for stopping Jarrett from being stung all over and for preventing the farm's owner, Dr Webb, from being sued, she assumed that Miss Quint was the mother of Arthur and Susan.

'Your youngsters are a credit to you,' said Pam, seizing Miss Quint's hand. 'I'm Pam . . . Pam Carruthers, by the way.'

'Mrs Carruthers! You're Mrs Carruthers? Woo-hoo! We've finally found you!' Arthur was so excited that he turned a cartwheel – badly – almost kicking Susan in the face.

Pam was somewhat startled. 'You've been looking for *me*?' she asked.

'Almost all morning!' said a beaming Miss Quint. Their handshake became more vigorous. 'We're friends of Mr Hardbattle, the owner of Hardbattle Books.'

At the mention of Mr Hardbattle's name, Pam's expression changed to one of elated surprise. 'Good gracious!' she said. 'The advert in *Farmers Weekly*! I should've guessed you were something to do with the bookshop when I met Susan! It's not every day you bump into a girl with magic wings!'

When all had been revealed, and Pam and Miss Quint had stopped laughing at Arthur's remark that their handshake might qualify as the longest one in history, Pam led them to a patch of woodland, which was out of bounds to the public. In a clearing in the middle of the spinney was a one-storey cabin where a woodsman had once lived. Dr Webb had had the idea to include the cottage in the tour of the farm, but it had been pointed out to him that lots of visitors traipsing through the spinney would upset the woodland creatures, and Dr Webb's idea, along with the planned renovation of the cottage, had been scrapped.

'What do you think of it?' asked Pam with a grin.

The woodsman's cottage was small, but its roof was in good repair and its unglazed windows had shutters to keep out the wind and the rain. There was a well behind the cottage and an outhouse, and a garden overwhelmed by weeds.

'Ooh! Isn't it dark?' said Susan when Pam pushed open the door and everyone trooped inside.

Arthur and Miss Quint made favourable comments as

they walked from one room to the next. Not having realised that they were looking for somewhere rundown, Susan was surprised to hear them rejoicing over the size of the spiders and laughing when a rickety old bedstead collapsed.

Their voices became livelier with every minute that passed and when they had completed their tour of the cottage and emerged into the sunshine again, Arthur and Miss Quint could not contain their jubilation.

'Talk about grotty!' said Arthur. 'That cottage was really dusty and there were hundreds of crawly things!'

'Quite unfit for human habitation,' said Miss Quint. She turned to Pam and hugged her. 'We're agreed: it's *perfect*!'

When possible dates for transferring the magic had been discussed, Pam borrowed the horse-drawn cart and took them to the bus stop, where they hopped on the express bus back to Plumford, which ran every hour. Sitting was uncomfortable for Susan so she stood in the gangway and clung on to a pole. She was envious of Arthur and Miss Quint. They had bagged a seat together and were talking about the cottage and the look of joy that was bound to appear on Mr Hardbattle's face when they revealed to him their marvellous news. Susan had to endure being stared at by all the other passengers. She was relieved when the bus reached the stop outside the toy store, which was only a short walk from Hardbattle Books.

'As soon as we get in, we'll unwish those dratted wings,' Miss Quint promised Susan as they stepped off the bus. 'The magic's been left to its own devices for the whole morning so it should be in a receptive mood.'

'I'll be jolly glad to be rid of them,' said Susan. She dragged her feet tiredly as she walked beside Miss Quint, 'but I feel very lucky to have had the chance to fly. It frightened me out of my wits, but it was grand all the same.'

Arthur was walking slightly ahead of the others because Scallywag had sensed that she was nearing home and had started to pull on the lead. 'I think you were very brave today,' Arthur told Susan over his shoulder.

'Do you?' said Susan. Her cheeks reddened. 'Gosh!'

'After we've unwished the wings, I suppose we'd better ring the police and tell them about Mr Hardbattle's van being stolen,' said Arthur, walking backwards for a few paces.

Miss Quint let out a groan. She had forgotten about the van. She had been on a high ever since she and Arthur had solved the problem of where to relocate the magic, and had even convinced herself that Mr Hardbattle might be persuaded to overlook the fact that wishes had been made in the shop, contrary to his instructions. Knowing how much Mr Hardbattle loved

his van, Miss Quint realised that no amount of good
news could make up for its disappearance. She was about
to agree with Arthur that the police should be called
when they turned into Meadow Street and saw a familiar
bottle green van parked outside the bookshop.

'Well, I never!' declared Miss Quint. 'The thieves
have brought it back!'

Chapter fifteen

Laying Down the Law

The van had a scratch on its bonnet, a dented hubcap and a muddy bumper. Miss Quint was appalled at these discoveries because she knew how highly Mr Hardbattle prized his vintage delivery vehicle. She guessed that it would take a great deal of detective work to find out the identity of the lowlife who had taken the van, but she turned out to be wrong. The culprits – there were three of them – owned up to the crime immediately without showing any remorse at all.

'But you're not insured, you don't know how to handle her and, more importantly, you didn't ask!' railed Miss Quint, her nose put out of joint.

The three law-breakers took no notice of her and continued with their card game. They had drawn up some chairs and were playing whist at Arthur's homework table.

'Which are trumps, again?' Mr Claggitt asked his companions.

'Clubs,' said Jimmy, fanning the cards in his hand.

Miss Quint reached between the two men and snatched up the keys to the van, which she had spied on the table soon after she had set foot in the shop.

'It's tantamount to stealing,' she told them sternly.

Mr Claggitt stopped examining his cards to give Miss Quint a cursory glance. 'Nonsense, woman!' he said. 'We only borrowed it!'

'Borrowing implies that you gained my permission, which you most certainly *did not*,' Miss Quint said. She broke off from giving them an irritated stare and stepped aside to let Arthur pass through the doorway and into the street. He had been instructed to fetch a sponge and bucket of water from the kitchen and to do what he could to restore the shiny appearance of the van's front bumper.

'Blimey, Missus!' said Jimmy, sorting his cards into suits. 'It ain't worth getting your pants in a twist! We brought your van back, didn't we?'

'You did, but not in the same condition,' Miss Quint pointed out, 'and, for your information, the van isn't mine. It belongs to Mr Hardbattle: the man who owns this shop.'

'All this palaver, and it ain't even hers!' Jimmy murmured to his friends, rudely rolling his eyes.

It was obvious from their behaviour that they did not believe that they had done anything wrong and were only too willing to forget the whole affair, but Miss Quint refused to be sidelined and would not let the matter rest. She insisted that the house guests should come clean and admit to her why they had taken the van.

'Claggitt here rose early and suggested that we should drive into the country,' said Mrs Voysey-Brown in her trademark drawl. A smile thinned her lips at the remembrance of their adventure. 'It was such fun being out and about when everyone else was tucked up in bed!'

'It's habit,' Mr Claggitt said. 'A good mountaineer's always up before sunrise. Finest part of the day.'

'But what did you *do*?' asked Miss Quint.

Mr Claggitt grunted. 'Stretched our legs. Looked at the scenery.'

'Had a shufti round some stately homes,' Jimmy said.

'And now we'd like to be left alone to get on with our game,' said Mrs Voysey-Brown, glaring coldly at Miss Quint, 'so why don't you stop being such a frightful bore and make us something to eat?'

The trio began their card game, and Miss Quint's fighting spirit faded. 'You're not to take it again,' she told them, pocketing the keys. 'Mr Hardbattle's due to arrive home this evening, and I want him to find his van exactly where he left it!'

Cheerfully swinging an empty bucket, Arthur re-entered the shop. He had scrubbed the front bumper of the van until it gleamed. When he had come to pour the dirty water down the drain, he had seen a glittering object in the gutter and picked it up.

'Anyone lost a piece of jewellery?' Arthur asked. He unfurled his fingers to show them his find. The brooch was in a bow shape, and set with round white gems.

'Ooh!' exclaimed Susan. 'Isn't it pretty!'

'Are those diamonds?' asked Miss Quint. She bent to get a closer look, but before she could examine the brooch, a hand shot out and grabbed it.

'It's mine!' said Mrs Voysey-Brown, and pinned it to her dress.

The card game continued until, crowing triumphantly, Jimmy took the final trick. He asked if anyone else wanted to join in the next game, and Arthur, who liked to play cards at school during break, told Jimmy to deal him in. He enjoyed playing whist, but was less enamoured with the game of fifty-two-card pick-up, which involved Jimmy throwing the whole deck of cards up in the air and telling Arthur to get down on the floor and pick them up. When they had first met, Arthur had thought that Jimmy was funny, but after enduring his pranks and jibes for three straight days, Arthur had begun to tire of him.

While Arthur played cards, Miss Quint escorted Susan to the kitchen, where she checked the child's skin for bee stings. Finding only one, Miss Quint daubed the sore spot on Susan's knee with cool, white cream. Then she progressed to the much more difficult task of unwishing Susan's wings. She guessed that they would have a greater chance of success if they concentrated their efforts in the areas of the bookshop where the largest, smelliest clusters of magic were to be found.

For their first attempt to get rid of the wings, Miss Quint elected to stand Susan in the bath, where magic could always be counted upon to make a nuisance of itself (pulling out the plug when someone was having a soak was a favourite prank). Despite their best efforts, unwishing the wings in the bath did not work so Susan and Miss Quint moved on to the pantry and afterwards to a corner of the landing which smelt particularly rank. They also tried to get into the attic, but found that it was padlocked.

It was only a matter of time before the magic began to interfere in the card games downstairs. Just as Arthur was about to put down an ace that would have won him the game, the ace changed itself into a two, and later when he had collected three queens, they skipped across the table and plunged back into the pack. Soon afterwards, Arthur lost interest in playing and went in search of Susan. He found her leaning against the couch on the landing, both wings still attached.

'I thought you were going to unwish those,' said Arthur, flopping down next to her. (Miss Quint had replaced the couch's seat cushions, fortunately.)

'We tried,' said Susan. 'We both did our darnedest.'

'Given up, have you?' said Arthur. 'Where's Miss Quint now?'

Susan flapped a hand in the direction of the kitchen. 'She's busy making sandwiches for Mrs V-B and the rest of them. She said that they didn't deserve to be fed and shouted at me when I tried to help.'

'Don't take it personally,' said Arthur to Susan. 'It's not you she's cross with, it's that selfish bunch downstairs.'

Stroking the ribbon on one of her plaits between her forefinger and thumb, Susan nodded solemnly. 'They're in her bad books because they went off in the van,' she said.

'Yes,' agreed Arthur, 'and she hasn't got much patience today what with Mr Hardbattle coming home soon.' He stared at Susan's wings and frowned. 'It's going to be awkward enough to tell him about his four extra house guests. Those wings of yours will be even more of a problem to explain. Let's try to get rid of them, shall we?'

Arthur was inspired to stand Susan on the stair that turned to custard from time to time, and it was here that the magic finally yielded to their demands and took away the wings. It was a long, drawn-out process, each wing vanishing a feather at a time. When her ordeal was over, Susan was left with gaping holes in the back of her dress, so they sought out Miss Quint, who fetched her needle and thread and sewed them up. She did the best job that she could, but the stitches looked untidy and they wrinkled the material. Miss Quint promised that after their meal, she and Susan would go to a thrift shop to choose Susan some new clothes.

'What time did Mr Hardbattle say he'd be home?' asked Arthur.

Miss Quint did not seem pleased to be reminded. 'His postcard said in the evening,' she said. Then she pulled Arthur to one side, and lowered her voice. 'I've been thinking, Arthur . . . I'm going to tell him that Susan is my niece, and the other lot are friends of mine from out of town.'

Arthur did not like the idea of lying to Mr Hardbattle. 'Couldn't we just tell him the truth? OK, he'll be annoyed when he realises that we've broken his rules, but when he sees the fine place we've found for the magic, he's bound to forgive us.'

Miss Quint was sceptical of Arthur's plan. 'We'll see,' she said uncertainly, 'but whatever we tell him, that little trio will have to improve their manners. Mr Hardbattle won't let them stay if they act all high and mighty.'

Having missed out on lunch, they had an early tea at half past three, which was eaten in a tense, strained atmosphere. When the last morsel had been consumed, Miss Quint asked for everyone's attention and unfolded a list of dos and don'ts that she had compiled after her conversation with Arthur.

'Just lately,' she told them, eyeing the adults stonily, 'I have noticed that certain members of the household have been getting rather above themselves. You may be staying as guests here, but that does not give you licence to ride roughshod over everyone else and do whatever you want.'

There was an uncomfortable silence. A bulging vein pulsed on Mr Claggitt's forehead. Next to him, Mrs Voysey-Brown inspected her nails. Further down the table, between Arthur and Susan, Jimmy attempted to balance a teaspoon on the rim of his cup, giving the impression that he was not listening.

'I've drawn up a list of rules,' Miss Quint said, 'which I will pin to the cupboard above the sink. It would be in your best interests to read them. You've had it easy for far too long. From now on, I'll expect you to help with the cooking and washing-up, and the making of the beds, and on no occasion will you be permitted to get behind the wheel of Mr Hardbattle's van.'

Miss Quint's announcement was greeted with several murderous looks. Then Mr Claggitt stood up. Muttering under his breath, he began to clear the table, scooping up armfuls of crockery and dumping them in the sink. He turned on the taps, and water poured from them in gleaming rods. Miss Quint's apron would not fit round his middle and the rubber gloves split as soon as he tried to put them on.

'Here's a tea towel for each of you,' Miss Quint said, handing a linen cloth to Jimmy and Mrs Voysey-Brown. Jimmy grinned and draped his round his shoulders like a cape, but Mrs Voysey-Brown was more reluctant and would only handle her towel with the tips of one finger and thumb.

Leaving them to their chore, Miss Quint led Arthur and Susan downstairs. The children were a little in awe of Miss Quint after her showdown with the three grown-ups, and hardly dared to open their mouths.

'What's up with you two? Cat got your tongues?' Miss Quint said when they reached the shop floor.

They both shook their heads and Susan giggled nervously.

'That was some talking-to you gave them,' said Arthur.

Miss Quint seemed flattered by Arthur's remark. She smiled self-righteously and primped her hair so that it curled neatly against the collar of her blouse. 'Yes,' she said. 'It went pretty well, I thought. It was high time I stopped pandering to those idlers and told them what was what.'

She walked to the door and unlocked it, then turned over the sign, which told the public that they were open.

Susan followed behind her as if she were Miss Quint's

second shadow and, when she had got up the nerve, she tugged on the woman's sleeve.

'Miss Quint,' she said, 'might we go shopping for my new outfit now?'

'Yes, I think so,' said Miss Quint. She glanced around the shop to check that it was tidy enough for customers to be able to browse with ease. 'Will you be all right on your own, Arthur?' she asked. 'We won't be more than an hour.'

Arthur assured them that he was perfectly capable of managing without them, and Scallywag banged her tail against a table leg to communicate that she would be on hand should her canine skills be required.

Arthur found that he was quite keen to be left in the bookshop on his own. It gave him a feeling of importance. At home he was the third of six children and he had siblings who were funnier, smarter and cuter than him. At school he felt even more ordinary. In a class of thirty-one, there was nothing about his average grades or his modest sporting talent to make him stand out. However, in Hardbattle Books on this particular afternoon, Arthur was solely in charge. It was possible, in the space of an hour, that a customer might come in and if they had a question, Arthur was the one who they would need to rely on to answer it. He felt calm, confident and ready for anything.

When the bell jingle-jangled, his reactions were even

faster than Trunk's. He jumped to his feet and waited to see if the customer would ask for assistance. Faintly, through the ceiling, he heard the sound of breaking china, which told him that the others had not yet finished the washing-up.

'I'm looking for a book,' said the customer, getting straight to the point. 'The title's . . . oh, my sainted aunt!' The man blundered forward and covered his mouth. 'GOODENOUGH!' he bellowed. 'WHAT, IN HEAVEN'S NAME, ARE YOU DOING BEHIND THAT DESK, BOY?'

Arthur came close to wishing that the ground would swallow him up. The customer that he had been so looking forward to helping out was none other than Mr Beaglehole, his least favourite teacher.

Chapter Sixteen

from Bad to Worse

Scallywag would not stop growling. She did not have to be told that the man who had come into the shop was not a nice fellow at all. She objected to the thumps that his boots made on the floor and the cloying, musky smell that oozed through his clothes. When he leaned over her master's desk and made loud, angry noises at the kind boy who took her for walks, Scallywag came very close to sinking her teeth into the man's leg.

'Steady!' murmured Arthur. He placed his hand on Scallywag's head and her growl acquired a less threatening tone. Mr Beaglehole was not the sort of man that you wanted to mess with. If Scallywag's teeth so much as brushed against Mr Beaglehole's jeans, Arthur had no doubt that he would drag Scallywag down to the police station, where he would insist that he had been savaged by a dangerous dog.

'Come out from behind that desk, Goodenough!'

commanded Mr Beaglehole, wrinkling his clean-shaven face into a sneer.

Arthur might have obeyed him if Scallywag had not been sitting, firmly and loyally, on his feet, preventing him from taking even the smallest step in any direction. 'I . . . I'd prefer to stay here,' said Arthur, which was the truth. It made him feel more secure to have a metre-wide piece of furniture between himself and his overbearing teacher.

Mr Beaglehole folded his muscular arms and shot Arthur a disconcerting smile. 'I suppose you think you can do as you please because we're not at school?'

Arthur found the courage to nod. As Mr Beaglehole had so helpfully pointed out, teachers had no power over their pupils outside the school gates. Arthur started to feel a bit braver. His teacher was not wearing his usual school attire of slacks, a short-sleeved shirt and a stripy tie. Dressed in jeans and a T-shirt, Mr Beaglehole was slightly less intimidating.

'Where's the real assistant?' barked Mr Beaglehole.

Arthur drew himself up to his full height. 'I can help you if you have an enquiry,' he said.

Mr Beaglehole snorted with laughter. 'You?' he said. 'A spotty little twelve-year-old?' Abruptly, Mr Beaglehole's scornful smile disappeared. 'I've changed my mind,' he said. 'I demand to see the manager. It's shameful to keep a customer waiting, and I'd also like a word with him about the smell in here. Rotten eggs, if I'm not mistaken. Very unhygienic.'

Scallywag continued to growl, her body trembling against Arthur's shins.

'The manager's away,' said Arthur coolly, 'and I'm minding the shop for Miss Quint because she had to pop out. Oh, and you got my age wrong. I'm thirteen.'

Mr Beaglehole breathed in sharply. 'Cheeky little pup!' he snarled. 'You won't be as flippant on Monday when I reveal the results of that last test I set you. In the meantime, I want to know if you have a particular book. It's called *The Future Is Nuclear* by Aidan Schmidt.'

Arthur was not prepared to unseat Scallywag in order to search for a book for a man he despised. 'We don't have that,' said Arthur as confidently as he could.

'I'd like it ordered in that case,' said Mr Beaglehole. He did not offer to pay up front, but moved towards the door instead. He paused on the doormat and glanced over his shoulder at Arthur. 'You are aware, aren't you, Goodenough, that it's against the law for a person your age to work in a shop?'

'Yes,' said Arthur stiffly. 'I'm not being paid.'

Mr Beaglehole's arrogant grin made Arthur feel anxious.

'I've got my eye on you, Goodenough,' Mr Beaglehole told him, and left.

As soon as he had crossed the threshold, Scallywag

ran to the door and barked to let the man know that he had not been welcome and would be wise never to come in again. Trunk ambled along his shelf to get closer to Arthur so that he could give him a look of deep sympathy.

'I know,' Arthur said with a sigh. 'It's just my luck to have a moron for a form teacher.'

Behind Mr Hardbattle's desk there were dozens of files, which listed most of the books that were still in print in England. Arthur sifted through them. When he found *The Future Is Nuclear*, he filled in an order form and put the lower half in an envelope ready for someone to post. He wondered if Mr Beaglehole had chosen that title on purpose to annoy him. Arthur did not approve of nuclear power. He thought that there were far better ways of making energy and had worked hard on a pre-sentation, which he had given to his geography class that term. He had gone into great detail about solar panels and wind turbines, and other amazing ideas and had been hopeful of being awarded at least a B. Predictably, however, Mr Beaglehole had failed to be impressed and had given Arthur a D minus minus, which was the lowest grade that he had ever handed out.

When the bell jingle-jangled for the second time that hour, Arthur stayed sitting down. Harbouring a vain hope that a friendly customer had just arrived, he glanced across to see who had come in and instantly experienced a jolt of panic. A policeman stood in the doorway and, if Arthur was not mistaken, it was the very same member of the force who had confiscated the knight's sword just a few days before. Arthur thought about hiding, but he was too slow off the mark. The policeman had already spotted him and was marching towards him in the manner of a soldier on a parade ground, swinging his arms stiffly and sticking out his chin. When the stout little officer halted with a *stomp-stomp* of his feet, Arthur half expected to be honoured with a salute.

'Young sir,' said the policeman, giving a nod. He took off his helmet and wiped his sweaty brow with a handkerchief.

Arthur stood up gingerly. His legs felt as if they had turned to cotton wool. 'Did Mr Beaglehole send you?' Arthur asked nervously. 'I'm not working, honest. I was just sitting in this chair because my legs were tired. I'm not an employee or anything like that.'

'What are you on about, lad?' the policeman said. 'Mr Beagle-who?' He unbuttoned his collar and scratched his neck. 'I was sent here by my sergeant. I've come to give you a warning.'

Arthur gulped. He had never been in trouble with the police before. He racked his brains to think what he had done in recent weeks that might have been construed as a crime. It was possible that he had ridden his bike on the pavement, and he remembered throwing an apple core under a hedge. Would he be given an ASBO? He dreaded to think what his mother would say.

The policeman stared at Arthur with a concerned frown. 'You've gone a peculiar colour, lad. If I were you, I'd open a window and get some fresh air in here. I've never seen a place so smothered with dust and there's a right funny pong an' all. Smells like tripe. Now where was I? Ah, yes. Shoplifting. There's been a spate of it in these parts. My sergeant has told me to put you shop-keepers on the alert. Had anything nicked in the last week or so, have you?'

'Er . . . no, I don't think so,' said Arthur, not wanting to mention the missing books in case it prompted some awkward questions. He smiled at the policeman, relieved that the purpose of his visit had not been to tell Arthur off.

'Well, keep your eyes peeled, won't you?' said the policeman. He put on his helmet and fastened his collar. 'If you clap eyes on anyone shifty, call the station, and ask for me. My name is Constable Chubb.'

Arthur assured PC Chubb that he would follow his advice, then he escorted the policeman to the door. The magic had kept a low profile whilst the policeman had been in the shop, but Arthur could not count on it to remain inconspicuous for very much longer. He did not know if magic was against the law, but he had a feeling that PC Chubb and his sergeant would not approve of it.

'Phew!' said Arthur when the policeman had gone. Arthur closed the door firmly and pressed his back against it, praying that no more customers would come in before Miss Quint returned. He did not think that his nerves could stand another shock in so short a space of time.

He checked his watch. There were fifteen minutes to go before the hour was up. He moved away from the door and wandered around the shop, looking for a book to browse through whilst he was waiting for the return of Miss Quint and Susan.

When the bell jingle-jangled two minutes later, Arthur ducked down and hid. From the innermost recesses of the children's section, he could not see round the corner to the doorway. However, if he stretched his neck and leaned to the left, he could get quite a good view of Trunk. The elephant's ears had raised themselves up like hoisted flags at the first clink of the bell, and Arthur watched as they fell into folds again as they always did when the newcomer did not prove to be his little girl. The elephant continued to peer in the direction of the doorway and then, instead of staying where he was, he set off at speed along his shelf and dived behind his flowerpot. Arthur knew that this did not bode well, and neither did the low rumbling sound which emanated from Scallywag. A quick glance told Arthur that her hackles were up and that she was baring her teeth. Whoever had just come into the bookshop had been scary enough to alarm a dog and a stuffed elephant. Arthur took off his belt, slipped it through Scallywag's collar and tied her securely to a table leg. He crouched low beside her and hoped that the person would think that the shop was not staffed and go away. Arthur heard the creak of shoe leather and the rustle of clothing, and then he almost jumped out of his skin when he heard somebody cough.

It was a dry, artificial sort of cough. Arthur knew that people only coughed like that in order to get somebody's attention – or to check whether anyone was around. Could the person who had just entered the shop be the shoplifter that PC Chubb had warned him about? While Arthur skulked behind shelves of children's books, was the mystery person filling carrier bags with Mr Hardbattle's stock?

Arthur realised that he could not hide any longer. He had been entrusted to look after the bookshop and it was his responsibility to guard against theft. Stealthily, Arthur stood up and tiptoed out of the alcove. If there was a thief in the bookshop, Arthur wanted to catch him red-handed.

The man who stood in the doorway did not strike Arthur as being the criminal type. He was young and had an open, friendly face. He wore overalls and

171

workman's boots, but his sideburns and his quiff of dark hair shaped like a shark's fin implied that he was more stylish than his clothes would suggest. Arthur could not understand why Scallywag and Trunk had taken such a dislike to the man. He looked harmless enough. He did not have any carrier bags or holdalls in which to stuff stolen goods, and he was not acting in a threatening or suspicious way. All the man was doing was standing on the doormat with his hands in his pockets, sniffing the air.

Arthur walked up to the man, without a shred of fear. 'Hello!' he said. 'Can I help?'

The man gave a lopsided smile and stepped forward to shake Arthur by the hand. He seemed to smell strongly of detergent.

'Afternoon,' he said. 'My name's Dexter Bland and no, mate, I don't need your help, but I think you could do with mine.'

Arthur was bemused. 'Oh, really?' he said.

'I'm in the extermination business,' said Dexter.

Not seeing how this affected him, Arthur said, 'Good for you.'

'Pest control's another name for it,' said Dexter. He reached into a pocket in his overalls and put on a pair of thick padded gloves. 'I had a report that Hardbattle Books had got an infestation – something making holes in the pages of your books – and by the smell of this place, I'd say you're knee-deep in cockroaches.'

Arthur took half a minute to digest what Dexter had said. He remembered that a fussy, middle-aged woman had brought back a book, complaining that its pages were riddled with holes. At the time, Arthur had been sure that the makers of the holes had been the drawing pins.

Trying to see the humour in the situation, Arthur gave a nervous laugh. 'You're mistaken,' he said. 'We don't have cockroaches here. Someone's been having you on.'

Dexter took up a determined stance. 'Don't give me any aggro, pal. This nose of mine has never been wrong. There's a mightily powerful stench in here, and I know roaches when I smell them.'

Arthur tried to explain that, although there was a smell, it was a misleading one and that what Dexter's nose could detect was actually magic. His rushed explanation made no impression on Dexter.

'Listen, buster,' Dexter said to Arthur. 'A shop full of roaches is a health hazard. They'll have to be got rid of. It's as simple as that.' He turned and walked out of the bookshop, but was back again within seconds. In his arms he held what looked like a gigantic vacuum cleaner with a suction hose and a telescopic tube. Arthur realised with a stab of horror that it was large enough to suck up all the magic in the shop.

'NO!' cried Arthur. He tried to push Dexter out of the door. 'You can't use that in here!'

'Oh yeah?' said Dexter, standing firm. 'Just you watch me, mate.'

Chapter Seventeen

The Pied Piper of Plumford

Arthur was not a lily-livered boy by nature, but he knew when he was beaten. One glance at the mammoth, cockroach-eating monster in the pest control man's grip was enough to tell him that he stood no chance against it on his own. He could have opted to run upstairs to ask one of the guests to intervene. Mr Claggitt was the obvious choice. A hulking, super-fit, barrel-chested mountaineer would undoubtedly cause Dexter to think twice before he switched on his machine. However, Arthur's instinct told him not to bother the guests upstairs. He felt that, in a crisis, it was probably best to enlist the help of people whom you judged to be the most dependable. It was purely for this reason and not because of any streak of cowardice that Arthur dodged past Dexter Bland and hared off up the street.

The panic which had built up inside him made Arthur sprint so fast that he reached the end of Meadow Street in one minute flat. He waited at the junction with Milestone Lane, where the pick of Plumford's thrift shops were to be found. Surrounded by a forest of much taller bodies, it was difficult for Arthur to see every person as they passed. To give himself a better view, he scrambled on to a postbox (which would have earned him a telling-off if PC Chubb had caught him). From Arthur's new vantage point, he looked in every direction, searching for the familiar faces of Susan and Miss Quint.

With each second that ticked by, Arthur grew more anxious. He tried to blot out a vision in his mind of Dexter Bland's machine consuming all the magic in the shop. Arthur's vision disintegrated when someone tugged on his trouser leg, and a man's voice cut through the hubbub on the busy street corner.

'Great Scott, Arthur! Why are you larking about up there?'

Fighting to keep his balance, Arthur glanced below him and saw a grey felt hat and a mackintosh draped over somebody's arm. On the pavement, next to a pair of snuff-coloured shoes, was a suitcase. Arthur closed his eyes and felt relief flood through his veins, then he sank to his haunches and grinned at Mr Hardbattle's upturned face.

'Crikey! Am I glad to see *you*,' said Arthur.

'And I you,' replied Mr Hardbattle, frowning, 'but the reason escapes me why you'd want to stand on a postbox of all things.'

'I didn't have a stepladder handy,' joked Arthur, his broad grin widening. Then, remembering Dexter Bland, his mood turned serious again. 'There's an emergency back at the shop,' he said, jumping down from the post-box. 'We have to get there right away. The magic is in danger.'

Seventy-year-old Mr Hardbattle proved in the next few minutes that he was no slouch when it came to taking to his heels. As they ran together along the pavement, dodging shoppers, Arthur revealed what had happened while he had been minding the shop.

'What a vexing chap!' Mr Hardbattle said of Dexter Bland as he panted and puffed in Arthur's wake, clutching his suitcase and raincoat. 'I shall turf him out of my shop. I'm the owner. He'll have to do what I say!'

Over his shoulder, Arthur expressed his view that that plan might not work. 'Dexter's very strong-willed. It's unlikely he'll take any notice!'

'Pig-headed blighter, is he?' said Mr Hardbattle, his fury increasing. 'How do you propose that we should stop this madman, then?'

'Don't know,' Arthur replied. 'That's why I legged it to fetch help!'

They slowed to a walk as they drew nearer to the bookshop, each of them thinking hard about how they could prevent the pest control man from emptying the shop of magic. Parked next to Mr Hardbattle's bottle green van was a much larger vehicle, which was dayglo orange in colour and had *PEST PULVERIZERS* painted boldly on its side.

Mr Hardbattle eyed Dexter's van with distaste. 'What a vulgar automobile,' he said.

Arthur cupped his hands around his eyes and peered through the bookshop's window to see what was going on. 'There's Dexter!' said Arthur. 'He seems to be crouching beside his machine. I can see his white overalls.'

'Overalls, eh?' Mr Hardbattle scratched his head. 'That's the sort of uniform they wear, is it? Hmm . . . Well, if this Dexter chappie won't heed the words of a lay person, perhaps he'll take notice of a pest control expert like himself.'

Arthur watched curiously as Mr Hardbattle knelt down on the pavement and rummaged around in his suitcase. The old man withdrew a pair of blue paint-spattered overalls.

'Here they are!' Mr Hardbattle said, shaking them out and unbuttoning them. 'I took them with me on my trip to protect my clothes. Thought that some of the places I looked at might be a little grimy.' Before he closed the lid of his suitcase, Mr Hardbattle folded his raincoat and put it on top of the rest of his things. Then, once he had fastened the clasps on his case, he got up from the ground.

'What's the plan?' Arthur asked him eagerly.

'I'm ruminating on it,' Mr Hardbattle said as he

stepped into the overalls and buttoned them over his shirt and trousers. 'I'll need an alter ego. What about Alan the Insect Man?'

Arthur regarded the old man in his scruffy new garb. 'I think you look like a Bert,' he said after a moment's consideration. 'What do you reckon to Bert the Bug Blaster?'

Mr Hardbattle frowned. 'Er . . . it's . . . well, it's . . .'

'Question is,' said Arthur, ignoring the fact that his suggestion had not been seized upon, '*how* do you blast the bugs? Where's your equipment? That bloke Dexter's got a ginormous machine.'

'Our approach? Yes, that's our stumbling block,' admitted Mr Hardbattle. 'We'll have to put on our thinking caps, and come up with something PDQ.'

After thirty seconds of unbroken silence, Arthur scowled and let out a sigh. 'It's those drawing pins' fault,' he complained. 'If they hadn't hopped all over that lady's book and made holes in it, we wouldn't be in the mess we're in now.'

'It's not the name Bert I object to,' mused Mr Hardbattle, who had seated himself on the doorstep of the shop. 'It's the method of dealing with the bugs . . . I mean, *insects*. I don't think I'd be capable of blasting them to pieces. Coaxing or cajoling is more my sort of thing.'

Arthur's heart sank. He glanced anxiously through the

window, and saw Dexter roaming the floor on his hands and knees. Mr Hardbattle's idea of impersonating someone from the pest control industry had been a good one, but if the old man was going to insist upon some namby-pamby method to get rid of the cockroaches, Arthur could not see how their plan would work. There was no way that Dexter was going to take a kind-hearted pest control expert seriously. Unless . . .

'If we'd had time, I could've popped home to borrow my sister's recorder,' said Arthur jokingly. 'You could've been like the Pied Piper of Hamelin from the fairytale.'

Arthur was taken aback when Mr Hardbattle slapped his hands on his knees and got up from the doorstep. He walked towards Arthur with shining eyes.

'Who needs a recorder?' said Mr Hardbattle, smiling. 'A penny whistle would do just as well.'

'Huh?' said Arthur. 'What are you staring at me for?'

'Your whistle,' Mr Hardbattle said, holding out his hand. 'I'd like to borrow it, if you don't mind.'

Arthur looked at him blankly. 'A whistle? I don't have one.'

'You don't?' Mr Hardbattle said, clicking his tongue against his teeth. 'Good heavens! What is the world coming to? When I was a boy, I was never without my penny whistle or my whittling knife or my catapult!'

'Sorry,' said Arthur. 'I guess times have changed.' He emptied his trouser pockets to prove that there was no whistle inside them, and Mr Hardbattle's eyes took in the collection of oddments on Arthur's palms.

'What's this?' Mr Hardbattle asked, pointing at a flat plastic toy with holes at either end.

Arthur squinted at the object, which was snarled in a rubber band. He had traded a bar of chocolate for it several days before and had completely forgotten about it until that moment.

'Um . . . it's a kazoo,' he said. 'It makes a noise if you blow through it.'

'May I?' asked Mr Hardbattle, taking the kazoo. 'It will serve very well. Now, here's what we're going to do . . .'

One minute later, Mr Hardbattle burst through the door of the bookshop in the manner of a cowboy walking into a saloon. His sudden entrance made the bell's clapper swing so sharply that its jingle-jangle sounded like a shriek. Dexter Bland's attention was seized immediately. He looked up from the floor of the shop where he was crawling about. In one hand he held a plug that was attached to a long length of cable. He appeared to be searching for an electric socket in which to fit his plug.

'Go, Arthur . . . now!' Mr Hardbattle hissed.

As swiftly as he could, Arthur slipped behind the old man and ran to Mr Hardbattle's desk, almost tripping over the coils of the suction device in his haste. Once he had reached the desk, he snatched up the carton of drawing pins and went to join Scallywag, who was sitting beside the table, still tied to its leg, and grumbling like a kettle that was coming to the boil.

'Have you seen a pest hereabouts?' was Mr Hardbattle's opening gambit.

Dexter Bland set his jaw. He narrowed his eyes and pinched his shark-fin quiff between his finger and thumb. 'Who's asking?' he said.

Mr Hardbattle grasped the knot of his tie and moved it a smidgen to the right. 'People in the trade know me as Marmaduke the Cockroach Charmer.'

'I've never heard that name,' said Dexter suspiciously. He got up from the floor and stood in a defensive pose in front of his cockroach-eating contraption. 'Your help isn't wanted, thanks. I've got this cockroach job all sewn up.'

'I beg to differ,' Mr Hardbattle said, venturing deeper into the shop. 'By the looks of it, you haven't even made a start!'

'Hey! This is my patch, old-timer,' said Dexter, shaking his plug at him threateningly. 'Go and do your cockroach charming somewhere else!'

'What's the matter, sonny? Afraid I'd do a better job?'

Mr Hardbattle's daring talk made Arthur hold his breath, but Dexter Bland did not seem fazed, and showed his contempt by snorting with laughter. 'There's nothing more efficient than my machine,' he said, setting aside the plug and grasping the telescopic tube with both hands. 'I put this nozzle in the cracks and crevices and suck out the roaches like milk through a straw.'

'Showy,' sneered Mr Hardbattle bravely, 'not to mention cumbersome. I find that the old traditional methods are the best.'

'How d'you do it, then?' asked Dexter, sounding a little less sure of himself.

'You must've heard of the Pied Piper of Hamelin?' said Mr Hardbattle. He squared up to Dexter and looked him in the eye.

'Sure!' said Dexter brazenly. 'Everyone in our line of work knows about the Piper dude. He's the most famous controller of pests that there has ever been. He lured a load of rats out of a town by playing on his pipe and led them to a river, where they drowned.'

'Go to the top of the class!' Mr Hardbattle said to Dexter. Then he wiggled his finger in his right ear, which was the signal for Arthur to begin the next stage of their plan.

Obediently, Arthur unfolded the flaps on the carton, which he had balanced on his knees, and began to whisper instructions to the drawing pins. This was made far easier because Scallywag had stopped growling as soon as she had recognised her master's voice, and the only sound that Arthur was obliged to compete with was the *swish-swish-swish* of her tail sweeping the floor.

'You're telling me you serenade the roaches?' Dexter said to Mr Hardbattle. He smirked. 'Boy, I'd love to see that! Where's your pipe, then? Let's have a tune! Put your money where your mouth is, Grandad!'

'Very well,' Mr Hardbattle said. 'Stand back and enjoy the show.'

The sound that the kazoo made when Mr Hardbattle put it to his lips and hummed through the narrowest end could not be described as melodic. It made the hairs on the back of Arthur's neck stand up. Dexter grimaced and placed his hands over his ears and Scallywag raised her muzzle to the ceiling and started to howl. No cockroaches appeared, which was to be expected, but as Mr Hardbattle continued to belt out his unrecognisable tune, there was movement in the corner of the shop where Arthur was sitting. The carton on his knees gave a wobble and then, like a snake emerging from a hole, the drawing pins jumped out of their carton and, in a long, wavering line, hopped on their little pin legs towards Mr Hardbattle.

'There are the cockroaches!' cried Arthur, running up and down beside them so that Dexter could not get a clear look at them. 'See, there they go!' he said, as they followed Mr Hardbattle's beckoning hand and hopped two by two, in a crocodile, out of the shop.

Dexter stood and gawped. 'I've never seen anything like it!' he said.

'Made it look like child's play, didn't he?' Arthur commented gleefully. 'That's experience for you, I suppose. Well, I expect you've got to dash off to your next appointment, Mr Bland . . .'

With a defeated sigh and a dispirited slope to his shoulders, Dexter began to coil his electrical lead and wind it around the top of his cockroach-eating machine.

Arthur was thrilled that he and Mr Hardbattle had pulled off their scam with such ease, but he did feel a twinge of guilt for tricking Dexter so slyly. 'You win some, you lose some!' he said to the pest control man as he helped him to carry his machine to his van. When Dexter had driven away, Mr Hardbattle emerged from behind a lamp post and gave Arthur the thumbs up.

'Worked like a dream,' said Mr Hardbattle, walking rather gingerly because his pockets were filled with drawing pins.

Arthur nodded and grinned. 'Marmaduke was a cool name to choose. Better than Bert by miles.'

'It's the name I was christened with,' said Mr Hardbattle, chuckling. 'I'm glad that it meets with your approval, Arthur!'

Chapter Eighteen

Miss Quint Is Dishonest

Once inside the shop again, Arthur took the drawing pins and tipped them into their carton, while Mr Hardbattle enjoyed a reunion with his dog. Not waiting to be untethered, Scallywag slipped out of her collar and streaked across the floor. When Mr Hardbattle bent down to greet her, she lathered his face with licks.

After a few minutes, Scallywag contented herself with lying at her master's feet, and Mr Hardbattle straightened up and dried his face with his handkerchief. 'What's become of my large-eared friend?' he asked, glancing at a shelf above his desk, which was Trunk's usual stamping ground.

'He's hiding,' said Arthur. 'He got scared.'

'Trunk, my boy!' Mr Hardbattle called, waving his handkerchief in the air. 'There's nothing to fear. That loathsome fellow has gone. Come out and say hello!'

It was unclear whether it was Mr Hardbattle's plea or

the jingle-jangle of the shop bell that persuaded Trunk to come out from behind his flowerpot. His trunk made an appearance first, followed by his tusks and his anxious, velvety face. Trunk's ears gave a twitch of delight when he saw that Susan and Miss Quint had returned from their shopping trip, but it was the sight of Mr Hardbattle that gave the elephant the most joy. He lifted his trunk to deliver a trumpet blast to welcome his old friend home, but unfortunately, by that time, the new arrivals in the shop had seized everybody's attention, and because he could not make any sound, Trunk's fanfare went unnoticed.

It had been Susan who had caused the bell to ring. She had skipped through the door ahead of Miss Quint, a blissful smile on her face. In one hand she clutched a carrier bag, and in the other a piece of pink paper. Her appearance made Arthur do a double take. Rather than wearing her drab gingham dress, Susan was attired in a T-shirt and shorts. Behind Susan lurked Miss Quint, who had stopped dead on the doormat, a look of panic in her eyes.

'You seem surprised to see me,' Mr Hardbattle said, raising his hat in a respectful greeting to Miss Quint.

'No!' Miss Quint said hurriedly. 'It's just . . . you're early . . . and I didn't realise it was you at first. That old get-up threw me. I thought you were an odd-job man!'

Mr Hardbattle looked down at his overalls, which he

had neglected to remove. 'I'm supposed to be in pest control,' he told her, and, with several interruptions from Arthur, he divulged the details of their recent adventure. While they chattered away Susan hovered by Mr Hardbattle's side, bursting with eagerness to introduce herself.

Eventually, Mr Hardbattle turned to speak to her. He pushed his horn-rimmed spectacles up his nose, and asked, 'Who might *you* be?'

'She's my niece,' Miss Quint said, getting in her explanation before Arthur could admit the truth. She put an arm around Susan's shoulders and ignored Arthur's reproving stare. 'Susan needed somewhere to spend her half-term holiday,' said Miss Quint. 'Her parents are too ill to look after her. They've got . . . Pollywolly Disease . . . quite badly. I didn't think you'd draw the line at Susan moving in.'

It was a struggle for Mr Hardbattle to look as if he did not mind that his home had been invaded by a second female. He was too flustered to speak at first. All he could do was smile unhappily.

'I don't eat much, and I'm helpful, aren't I, Aunt Beatrice?' Susan said.

Arthur glowered at Miss Quint even more intensely. It was plain that she had taken Susan into her confidence and persuaded the girl to go along with her deceitful ruse. Perhaps Susan's new clothes had served as bribery.

Turning Susan into a liar was not something that Arthur approved of; neither was trying to pull the wool over Mr Hardbattle's eyes.

'Pollywolly Disease . . .' murmured Mr Hardbattle, frowning. 'I haven't come across that. It doesn't sound nice.' He gazed at Susan pityingly, and his voice became gentler. 'Poor little girl! Of course it's all right if you remain here.'

After blowing out her cheeks with relief, Miss Quint clapped her hands. 'That's settled, then. Arthur, have you told Mr Hardbattle our good news?'

Arthur stopped lolling against a bookshelf and took his hands out of his trouser pockets. 'No, there hasn't been time,' he said. Aware that he sounded sullen, Arthur tried to shake off his sulky mood, and made an effort to sound glad. 'We've found a brilliant place for your magic, Mr Hardbattle! It's an old cottage in a wood, and it's got *loads* of cobwebs!'

Mr Hardbattle's cheeks turned a rosy shade of pink, and he clapped Arthur on the shoulder with immense pride. 'That *is* a load off my mind! How splendid! Clever you! The places that I looked at weren't really up to scratch. The best of the bunch was a hayloft in Devizes, but horseshoe bats and barn owls had already set up home there, and bats, owls and magic wouldn't make good bedfellows.'

'The cottage is at Down-the-Ages Farm,' said Miss

Quint. 'Pam Carruthers suggested that we might move the magic in this weekend.'

'But not Saturday,' said Susan, her eyes widening with worry.

Arthur hesitated. 'What's happening on Saturday?'

'This!' said Susan, holding up a pink flyer. 'A man was handing these out in the street. He was taller than a tree!'

Arthur was baffled by Susan's description of the flyer man until Miss Quint explained that he had been wearing stilts.

Arthur took the flyer from Susan and read it. Almost immediately his face broke into a smile. 'Oh yeah!' he said. 'I'd forgotten that it's the carnival this weekend.'

'The high spot in Plumford's cultural calendar,' Mr Hardbattle said. 'Naturally, you children mustn't miss it. I'd be more than willing to move the magic on Sunday.' His eyes grew round and bright as a thought occurred to him. 'That's the one day the shop isn't open so I shan't lose any trade!'

Mr Hardbattle took off his trilby hat and threw it with enough precision for it to alight on the hatstand. 'My bookshop is saved! This calls for a celebration!' he cried. Then he picked up his suitcase and walked spryly towards the stairs.

With a squawk of alarm, Miss Quint moved like lightning to head him off. 'Stop!' she shrieked. 'You mustn't!'

'What do you mean, I mustn't?' Mr Hardbattle asked.

He tried to pass Miss Quint, but she prevented him from doing so. 'I'm only going upstairs to put the kettle on!' he said, frustrated by her awkwardness.

'I can do that for you!' said Miss Quint soothingly. 'You've been travelling all day. You must be exhausted!' She placed her fingers around the handle of his case. 'Let me take your bag!' she said, trying to tug it from his grip. 'I'll make the tea while you sit down and put your feet up!'

Mr Hardbattle had to admit that Miss Quint was right about one thing. He had been on the go all day, and was certainly too weary to argue the toss. Without another word of protest, he let Miss Quint relieve him of his suitcase, and made straight for the nearest chair.

While Miss Quint was upstairs making tea, Arthur sat and fidgeted. He tried to join in the conversation with Susan and Mr Hardbattle, but he could not prevent his mind from straying on to other things. He had a fair idea why Miss Quint had been anxious to go upstairs. She had wanted to talk to the house guests before Mr Hardbattle met them. She was probably asking them to pretend to be her old pals, just as she had prevailed upon Susan earlier.

Arthur looked over at Mr Hardbattle, who was sitting contentedly in a chair with one of the bookends on his lap. Arthur yearned to tell the old man the truth, but he did not dare to reveal all while Susan was in the room. He got up from his perch on the arm of a chair and paced the floor restlessly.

Within the space of ten minutes, Miss Quint returned with a tray. Behind her, trotting down the staircase like obliging sheep, came Jimmy, Mrs Voysey-Brown and Mr Claggitt.

Mr Hardbattle heard the clatter of footsteps and glanced at the stairwell, aghast. 'Miss Quint! Who in the world are these people?' he asked. 'Are these your family too?'

'No!' said Arthur loudly. He planted his hands on his hips. 'And they're not her friends either. They're –'

'They're relatives of Arthur's,' interjected Miss Quint. She turned and nodded at each of them as they stepped off the final stair. 'This is his Uncle Jim . . . and Aunt Dolores . . . and Uncle Sidney.'

Arthur was so cross with Miss Quint that he left the bookshop immediately after she introduced the three house guests as his relations, and did not come back until the following afternoon.

He still had a little homework to finish over the half-term break, and tried to fill his time by concentrating on it. As usual, however, this was anything but easy. Everywhere he went in his house, he was confronted with loud music, arguments, giggling or his cockatiel, Bubbles, who had developed the habit of sitting on

Arthur's head. The back garden was Arthur's usual sanctuary but, because of the good weather, his family had taken this over too. When Arthur sat at the bottom of the garden, his brothers started a kickabout and clobbered him with their ball, and when he moved to the patio, Arthur's bikini-clad sisters got on his nerves by squealing as they ran past the sprinklers on the lawn.

It was late on Wednesday afternoon when Arthur admitted to himself that the only place to study was the bookshop. He moaned and grumbled about it as he packed his schoolbooks into his bag, but secretly he was glad to be returning, having missed his friends.

When he pushed open the door of the shop, Arthur discovered, to his disappointment, that Mr Hardbattle was not there.

'He's gone in his van to Down-the-Ages Farm,' explained Susan, who had leaped up from her chair as soon as Arthur had entered the shop. She had been reading a book, but had thrown it aside to greet him.

Miss Quint was sitting behind a sewing machine at Mr Hardbattle's desk. The machine was an odd-shaped contraption, topped with a cotton reel. As Miss Quint turned a handle, a needle dipped in and out of some cloth at speed.

'He wanted to meet Pam Carruthers, and to see the woodsman's cottage for himself,' said Miss Quint over the whirr of her sewing machine. 'Mr Hardbattle's such an old fusspot! Let's hope he doesn't find fault with it!'

She stopped turning the handle of the sewing machine, whipped the material out from underneath the presser foot and inspected the stitching. Arthur saw that the garment was a child's skirt and that Miss Quint was altering its length. Plainly, shorts and a T-shirt were not the only clothes that had been purchased for Susan the day before.

Arthur had made up his mind not to speak to Miss Quint, but found that he could not bring himself to be quite so rude.

'I've come to do some schoolwork,' he said gruffly. 'It was too noisy to get much done at home and the library's too crowded in half-term week.' He lifted his head and listened, but there were no sounds from upstairs. 'It seems quieter than usual,' he said. 'Where are the three musketeers?'

Miss Quint smiled to herself. 'You mean, your aunt and uncles, Arthur!'

'That's *not* who they are,' snapped Arthur, 'and you shouldn't have said it was!' He threw his school bag on the floor in a fit of pique.

Miss Quint abandoned her needlework to glare at him. 'You didn't give me much option, did you? I was all set to follow Plan A but, thanks to your little outburst, I had to invent a Plan B on the spot!'

Arthur was amazed that Miss Quint seemed to think

that he should say sorry for inconveniencing her. He curled his hands into fists, and fumed silently.

The handle of the sewing machine revolved again. 'They're out, if you must know,' said Miss Quint. 'I advised them to make themselves scarce. Mr Hardbattle wasn't best pleased to be lumbered with three more house guests. I told him that your parents' house was too packed to accommodate them. He's agreed to let them stay here for now.'

Arthur grunted and started to clear a space on his homework table. He laid out his pencils and exercise books, and Susan picked up the nearest book and leafed through the pages.

'What does "abysmal" mean?' she asked, peering at a teacher's scrawl.

Arthur snatched the book back and told her not to be so nosy. Startled by his hostile manner, Susan decided to leave him alone. She went back to the book that she had been reading when Arthur had come in. It was called *Emil and the Detectives*.

Half an hour passed without another word being spoken. The only noises were the whirr and trundle of Miss Quint's sewing machine and the twangs of rubber bands as they competed in a contest to see which one could fling itself the furthest across the room. Susan read her book and Arthur gnawed his pen and tried to get on with his homework, but he found the going hard. Apart from having impossible questions to answer, there was also the distraction of the temperature. It was the first day of June and the weather was cloudy and close. Inside the dusty, airless bookshop, Arthur felt uncomfortably warm. He had untucked his shirt and taken off his shoes, but neither action had made him feel much cooler.

At a quarter to five, he sighed and put down his pen.

'How's business been?' he asked.

'Quiet,' said Miss Quint. She had finished altering Susan's skirt and was trying to put her machine away, but the bobbins had escaped from their compartment and were racing each other across the desk. 'Come back here, you!' she said to the fastest bobbin, which was wound with black thread and nearing the table's edge.

'Have you had a visit from that shoplifter that PC Chubb told me about?' asked Arthur.

'No,' answered Miss Quint, snatching at bobbins to the left and right.

Arthur wiped the sweat from his forehead with his sleeve. 'I bet that other bookshop in town has had loads of customers. When the magic's gone, Hardbattle Books will be much busier . . . won't it?' His tone was faintly anxious.

Miss Quint slammed down the lid on the last errant bobbin. 'Are you sure that's what you want?' she said.

'For Mr Hardbattle's bookshop to be successful? Of course it is!'

'But where will you do your homework?' Miss Quint asked.

Arthur smiled. He checked his watch, then closed his books and began to place them in his bag, but before he could leave for home, Mr Hardbattle returned.

He was in a jovial mood, having been greatly impressed by the woodsman's cottage. He bid Arthur a hearty hello and handed Susan a warm bundle wrapped in newspaper, which had a fishy, mouth-watering smell.

'Haddock and chips!' Mr Hardbattle said. 'You'll stay for some, won't you, Arthur? And afterwards I wonder if you'd help me fetch down some packing cases from the loft. I've got three or four of them, and each one's dusty and dry as a bone. They'll be perfect for transferring the You Know What when I drive it to Thornwick.'

Arthur nodded. 'Sure thing!'

Declaring that the fish and chips smelled scrumptious, Susan hugged the parcel to her chest while Miss Quint went upstairs to fetch some plates and cutlery.

Arthur helped to unwrap the takeaway meal and share out the portions of haddock and chips, and as he peeled away the layers of the *Plumford Gazette*, his eyes were drawn to a photograph of PC Chubb underneath a headline that warned: *ROBBERS RUN AMOK IN PLUMFORD*. Arthur read the start of the article, which revealed that burglaries were on the rise in the area as well as theft from shops. The others did not have the patience to wait for him to finish reading the entire story so Arthur folded up the page of newsprint and tucked it away in his pocket to read later.

Once their appetites had been appeased, and Miss Quint and Susan had trooped off to the kitchen with the greasy paper and dirty plates, Arthur and Mr Hardbattle fetched a stepladder from the shed. Between them they carried the ladder upstairs and stood it under the hatch to the attic. Then Arthur remained at the bottom, holding it steady, while the old man climbed up the steps. When Mr Hardbattle reached the top step, he gasped and gave a cry.

'Well, that's a funny thing!' he said, staring at a large brass padlock a matter of inches from his nose. 'I don't remember fitting a lock on this hatch! Where could I have put the key?'

After an hour of Mr Hardbattle emptying drawers and finding every sort of key except the one that fitted the padlock in question, it was decided that they should postpone their packing case forage until the next day. It made no odds to Arthur. He got on his bicycle and rode home.

Much later on at Hardbattle Books, when night had fallen, beds were occupied and every light had been switched off, a bumping noise startled Susan awake.

Scallywag, who had taken to sleeping on Susan's bed, woke up too. Susan put out her hand to touch the dog's shoulder and felt her stiffen. The next moment, she started to growl, and then, without warning, Scallywag jumped off the bed and disappeared through the door. Susan sat on her own. She clutched her eiderdown tensely. More noises banged above her head, similar to the first. It sounded as if someone were dropping rocks and boulders on to the roof. Susan suddenly wanted the company of Mr Hardbattle or Miss Quint. She threw back her feather quilt and got out of bed, but before she could reach the door of her room, somebody slammed it shut and a key turned in the lock. Susan tried the door handle, and her worst fears were realised. The door would not open. There were more thumps from above.

'Miss Quint?' called Susan. She raised her voice. 'Mr Hardbattle? This is Susan speaking! What's all that banging, and why have you locked me in?'

She rattled the door handle once again, but stopped when her ears caught a muffled shout. Susan listened more intently and heard the cries of the same two people that she had called out to a moment ago. Both were demanding to be freed from their rooms. Susan gulped when she realised that all of them had been locked in.

The situation did not make any sense to Susan at first, then she remembered the article in the paper that Arthur had been reading. Perhaps there were burglars in

199

the house, and they had locked everyone in their rooms so that they could steal Mr Hardbattle's books without risking capture. Susan's imagination began to run wild. She fretted about the books that would be lost and the damage that the burglars might do to the shop, but mostly she got herself into a state about Scallywag, who had sped off bravely to scare away the robbers and had not been heard of since. What could be done? Susan racked her brains. Arthur would know, but how could she contact Arthur when she was locked in her room? If only she could think of a way to escape!

The room's only window was already open a crack. Susan hoisted it up and leaned out over the sill. Even in the dark she could tell that attempting a jump to the ground would be madness. She would not be able to fetch help with a couple of broken legs! Something moved a few metres away, and Susan saw a shadowy trunk and a branch with quivering leaves. It occurred to her that if she knelt on the window ledge and stretched out an arm, she might be able to swing on to the branch and climb down the tree.

But not in my bare feet, wearing nothing but my petticoat, she thought, and hastened from the window to get dressed.

Chapter Nineteen

A Walk in the Dark

Once she had pulled on a skirt and jersey, Susan was ready to go. In her skirt pocket she had shoved a one pound coin and a torch that Miss Quint had been kind enough to give her. With the utmost care, Susan climbed on to the window sill and peered out into the night.

The most frightening part of the whole exercise proved to be at the start, when she shuffled along the window ledge on her knees and made a lunge at the branch. Dithering was not an option. Having made her move, she was forced to leave the window ledge completely and swing from the branch by her arms. For a few anxious seconds, while she found a foothold on the tree, Susan dangled in mid-air and tried not to look down. She felt that hanging from a tree was not half as pleasurable as being on a swing or flying through the air.

When she had anchored herself, the actual climb was not too bad, although she was torn between shinning down the tree at speed and taking things slowly so as not to risk tearing her new clothes. She plumped for climbing quickly and guessed that Mr Claggitt would not have approved of her technique. It was more of a slither than a measured descent, but Susan's lack of expertise did not seem to matter and she reached the ground without so much as a scraped knee.

Although the moon was out, the back of the house was draped in darkness so she switched on her torch and directed its beam down the yard. Susan's torch beam missed the side-gate, but picked out the tool shed, a dustbin, a washing line and a high fence.

Intending to clamber over the fence, Susan walked down the garden path, which took her past the shed. As she drew closer to the shed, she heard a scrabbling noise coming from inside it. Susan was tempted to hurry by, but her inquisitiveness prevailed, and, with the aid of the torch, she found the shed door and lifted the latch. Thrusting her torch beam inside, she saw that the maker of the noise was none other than Scallywag, who had been tied to a workbench and muzzled with a scarf. Susan was overjoyed to see that Scallywag was unhurt. She released the excited dog quickly, untying the rope and freeing her bound nose, then, using the rope as a dog lead, Susan ushered the dog out of the shed and continued towards the fence.

It was Scallywag who found a way out of the garden. She went straight to a loose board and prodded it with her nose. The board swung backwards and Scallywag slipped through. Tugged by the rope lead, Susan had no choice but to follow where Scallywag had gone. In order to get through the gap, she was obliged to squeeze through sideways whilst breathing in. Being fairly slim, she managed it.

Fighting her way through brambles was more testing, but eventually, covered in scratches, Susan crawled out on to a patch of waste ground next to a retail park. Keeping a firm hold on Scallywag's lead and pointing her torch at the ground, she made her way over a bumpy terrain of rubble and weeds. Her torch beam fell for a moment on a fox whose eyes shone like foil bottle tops in the unnatural light. Then with a flick of its bushy tail, it was gone. Scallywag yanked Susan's arm, yearning to go after it, but Susan did not intend to be waylaid even for a moment.

Once she had reached a pavement, Susan switched off her torch. The amount of light thrown by the street lamps was more than adequate to enable her to find her way. She walked along the street, which was flanked by terraced houses, searching for a telephone box.

Susan had no clue where Arthur lived. She had thought that she might walk the streets of Plumford until she encountered a person who knew him, but she had quickly dismissed this idea as time-consuming and likely to fail. The plan that she had settled upon was infinitely better. She had remembered being told about telephone boxes and the books called directories, which could be found inside them. These directories were huge, and held the name, address and telephone number of everyone who lived locally. All she had to do was find Arthur's number in this book, and ring him up.

It did not take Susan long before she spotted a telephone box. There were a few glass panes missing from it, but the all-important directory was there. Standing on tiptoe to reach the shelf on which the book sat, Susan took it down and flicked through it, searching for the surname Goodenough. Luckily, it was not a common name in the Plumford area, and there were only two Goodenoughs listed. Goodenough, G was a doctor and his address was at a surgery, so she knew that Goodenough, I was the one that she wanted.

Susan got out her pound coin. She read the instructions on the telephone carefully; lifting the receiver, putting in her money and dialling the number in the order that it said. The telephone on the other end rang and rang for a long time.

Susan's heart pounded. Why wouldn't anyone answer?

'Hello?' said a sleepy voice at last.

Susan perked up. 'Is that you, Arthur?'

'No, it's Arthur's mother,' said the voice. 'Who are you? What do you want? Don't you know what time it is?'

Susan did not have a wristwatch, and anyway she did not see that it mattered what the time was when there was an emergency to report. 'My name's Susan,' she said, 'and it's really, really ever so important that I speak to Arthur right away.'

'Well, you can't,' said Arthur's mother in a not-to-be-messed-with voice. 'He's in bed, and if *I* were your mum, Susan, *bed* is where I would have sent you *hours* ago. It's ten minutes to midnight! Call back when the sun is up! Goodbye!'

The receiver on the other end of the line was put down with a clunk and Susan was left listening to silence.

Murmuring 'Bother!' under her breath, she replaced her handset too and heard her pound coin drop in the box. 'So much for that idea, Scallywag.'

Although she had received a setback, Susan was not prepared to give up. She decided that there was nothing for it but to memorise Arthur's address and to try to find his house. The only problem with her new plan was that she did not have the faintest idea where she might find Willow Road. She would need to rely on the help of a passer-by.

As Susan made her way through Plumford, she was struck by how eerily quiet it was. Most of the roads were deserted and the houses that she passed had their curtains drawn, but plenty of windows were open, it being such a sultry night. Through them, from time to time, Susan heard snatches of laughter, raised voices and the tinny blare of music. A cat or hedgehog crossed her path occasionally, but the presence of Scallywag kept most creatures at bay. Not knowing in which direction she should go, Susan asked everyone she met for assistance. A couple strolling arm in arm had never heard of Willow Road, and a bunch of boisterous youths were more interested in pulling her plaits than providing helpful advice.

Finally, Susan's persistence paid off when she stopped at the door of a curry house and spoke to a man called Vijay who had driven cabs before he became a restaurateur. He gave Susan detailed instructions to get to Willow Road. He even drew her a map on a napkin and gave her some Bombay mix to eat on the way.

Willow Road, where Arthur lived, was part of a new estate. All of its roads had been named after trees, shrubs or flowers. When Susan turned into Dahlia Drive she felt a great sense of relief. She followed the pavement, which wound its way through a maze of roads. Those with the grandest names were lined with smart, detached houses that had garages tacked on the side and neat front lawns. In the plainer-sounding roads, the buildings were jam-packed and had an altogether shabbier look.

Susan's belief that she would find Willow Road started to fade when the rain began to fall. The drops were light at first, and Susan mistook them for winged insects landing in her hair, but soon they grew plumper and fell to earth in a rush. Getting wet did not dismay Susan as much as the knowledge that her napkin map was softening, and Vijay's carefully written words were being turned into splodges of ink. Within seconds the map was unreadable.

A distant rumble in the sky filled Susan with even more anguish, and Scallywag answered the noise with a rumbling growl of her own. To prevent them both from getting soaked to the skin, Susan looked for a place where they could hide from the rain. She spotted a tree in someone's front garden and ran to it. She felt drier beneath its branches, but she also felt a sense of despair. Having come so far, it seemed that she would have to spend the rest of the night under the tree or trailing around the housing estate, getting increasingly lost.

The next moment a car swept past, its windscreen wipers flitting back and forth at speed. Susan was caught in the car's headlights and raised her hand too late to shade her eyes against their glare. She was still blinking to get rid of the brightness when she heard a squeaking noise and the sound of a skidding wheel.

A voice called out, 'Why are you standing there, dopey?'

Susan looked up and thought, for a moment, that she must be dreaming. A metre or two in front of her, sitting astride his bike, was Arthur. He grinned at her and pushed his long fringe out of his eyes. 'Don't you know that sheltering under a tree in a thunderstorm is one of the stupidest things that you can do?' he said. 'If lightning strikes that tree, you'll be frizzled to a crisp!'

His words were lost on Susan, who had not yet recovered from the shock of Arthur appearing. 'How'd you know I was here?' she asked.

'I used my psychic powers!'

Scallywag whined to be stroked and Arthur leaned down to oblige. 'Stumbled on you, didn't I?' he said. 'You woke up the whole house with your phone call, Suze. I heard Mum say your name and guessed that something weird – and maybe bad – had happened at the shop. I waited till the coast was clear and then made tracks!'

'There *is* something wrong,' said Susan, feeling tearful all of a sudden. 'Someone locked us in our rooms . . . I had to climb down a tree to get out!'

Arthur's eyebrows shot up his forehead. Instead of asking her to explain, he gestured that she should get on his bike. 'Sounds like we'd better get there super-fast!' he said.

Susan revealed more details as they rode along the streets of Plumford on Arthur's bicycle. Susan had never ridden a bike so she sat on the saddle whilst Arthur stood up and pedalled, leaning his weight on the handlebars.

Scallywag was too big to fit in Arthur's saddlebag, so they took off her rope lead and she ran alongside.

They were an odd-looking pair; Arthur in long shorts and a pyjama top and Susan with her ribboned plaits flying out behind. The bike wobbled and wavered, sent off course by the weight of two riders instead of one, but Arthur was a capable cyclist and managed to keep his bike from falling over.

'*Burglars?*' said Arthur as they left the road and freewheeled down a narrow, unlit footpath close to his school. Wet nettles and cow parsley brushed against their legs.

Susan clung to the crossbar tightly. 'That's who I thought they must be. What do you think they've come to steal? Mr Hardbattle's books?'

Arthur pulled a face, and turned the handlebars sharply to avoid a fallen branch. 'Mr Hardbattle's books can't be worth *that* much,' he said. 'And he isn't rich. The till drawer's practically empty, and he doesn't have any signet rings or gold medallions or things like that. He hasn't even got a TV!'

Susan struggled to stay in the saddle as they went over a hump in the path. A loud, crackling rumble followed a flash in the sky, and made her squeal.

'It's just a thunderstorm. You'll be OK,' said Arthur, pedalling faster.

Arthur's spurt of speed and his knowledge of short

cuts saved them from getting totally drenched. They were fairly damp, but not dripping, when they arrived outside Hardbattle Books. They dismounted clumsily as another lightning flash lit up the sky. A crash of thunder swiftly followed.

'Electricity in clouds,' whispered Arthur. 'Nothing to be scared of, Suze.' He crept towards the shop and put his finger to his lips. 'Shh!' he said over his shoulder.

Susan reattached Scallywag's lead, and Scallywag sank to the ground, worn out from having run several miles across town. Her tongue lolled from her mouth and her sides heaved. She was so tired that the thunderstorm failed to trouble her.

Arthur examined the frontage of Hardbattle Books. None of the windows had been broken and the lock on the door had not been tampered with. At first glance the interior of the shop seemed dark, but when Arthur peered through the window, he saw glimmers of deep gold light at the very back of the shop.

'Someone's there!' he whispered to Susan. 'But it beats me how they got in. There isn't any sign of a break-in as far as I can see.'

Susan tweaked Arthur's pyjama sleeve. 'Whose car is that?' she asked.

Next to the kerb, in the space in front of Mr Hardbattle's van, was a battered old Land Rover. As Susan and Arthur stared at it, bewildered, they heard the creak of a bicycle, which sounded as if it needed oiling, and saw a man in a deerstalker hat pedalling quickly in their direction. Arthur pulled Susan away from the portion of pavement that was lit up by a street lamp. They goggled at the cyclist from the shadows as he pressed his brakes and came to a stop. Alighting from his bike, the man retrieved a briefcase from a pannier, looked around him to check that no one was watching and walked straight up to the bookshop's door. There, he knocked in a sequence: once, three times, twice, and four times more. He turned up the collar of his raincoat and cast furtive glances over his shoulder as he waited to be let in. The door opened a crack and there was a murmur of voices. When the man was ushered into the shop, they heard the bell jingle-jangle. The door was closed firmly behind him.

'That was just plain odd!' said Arthur, not altogether convinced that what he had just witnessed was the typical behaviour of a burglar. 'Who do you think that man was, Suze?'

'I don't know, but I thought he looked shifty,' Susan whispered in reply. 'Not the sort of man that Mr Hardbattle would be chums with. I do wish we could see what was happening inside the shop!'

'The way that Mr Shifty rapped on the door was strange,' commented Arthur. 'It was almost as if he was giving a secret knock! Even if we copied it, I'm not sure that we'd be let in . . .' He hesitated while he thought about what they should do next. 'Perhaps we should try round the back,' said Arthur. 'If the burglars didn't get into the building from the street, they must have broken a window or jemmied the door at the back of the house. There's a footpath somewhere that leads to a gate in Mr Hardbattle's yard. Come on, Suze! Let's try to find it!'

They had started to sneak along the row of houses in search of a path that linked all of their backyards, when the sound of another vehicle approaching caused them to stop in their tracks.

This time it was a van which was the size of a small truck. Its driver parked in front of the Land Rover, and three stocky men got out. They hunched their shoulders against the wet weather and, hands in their pockets, walked up to the door. One of them lifted his fist to deliver the secret knock.

'Change of plan!' whispered Arthur to Susan, turning on his heel and tiptoeing back towards the bookshop. He paused by his bike and removed the pump. 'I've just had an idea!'

Chapter Twenty

Shady Dealings

Arthur dropped to his hands and knees when he passed in front of the shop so that his head did not show above the window sill. Taking care to keep to the shadows, Susan crawled behind him, and a panting Scallywag brought up the rear. When they were a stone's throw from the three men, Arthur called his stalking party to a halt, signalling by raising his hand. He and Susan crouched together, not even daring to whisper, waiting for the door of the bookshop to open.

The men did not appreciate being made to hang around outside in the rain. They buttoned up their donkey jackets, and grumbled about getting wet. When the door creaked ajar they squashed into the doorway, eager to get into the dry, but an unseen person drove them back.

'Password first!' the person said.

'We got ourselves a right stickler 'ere!' complained one of the men, turning to his two pals. 'What's the flamin' password, lads? Anyone remember?'

Both men shrugged, then one of them had a flash of inspiration. 'Some geezer's name, weren't it? A Mafia Mr Big, it sounded like . . . Poppa Peddle or someone . . .'

'Popocatépetl,' said the man behind the door, but judging their effort to be close enough, he allowed the three men to enter.

Arthur readied himself as the men trooped over the threshold, waiting for the moment in which to make his move.

When the door was a split second away from clicking shut, Arthur sprang into action. Leaping forward, with one arm outstretched, he lodged his bicycle pump in the gap between the door and the doorpost. His aim was true, and the pump did its job, keeping the door of the bookshop open. Arthur waited to see if it had been noticed that the door had not closed properly, but he did not hear any utterances of annoyance, and the door remained ajar.

Arthur was so pleased that his plan had worked and so keen to discover what was happening within the shop that he did not give a second's thought to the bell above the door. Susan whispered a warning in his ear just in time.

They concluded that their entry would have to coincide with a thunderclap, which, with luck, would cover the clamorous jingle-jangle of the bell. A flash of lightning gave them their cue, and the instant they heard the first crackle of thunder, Arthur and Susan nudged the door open and sneaked inside the shop. Before closing the door behind him, Arthur retrieved his bicycle pump, then he ran to join Susan and Scallywag, who had taken refuge behind a tall bookcase. They huddled there in the dark, their hearts thumping wildly.

When Susan and Arthur were satisfied that their entrance had not been detected, they left their hiding place behind the bookcase and crept through the warren of books towards the hum of voices. As they ventured deeper into the shop, their surroundings grew lighter so that they could see the outlines of books on the shelves and very nearly read their spines. Somewhere, in a hidden recess of the shop, a source of light was brightening the gloom.

'Over there!' hissed Arthur to Susan, pointing with his bicycle pump. 'Candles and a whole load of people! Look!'

Both children peered round a bookcase and saw a gathering of twelve or more people who were standing in pools of light thrown by the wavering flames of six stout candles.

'Are *all* these people burglars?' Susan asked. She had expected to be afraid, but found that she was more puzzled than scared. 'Golly, Arthur! Aren't there a lot of them?'

The 'burglars' were milling around a table display of some kind. Amongst them were the three broad-backed men, Mr Shifty, who had taken off his deerstalker hat but was still sporting his bicycle clips, and a woman in a green paisley headscarf and wellington boots. When Arthur spotted Mrs Voysey-Brown and Jimmy amongst the throng, he started to think that Susan had been mistaken, and that the people in the shop were not burglars at all. He saw someone flaunt a wad of twenty-pound notes and hand a thick sheaf of them to Jimmy. A sale seemed to be going on. It was not unlike a tabletop sale, of the sort that was held in the playground at Arthur's school at weekends. Were the three house guests selling Mr Hardbattle's books and pocketing the proceeds? Arthur trembled with outrage, alerting Scallywag that something was wrong. A growl started in the dog's throat, and instinctively Susan tightened her grip on Scallywag's lead to prevent her from rushing into the small crowd of people.

A well-to-do voice raised itself above the commotion: 'These rugs are exuding a strong smell of garlic! Or is it these opera evening gloves? The wretched smell seems to be floating right underneath my nose!' The woman in the headscarf replaced the soft leather gloves on the table and, in her prissy voice, continued to complain.

'Must we view these artefacts in such poor light? Surely, we could switch on the electric lights and do away with these candles!'

'And have the rozzers sniffing round 'cos a shop's open after hours?' said one of the thickset men beside her. ''Ave some sense, love! Blimey!'

'They aren't buying books, Arthur!' Susan said, as more money changed hands and somebody walked out with an umbrella stand and a porcelain vase. Arthur and Susan watched, bemused.

'It's expensive junk, that's what it is!' declared Arthur. 'Where can it have come from? I've never seen any of it before!'

Every so often, Mr Claggitt made an appearance, tramping downstairs in his hiking boots, his arms laden with paraphernalia.

'Where's he getting it all from?' murmured Arthur, daringly leaning round the bookcase to get a closer look.

Susan remembered the banging noises that she had heard in her room prior to her tree-climbing escapade. At the time, she had thought that the sounds had originated on the roof, but it seemed more likely now that they had come from the attic instead. She shared her new theory with Arthur.

But if Mr Hardbattle had all this valuable stuff in his attic, why didn't he flog it to help him keep his business afloat? pondered Arthur, feeling more confused by the minute.

217

Before he could try to make sense of it all, Arthur became distracted by an argument over an item of jewellery.

'Five thousand pounds?' Mr Shifty snorted. 'My good woman, I wouldn't give you five *hundred*!' He scrutinised a bow-shaped brooch through an eyeglass, shook his head and handed it back to Mrs Voysey-Brown.

Extremely unimpressed to be offered a tenth of her asking price, Mrs Voysey-Brown resorted to calling Mr Shifty names, including a crooked old goat, a swindler and a rip-off merchant. 'You know damn well,' she said, 'that this diamond brooch is worth a mint. You can't expect me to believe that a *lady* would wear *paste*. And when I say "lady", I mean the wife of a *lord*!' Mrs Voysey-Brown looked down her nose at Mr Shifty. 'These gems are genuine, and you shan't convince me otherwise, you foul, insipid little upstart of a man!'

Before Mrs Voysey-Brown could close her fingers over it, Arthur got a good look at the brooch, and realised that it was the very same one that he had found in the gutter outside the shop on the day he had cleaned Mr Hardbattle's van. He frowned. Something was bothering him. How had Mr Claggitt managed to get into the attic? Despite searching for ages, Mr Hardbattle had not been able to find the key to the padlock. Could it be that the house guests had put all the antiques in the attic themselves and fitted the padlock to stop anyone else from finding their haul? Where had the three of them been in the hours before Arthur had found the brooch? Touring stately homes, they had said.

Arthur gasped. He delved inside his pocket and found the newspaper article he had ripped from the *Plumford Gazette*. Tilting it towards the light, he read the whole thing. It mentioned the outbreak of shoplifting and various burglaries in the town, but the article concentrated on the plundering of stately homes on the thirty-first of May. Amongst the items stolen were statues, a silver teapot, vases, figurines, paintings, oriental rugs, and a diamond brooch identified as missing by Lady Smythe-Hughes. In one fell swoop the mystery had been solved!

'Crikey, Suze!' said Arthur, shoving the article under her nose. 'All that stuff is nicked! And these people – Mr Shifty and the rest – they must be dealers . . . dodgy ones who aren't fussed about buying stolen goods!'

There was a loud bump and a discordant series of clangs and tings, which sounded as if somebody had dropped a cutlery set on the floor. Moments later, a flash of sheet lightning lit up the shop, and Arthur and Susan ducked behind their bookcase, but not before they had glimpsed Mr Claggitt emerging from the stairwell, with his arms full of silverware and his boots caked in yellow gunge.

'Had a bit of an accident,' they heard Mr Claggitt say.

'I'm no stranger to those, of course. Fallen down a fair few crevasses in my time, but I've never come a cropper on a staircase.'

Arthur and Susan froze when they heard Mr Claggitt's words and saw the vibrant colour of his boots. They both guessed immediately that the second to last stair had turned to custard, which meant that, in the next few minutes, the magic would go haywire.

Torn between wanting to see the magic misbehave and getting out of the shop to a place where their safety could be assured, Arthur and Susan waited to see what would happen.

'How much for this?' The woman in the headscarf had had the cheek to remove a picture from the wall, which belonged to Mr Hardbattle. As she thrust the painting of Lake Tahoe at Mrs Voysey-Brown, a flock of ducks circled the lake and flew straight out of the painting. They flew in a 'V' formation all around the shop, emitting loud quacks with every flap of their wings.

'Where'd they come from?' One of the beefy men shielded his head with a silver tea tray as the flock of ducks careered past. 'Ruddy 'ell! They'll wake the neighbours! Hilary, don't you usually carry a shotgun in your boot?'

'Yes, I do,' the woman in the headscarf said. 'I've got my twelve-bore in my Land Rover, but I couldn't possibly shoot these ducks! It's not duck-shooting season till September!'

The man put down the tea tray and called out to his mates. 'Come on, fellas! We should go! In five minutes, the rozzers are gonna be crawling all over this joint!' Buttoning his jacket over a carriage clock and a marble bust, the man set off at a jog towards the door.

At the mention of the police, everyone seemed to agree that they had spent enough and that they had no room left in their vehicles or in their briefcases for anything else. Purses were put away and wallets were snapped shut. Unnerved by the ducks, which they seemed to regard as some sort of booby trap, all of the dealers gathered together their purchases and fled.

'We ought to scram too,' said Arthur to Susan. He knew from Mr Hardbattle's instructions that it was not wise to stick around when the magic was about to lose control, and besides, they had seen everything that they needed to see. As they turned to leave the shop, Susan trod on Scallywag's paw.

The dog's yelp of pain was shrill, and in seconds Susan and Arthur had been discovered and surrounded.

'Well, well, well . . . what have we here?' said Mr Claggitt, holding a candle aloft so that its golden light fell on their horror-stricken faces.

'I could've sworn I put that pooch in the shed,' muttered Jimmy, 'and how the hell did Susie get out of her room?'

Mrs Voysey-Brown eyed Jimmy coldly. She looked the most displeased to have found out that they had been spied upon. 'Susan can't have been in her room when you locked it, you fool!' she snapped.

As well as feeling mortified that they had been caught, Arthur and Susan were also disturbed by the change that they could detect in the air. The magic's energy was building, and it was unlikely to be long before the magic let rip.

Standing close together, they weighed up their chances of dodging past the three grown-ups and reaching the door to the street.

'We should at least try,' whispered Susan.

Arthur nodded. 'Yeah. Ready? After the count of three . . .'

A noise like a popping cork caused Arthur and Susan to glance at each other, and their uneasiness turned to fear when a few seconds later, the floor of the bookshop began to vibrate. After a similar interval, the bookcases started to tilt and books drummed on to the floor, sending up clouds of choking dust. If Mrs Voysey-Brown had been auditioning for a horror film, the scream that she gave would have earned her the part. Everyone else doubled up, coughing, but when the air had cleared a little, Susan and Arthur seized their chance to escape.

They darted past the three grown-ups, intending to race as fast as they could through the shop until they reached the way out. If their route had been straight and their path unobstructed, they might have achieved their aim, but the shop was like a labyrinth and Arthur and Susan had to keep changing direction to weave in and out of the alcoves. Their goal was not made easier by having to swerve to avoid falling books or being forced to scramble over mounds of them.

Without Susan's torch, they would have been very lucky to stumble on the exit, but even with its beam they found that they kept hitting dead ends. Every time that they had to turn round and go back, they grew more panicky, conscious all the while that their pursuers were right on their tail.

The turning point came when the books joined in the chase. Finding themselves at the mercy of Mrs Voysey-Brown (who could run like a gazelle when she felt like it), Arthur and Susan thought that their number was up. However, their view changed when a heap of books nearby sprang to life and formed a staircase that the children eagerly scurried up. (The lower part collapsed when Mrs Voysey-Brown tried to do the same.)

As the chase progressed, Arthur and Susan were saved over and over again by the books. As well as more stair-cases, the magic conjured up bridges, slides, and on one occasion, a travelator.

All this exertion meant, however, that the magic tired itself out. Before half an hour was up, the floorboards stopped vibrating and the books lay still. Silently, the ducks glided back into their painting, landing on Lake Tahoe with a waggle of their tails.

Youth was on their side, but Arthur and Susan did not turn out to be the fittest in the shop. Drawing on his impressive reserves of stamina, it was Mr Claggitt who emerged from the wreckage, triumphant, with a child in each hand and Scallywag hanging off his trouser leg. Years of clinging on to rock faces with his fingertips had made Mr Claggitt's grip incredibly strong and, although they tried their hardest, neither Arthur nor Susan were able to free themselves.

A candle was found and relit, and a couple of chairs were recovered from underneath a pile of books. Mrs Voysey-Brown and Jimmy sat down on the chairs, while the others perched side by side on an overturned bookcase. Everyone looked exhausted and the worse for wear.

'We know you're behind all the burglaries in the papers!' burst out Arthur, aiming a kick at Mr Claggitt's shins.

Mrs Voysey-Brown smiled. 'Is that so?'

'It's wrong to steal,' said Susan. 'I think it might be against the law.'

'So, what you gonna do, pipsqueaks?' Jimmy said, smirking at them. 'Hand us over to the cops?'

'Maybe we will!' said Arthur boldly, sticking out his chin.

Clenching the collar of Arthur's pyjama top, Mr Claggitt gave him a shake.

'No, you won't, sonny boy,' he said, 'and I'll tell you why. You and little Susie here are in this up to your necks –'

Before Mr Claggitt could expand on why Susan and Arthur would be unwise to involve the police, there was a noise on the stairs and Miss Quint appeared at their foot in her dressing gown and slippers. She looked cross and also a little bit smug.

'I've a hunch it was *you*!' she said, pointing a finger at Jimmy. 'You're the sort of prankster who would lock us in our rooms. Thought it was hilarious, I'll bet! Well, as you can see . . . I'm not easily beaten. You'll have to try harder than that to get the better of Beatrice Quint!'

Having decided that Jimmy was the culprit who had locked her in, Miss Quint proceeded to tell them how she had engineered her escape. Not possessing the sort of shoulders that could knock down a door, she had settled on attempting to pick the lock. After hours of trying, she had finally found the winning combination of a nail file and a kirby grip.

When she had finished blathering on about how resourceful she had been, it dawned on Miss Quint that Arthur should have been at home in bed, and that the shop looked as if a herd of wildebeest had rampaged through it.

'The magic's gone crazy again,' said Arthur, seeing the look of surprise on her face.

Slowly, Miss Quint began to accept that she had probably made a mistake. Too proud to ask the others to explain what had happened, she tried to hide her embarrassment by burbling at top speed. 'I was about to insist that you let Mr Hardbattle out of the bathroom, but I heard him snoring as I came past the door. It would be kinder to let him sleep, I think, all things considered. So that's why you locked us in our rooms! You wanted to keep us safe while the magic caused a rumpus. Well, why didn't you say?'

'Actually –' began Arthur, but Miss Quint would not listen. She fancied that she had solved the conundrum of why five people were gathered downstairs in the wee small hours.

'It's sweet of you to tidy up the mess,' she interrupted, keen to make amends for her blunder earlier when she had accused Jimmy of playing a practical joke. 'It's kind . . . very kind, but Arthur and Susan should be in bed. The clear-up can wait until tomorrow, don't you agree?'

Arthur could not believe his ears. He wondered if it was sleepiness rather than stupidity which had caused Miss Quint to misinterpret what was going on.

'But, Miss Quint –' began Arthur.

'There's something we ought to tell you!' said Susan.

Miss Quint wrinkled her nose with displeasure and

intimated that they should be quiet.

'Whatever you children have to say, I'm sure it can wait until morning,' she said. 'Arthur, did you arrive on your bike? Well, what are you waiting for? Off you scoot!'

Chapter Twenty-One

After the Storm

By morning, the sky had been wiped clean, the rain clouds had moved on and the thunderstorm's bequest to the new day was a cool, fresh breeze. Puddles shone, grass gleamed and birdsong pierced the air.

Outdoors, all was right with the world, but inside the bookshop, it was a different story. There were books and furniture strewn everywhere, and Susan was having an awful job trying to make Miss Quint see reason.

Both had risen early. Miss Quint had wanted to get up at first light so that the bookshop could be restored to a half decent state by the time that it was due to open, and Susan, who had barely slept a wink, had wanted to tell Miss Quint as soon as she was able that Jimmy, Mr Claggitt and Mrs Voysey-Brown were a band of thieves.

As soon as she had heard the joggling of a doorknob and the creak of the broom cupboard door opening wide, Susan had jumped out of bed, pulled on some shorts and followed Miss Quint downstairs.

Miss Quint had already begun to clear up when Susan made an appearance, and refused to take a break from sweeping the floor to focus on what Susan had to say. While Miss Quint's indifference was discouraging, Susan did not let it deter her from launching into her account of what had happened during the night. She explained about her trek across town, Vijay's map, her ride on a bike, the secret knock and the sale of stolen antiques.

When Susan had finished, Miss Quint straightened up and examined the head of her broom. 'This could do with having stiffer bristles,' she observed.

'You do believe me, don't you, Miss Quint?' asked Susan, wondering if Miss Quint had listened to a word she had said.

Having had her eyes fixed firmly on the floor during Susan's lengthy narration of events, Miss Quint looked up and gazed directly at her. 'It sounds far-fetched,' she said. 'Might you have dreamed it?'

Susan was indignant. 'Of course not!' she said.

'You expect me to believe that the people lodging here – my guests – are a band of scheming crooks?' asked Miss Quint. 'Jimmy's just a normal lad who likes to play the fool and you can't think a respected mountaineer like Mr Claggitt would be involved in anything underhand! As for Mrs Voysey-Brown . . . have you ever heard of a film star leading a life of crime?'

'But it's true!' insisted Susan.

'True, she says!' muttered Miss Quint, shaking her head in disbelief. She turned her broom the right way up, propped it against a bookcase and knelt down on the floor to gather up some books.

Susan did not offer to help straight away because Miss Quint had riled her, but standing by and watching while someone else worked made Susan feel increasingly embarrassed, and after a couple of minutes, she offered to lend a hand.

It was only when they happened upon some antiques amongst the debris that Miss Quint began to believe that Susan might be telling the truth. They collected together a brass doorknocker, a picture of fruit in a bowl, a silver tea tray and an ornamental lion. Miss Quint locked them all in the cupboard under the stairs, and apologised to Susan for doubting her.

'It's quite *incredible*, but it does make sense,' Miss Quint conceded, weighing up all the evidence in her mind. Crime had never been a major problem in Plumford. It was only after she had wished for the book characters to be real that the incidents of burglary and shoplifting had soared, and on the day that antiques had been filched from stately homes, Jimmy, Mr Claggitt and Mrs Voysey-Brown had admitted to driving into the country in Mr Hardbattle's van.

Miss Quint praised Susan's pluck and ingenuity, and then subjected her to a telling-off. Climbing down a tree in the dark Miss Quint described as 'reckless', and roaming the streets of Plumford on her own she summed up as 'foolhardy'. Finally, she secured Susan's word that she would never go off by herself at such a late hour again.

They wrestled with a bookcase and managed to stand it upright.

'What should we tell Mr Hardbattle?' asked Susan as she started to fill the empty shelves.

'I'll tell him that it was me who locked him in,' said Miss Quint, 'and that I did it for his own safety because the magic was set to go wild.'

Susan picked up another stack of books from the floor. 'Shouldn't we mention that he's got some burglars living under his roof?'

'No, we certainly shouldn't!' said Miss Quint. She noticed that Susan looked troubled about keeping this information from Mr Hardbattle, and thought of a way to mollify her. 'I'll tell you what,' said Miss Quint, squeezing Susan's arm and speaking in a gentle voice. 'While Mr Hardbattle's opening up, you and I will whizz upstairs and speak to those three scoundrels. We'll make them see that what they've done is wrong and tell them to give back all the things they've stolen. There won't be any need to bother Mr Hardbattle once this mess has been sorted out. He's got enough on his plate, poor man, what with arranging the rehoming of the magic.'

The plan met with Susan's approval, and they carried

on with their wearisome task, but had to suspend their tidying temporarily when, at seven thirty sharp, the phone began to ring.

Miss Quint snatched up the receiver. It was Arthur. Having had a restless night like Susan, he had woken up at six a.m. and waited until a civilised hour before telephoning the shop.

'So, Suze has told you everything?' said Arthur.

'She has,' replied Miss Quint. 'Though I'll admit I was sceptical at first. It beggars belief that our guests are involved in the burglary business!'

'Yes, it does,' said Arthur curtly, 'but they are.'

Creaks were heard through the ceiling, and Miss Quint panicked and almost dropped the phone. Worrying that Mr Hardbattle had woken up, and might come downstairs and overhear their conversation, she insisted that they should end their call immediately. Arthur agreed to meet Miss Quint and Susan later on that morning at an eatery in town where they would be able to talk freely.

At ten o'clock, Arthur, Susan and Miss Quint convened at The Blue Wisteria Tea Rooms. They sought out a table in the darkest, most secluded nook.

'The question is, what are we going to do?' said Arthur, perusing the menu while he waited for an answer.

No one spoke, but Miss Quint made a high sound in

her throat. She seized a paper napkin and dabbed away the tears, which were welling in her eyes.

'Oh, Miss Quint!' said Susan, overcome with sympathy.

Arthur looked up from the menu and was surprised to see Miss Quint in such a wretched state. He was just about to ask what had caused her to get so upset when he saw a waitress approaching with a notepad in her hand. He thrust the menu at Miss Quint and she hid her tear-streaked face behind it.

Arthur ordered for the three of them, and when the waitress was out of earshot he whipped the menu out of Miss Quint's hands.

'What on earth's the matter?' he asked.

'You'd think, wouldn't you,' Miss Quint said, her voice cracking slightly, 'that when someone's been accused of stealing, they'd try to deny it or be ashamed of what they'd done! Not our bunch of miscreants! They confessed to the thieving just like that!' Miss Quint snapped her fingers, then her bottom lip trembled and more tears flowed. 'And were they repentant?' she said. 'Not a bit of it! They boasted about how clever they'd been and wouldn't hear of bringing an end to their crime spree, let alone returning what they'd already taken.'

Arthur took a deep breath. 'Then we'll have to go to the police.'

'We can't!' said Susan. 'We're part of the gang! We've

handled stolen goods! And we haven't just handled them, we've eaten them!'

'What *are* you talking about?' asked Arthur.

'The ices!' said Susan, gripping the edge of the table earnestly. 'We each had one on that day we went to Plentiful Sands!'

Arthur was appalled. 'You mean those ice creams were *stolen*?'

'*And* the plastic ball *and* the deckchair *and* the sun hats *and* the bucket and spade,' Miss Quint revealed. 'Jimmy pilfered all of them from people on the beach.'

Arthur's mouth sagged open in shock. He had remembered the shopping trip that Jimmy, Mr Claggitt and Mrs Voysey-Brown had made when they had first arrived. On that occasion they had come back with a scarf and two gold watches. At the time their purchases had not aroused Arthur's suspicions, but once he had found out about their criminal tendencies, he realised that the items had probably been pinched. However, he had forgotten all about the trip to the beach, and was dismayed to think that he had gobbled down somebody else's ice cream.

'It seems that it was Jimmy who led the others astray,' said Miss Quint. 'He told Susan and me that he'd been thieving since he was a tot, and that he only took the job as a bellhop so that he could steal from the hotel's wealthy guests!'

Arthur urged Miss Quint to change the subject swiftly when he spotted the waitress coming towards them, carrying a tray. They smiled politely when the woman placed their order in front of them. Arthur had asked for two cherryades, a pot of tea and a plate of cream cakes.

'What *I* don't understand is why they did it,' said Arthur. 'Mr Claggitt's so obsessed with mountains, I wouldn't have thought that he was the money-grabbing type.'

'He's the most enthusiastic burglar of the lot!' said Miss Quint.

'He likes scaling walls,' explained Susan as she reached for a cream tart with a raspberry on top.

Miss Quint wholeheartedly agreed. 'Mr Claggitt told us that his grappling hook had seen more action in the past few days than it did when he went up Mount Everest!'

'What are they planning to do with the money?' asked Arthur.

'They're using it to finance their new life,' said Miss Quint, pouring herself a strong cup of tea. 'Free bed and board at Mr Hardbattle's house is like living in squalor, according to them.'

'They're leaving Plumford,' said Susan, 'and going abroad!' To an untravelled person like Susan, the idea of journeying to another country was almost as exciting as going to the moon. 'Isn't that awfully daring, Arthur?

Abroad is very different from here, you know. They speak in languages you can't understand and the food is inedible, so Miss Quint said –'

'Jimmy and the rest have got their hearts set on Switzerland,' cut in Miss Quint. She sounded resentful.

'Why Switzerland?' asked Arthur, helping himself to a cream slice.

'It suits their requirements, doesn't it?' Miss Quint snapped, bitterness drawing her lips into a thin line. 'Mrs Voysey-Brown's a cut above the rest of us, being an actress in films. She's got expensive tastes. She's used to fine dining and glitzy resorts, and those sorts of places are right up Jimmy's street as well because of the rich clientele they attract. Switzerland's awash with posh hotels and, more importantly, it's got the Eiger.'

'What's that when it's at home?' Arthur asked.

'It's a mountain,' Susan told him. 'Mr Claggitt said it's terribly big and its north face is a real stinker to climb.'

Arthur could not quite get his head round the fact that the three book characters had mustered a large enough pot of cash to leave the country. 'Won't it cost a lot to get to Switzerland and pay hotel bills and climb up the Eiger? Have they got that kind of money?' he asked.

'They're a few thousand short, apparently,' Miss Quint informed him.

'If only we could go to the police and get them arrested!' said Arthur.

'If we hand them over to the police we'll be taken into custody too, as accessories,' Miss Quint told him briskly, 'and anyway, the police would realise they're not British citizens . . . or any kind of citizens come to that, and then I'd have to explain where they came from . . .'

'The police would find out about the magic!' said Arthur, his heart sinking rapidly. 'They'd raid Mr Hardbattle's shop!'

'You see?' said Miss Quint. 'Our hands are tied.'

Arthur groaned, and fell back limply in his chair. 'Things couldn't possibly be worse!' he complained.

'Oh, yes, they could!' objected Miss Quint. 'Yours wasn't the only telephone call we had this morning.'

Arthur clasped his forehead in despair. 'Who else phoned?'

'Mrs Carruthers,' said Susan. 'Her voice sounded funny so I didn't know it was her at first. I asked her how her bees were, but she didn't have time for small talk. She said that she needed to speak to Mr Hardbattle and that it was urgent. He was in the bathroom. It took me ages to find him. He had creamy white soap all over his chin. When I told him who was on the phone and what she'd said, he ran downstairs without rinsing his face or anything!'

Fearing that Pam Carruthers had been the bearer of unwelcome news, Arthur asked Susan what she had said.

'I couldn't hear,' Susan replied, 'but Mr Hardbattle

kept saying, "Oh, no!" and "Oh, how awful" over and over again.'

Arthur looked to Miss Quint for an explanation.

'A tree fell down last night,' she told Arthur solemnly. 'The tree got struck by lightning in the storm. It landed on that dear little woodsman's cottage and reduced the place to rubble.'

'He's acting like he's given up!' said Arthur as he and Susan stared across the shop at Mr Hardbattle. The old man sat behind his desk, benumbed and sorrowful, his shoulders hunched. In front of him sat a cup of cold tea that Miss Quint had made for him and which he had not touched.

The news that the woodsman's cottage had been badly damaged had been a blow to them all, but while the others had vowed not to let it defeat them, Mr Hardbattle had sunk into a deep depression. Arthur, Miss Quint and Susan had tried to rouse him out of his stupor-like state, reminding him that there were eight days left before the rent was due, but Mr Hardbattle would not be cheered up. He had made up his mind that their undertaking to rehouse the magic was hopeless, and had resigned himself to losing his business and his home.

Seeing Mr Hardbattle so down in the dumps was very upsetting for Arthur, and he longed to throw himself into the task of finding another home for the magic. However, Arthur was prudent enough to recognise that the problem of the three burgling house guests was more pressing just at that moment.

In The Blue Wisteria Tea Rooms, Arthur, Susan and Miss Quint had decided that they would have to put a stop to the thefts themselves. By turning detective, they aimed to discover how Jimmy and his gang were planning to add to their haul, and to stop them from doing so. In the space of a few days, the three artful thieves had amassed a small fortune, but they needed even more money to cover the cost of their adventure abroad. They would have to fork out for forged passports, luggage and aeroplane tickets, and once they had left England they would need a nest egg large enough to fund their new lives.

'One more big job, that's what they said,' revealed Susan, when she, Arthur and Miss Quint met up in the park to walk Scallywag on Friday afternoon. Susan was their eavesdropping champion. She was adept at finding places to hide in order to listen to conversations without anyone knowing that she was there. 'And they plan to 'pull it off on Saturday.'

'Saturday? You don't mean tomorrow?' said Miss Quint.

'The day of the carnival!' said Arthur. 'Of course! While the whole town is watching the parade, it should be simple for Jimmy's gang to steal loads of stuff! What kind of thing are they planning, Suze?'

Susan bit her lip. 'I didn't hear that part.'

The gang's preferred meeting place was Mrs Voysey-Brown's room. It was the largest bedroom in the house. Before Mrs Voysey-Brown had moved into it, Miss Quint had commandeered it for herself, and before that, the room had been the chosen sleeping quarters of Mr Hardbattle (who had not liked to turf out a relation of Arthur's and had said that he would sleep in the bath instead).

On Friday evening after supper, Susan managed to sneak inside the room and find a suitable hiding place. She chose the wardrobe and crouched down in a corner, concealing herself behind a long winter coat. Leaving the wardrobe door ajar, Susan was able to listen to the plans of the gang when they held one of their hush-hush meetings half an hour later.

'The jeweller's on Twopenny Lane!' she said to Miss Quint, after gulping down a large glass of water (it had been stifling in the wardrobe and she had been in there for over an hour).

'Right,' said Miss Quint, stern-faced and businesslike. 'I'll telephone Arthur, and then we should go to bed, Susan. It's crucial that we get a good night's sleep. We'll have to have our wits about us tomorrow if we're to foil their plans!'

Chapter Twenty-Two

Brass Bands and Bunting

When Arthur rode his bike through Plumford on Carnival Day, he saw that council workers had been busy overnight. At the edge of pavements, barriers had been put in place to keep members of the public from crossing the street once the carnival procession had got under way, and zigzagging from one side of the street to the other were several hundred metres' worth of bunting. The triangles of yellow, red, white and blue flapped lazily in the breeze as Arthur pedalled his bicycle beneath them.

It was eight o'clock in the morning and the weather was as glorious as the organisers of the carnival had hoped it would be. The sky was lapis lazuli blue and the sun was far too bright to look at. As Arthur whizzed along on his bike, he passed plenty of early risers like himself who were all busy with some job or other which would contribute to making Plumford Carnival go with a swing. Litter collectors and road sweepers made the streets look spick and span; a frowning pair with clipboards checked the timetable of events, and ladies from Plumford's Flower Arranging Society swarmed over a booth in front of the library which had been erected for the purpose of providing a sheltered seat for the judges of the parade. The judges' job was to award a prize to the most impressive float. Last year's head judge had been the town's bank manager, but this year the Plumford Carnival Committee had set their sights a little higher. It had been something of a coup when Lady Felicity Smythe-Hughes, who was the wife of a poultry tycoon, had agreed to preside over the panel of judges.

When they had learned that an aristocrat was to officiate, the ladies of Plumford's Flower Arranging Society had determined to dress the booth with expensive blooms, which to their minds was the sort of lavish gesture that a personage of blue blood merited.

There were bollards everywhere and most of the roads in the centre of town were closed off to traffic but, luckily, no one bothered to remonstrate with one young boy on a bike.

When Arthur reached Hardbattle Books, Miss Quint, Susan and Scallywag were waiting for him on the pavement outside. Miss Quint had packed a holdall with three rounds of sandwiches and two large bottles of lemonade to satisfy their appetites while they kept the jeweller's shop under observation. Miss Quint's choice of attire was usually smart and a little eccentric, but today she had dressed down. Her outfit of a pair of culottes, a vest top and sunglasses had been carefully selected to help her to merge into the crowds. Around her neck she wore Mr Hardbattle's old binoculars, which he had used on his holidays to watch herons on the Norfolk Broads. Miss Quint had no interest in birds. She intended to use the binoculars to look out for the arrival of thieves.

Susan had changed into something new: a pair of three-quarter-length trousers and a T-shirt with sequins sewn on to its front. She had also unravelled her plaits so that her hair fell loosely down her back. For the first time since she had arrived in Plumford she did not look peculiar. Arthur thought that she could easily have passed for a girl in his class or one of his sisters' friends.

'All set?' asked Miss Quint.

'Did you remember the things?' pressed Susan.

Arthur dismounted from his bike. 'Yes,' he answered. 'I've got my kazoo and the ball of string.'

'Excellent,' Miss Quint said, patting each child's shoulders. 'Let's go, team!'

The jeweller's shop was in Twopenny Lane, not far from the library and the junction with Swan Street, which were both on the route of the parade. It took them twenty minutes to walk there, and once they had arrived they looked closely at the shop, which was owned by a woman called Geraldine Jennings. Arthur and Susan gaped at all the treasures in the window, pointing out trays of gold necklaces and rings set with enormous gems, while Miss Quint got out her tape measure and noted the width of the doorway. She also counted the number of steps leading up to it (three) and saw that a paving slab outside the shop was liable to tip if its top left-hand corner was trodden on.

When they had carried out their inspection, they crossed the road and sat down on a bench which was positioned in an alcove, not far away from Jennings the Jeweller's. Miss Quint delved in her bag and drew out two comics, which she handed to Arthur and Susan. Next, she produced a newspaper for herself. Behind their periodicals, they went over their plan.

'Are you clear about what you have to do when the gang gets here?' hissed Miss Quint.

'I'm to slip inside the shop unnoticed,' said Susan, 'before the thieves have got out of Mr Hardbattle's van.'

'With my kazoo,' reminded Arthur, handing it to her behind his open copy of the *Beano*.

'What will you be doing, Arthur?' Miss Quint prompted.

'I shall be unwinding my ball of string,' Arthur said, 'and positioning myself on one side of the doorway and you'll be on the other side, won't you, Miss Quint?'

'I will,' confirmed Miss Quint. 'Top marks so far. Well done!'

Susan lowered her comic and grinned. 'I'm to wait until they've grabbed all the jewellery they want, and then when they're ready to leave, I must blow on the kazoo.'

'At which point,' said Arthur, turning to Miss Quint, 'we raise the string above the doorstep and hold on tightly . . .'

'And the whole dratted lot of them tumble down the steps,' finished Miss Quint with an air of supreme satisfaction.

'Then I grab the jewels and take off on my bike,' said Arthur, 'only returning when the coast is clear.'

'Quite right,' said Miss Quint. 'And when we hand them back to Mrs Jennings the jeweller, she offers us a huge reward!'

Miss Quint's final comment made them all laugh and they felt confident enough to revel in how simple, and yet ingenious, their plan was.

'And if one of them hops over our string, they'll land on that loose paving slab and fall flat on their face,' said Miss Quint delightedly. 'Our plan is foolproof. I can't see how it could go wrong!'

The morning wore on. Underneath the bench, Scallywag rested her head on her paws and went to sleep. Susan, Miss Quint and Arthur swapped their reading matter and got up occasionally to stretch their legs. The shops in Twopenny Lane opened their doors and the volume of pedestrian traffic increased. From their seat on the bench, they could see the top of the road where crowds were beginning to gather to view the carnival procession, which was due to start at eleven o'clock. Arthur saw his father walk past with his youngest sister, Tilly, in tow. He was hidden behind Miss Quint's newspaper at the time and so his father and sister did not spot him, but he watched them walk the length of the lane to Swan Street and claim their place in the front row, directly behind the barriers.

'I expect the gang won't get here until the parade starts,' said Miss Quint.

'That makes sense,' said Arthur.

They waited for another half an hour. Jimmy's gang did not show up.

At the top of Twopenny Lane the crowds continued to swell until there was no room left on the pavement. In the distance, Miss Quint, Susan and Arthur could hear a brass band striking up a tune. Fainter still were the whine of bagpipes and the steady pounding of drums. The carnival procession had started.

'It would've been fun to see all the floats,' said Arthur with a pang of regret.

'I should have been on one!' said Miss Quint, sounding put out as well. 'The Women's Institute has got the honour of leading the whole procession this year. They're dressing as Hawaiian hula girls and the float's all decked out like a tropical island with palm trees and coconuts and everything.'

Two children walked past at that moment, both licking ice creams draped with raspberry sauce.

'They look smashing! May I have one of those?' asked Susan, gazing beseechingly at Miss Quint.

Yielding to Susan's request, Miss Quint opened her purse and placed a five-pound note in her hand. 'Oh, very well, poppet! Could you fetch us all a cornet? There's a shop around the corner, behind the library, that sells them. It's called Clements. Off you go!'

'But, Miss Quint . . .' protested Arthur.

Susan picked up Scallywag's lead, and said, 'Scally! Walkies!' before setting off down the lane with the dog trotting beside her.

Arthur turned to Miss Quint reprovingly. 'What if the thieves turn up?' he said. He thought that an ice cream was a nice idea, but he viewed Miss Quint's decision as a poor one.

'We'd have to be very unlucky for them to come in the next three minutes!' scoffed Miss Quint. 'Stop worrying, Arthur! Susan won't be long.'

They waited patiently at first, but after Susan had been gone for more than five minutes, they both began to feel anxious. It was agreed that Arthur should go to the ice cream shop to see why Susan had been delayed, but before he was able to take more than a few paces, Scallywag appeared at a run, trailing her lead along the ground.

Arthur's stomach gave a lurch. He guessed, immediately, that something had happened to Susan. Without securing the opinion of Miss Quint, he flew off down the street, almost colliding with a lady and her shopping trolley as he turned the corner into Oldbrook Road.

'Susan! Susan! Where are you?' he yelled. His eyes darted from one side of the street to the other, and his heart did gymnastics in his chest. Hearing the squeal of tyres, he raced ahead and was just in time to see the rear of a vehicle vanishing round a corner. Arthur stamped his foot with frustration and felt something soft and gooey under his shoe. He lifted up his foot and saw that three ice creams had been dropped on to the pavement. Their cones had been flattened and their creamy scoops were a partially melted mess. He could see the mark that his shoe had made on them. A second footprint was visible too. It was much larger than Arthur's and had chunky treads that were commonly found on sturdy footwear. Arthur realised with a jolt of horror that it was the print of a mountaineer's boot.

Arthur started to run back the way he had come, knowing that he would need to fetch his bicycle to have any chance of rescuing Susan. Now that he had seen the boot-print he was convinced that the vehicle that had sped out of sight had been Mr Hardbattle's van and he had no doubts that Susan had been bundled into it.

Arthur raced past the shop called Clements and the rear of the library. When he turned into Twopenny Lane, he found that he had to dodge through a cluster of gossiping shoppers to get to Miss Quint. She had hitched her bag on to her shoulder and was holding Scallywag on her lead, a look of agitation on her face.

Not waiting until he drew close, Arthur shouted out the news, 'She's gone, Miss Quint! They've taken her!'

When Arthur heard the far-off whine of police sirens, he thought for a moment that he must be imagining them. There was a buzzing noise as well. Everyone around him seemed to be talking at once.

'Yes, isn't it dreadful?' said a woman, responding to Arthur's announcement. 'Kidnapped in broad daylight, right under the noses of all the local bigwigs. They found a ransom note pinned to the library noticeboard. A hundred thousand pounds, they've asked for!'

'What?' said Arthur, baffled by what the woman had said. He was amazed that the news of Susan's kidnap could have travelled so fast, and to ask for a ransom of a hundred thousand pounds seemed incredible. How could the gang have thought that he and Miss Quint could possibly raise that amount?

'Of course, if they'd known how much her husband

was worth, they might have asked for a million,' the woman gabbled excitedly.

'A million?' said Arthur, confused. 'Whose husband? What has all this got to do with Susan?'

The woman gave Arthur a scornful look. 'She's not called *Susan*,' she said. 'Lady Smythe-Hughes's first name is Felicity!'

Chapter Twenty-Three

In Hot Pursuit

'Those devious old so-and-sos!' spluttered Miss Quint when she and Arthur had had a quick confab and had started to piece together what had gone on. 'They never had any intention of robbing the jeweller's shop. It was all a ruse to throw us off the scent.'

Arthur was filled with anger and his hands were shaking so badly that he could not manage to unlock his bike. 'I'll bet they knew that Susan was listening in to their plans,' he said. 'They fed her a load of lies when she was hiding in that wardrobe. They're probably laughing up their sleeves at us!'

Miss Quint tried to help Arthur by holding his bicycle steady while he knelt beside the front wheel and wrestled with the lock.

'They must have thought that Christmas had come early when they found out that the chief judge of the carnival belonged to the nobility!' she ranted, gripping the handlebars tightly. 'If Jimmy and those rotten cronies of his get their hands on that ransom money they'll be hotfooting it to the Swiss Alps before you can say "Cuckoo Clock".'

'There!' Arthur announced with relief as he twisted a key and his lock snapped open. 'Now I can get after them!'

'I wonder why they needed to take Susan?' reflected Miss Quint. 'I suppose she might have seen them in the process of shoving Lady Smythe-Hughes into their van. They must have smuggled old Posh-Drawers out of the library's rear entrance.'

Arthur leaped on to the saddle of his bike and placed his foot on the pedal, ready to speed away.

'You haven't really got a hope of catching them, you know,' Miss Quint felt obliged to point out. She strained her neck and looked towards Swan Street, where people in the crowds were jostling to get a good view of the parade. The carnival procession still seemed to be going on despite the abduction of one of its judges. 'It's a shame we can't find ourselves a better mode of transport,' she commented.

Suddenly, Miss Quint twisted Arthur's handlebars, forcing his front wheel to face the crowds at the top of Twopenny Lane. 'I've got it, Arthur!' she cried, running up the slope towards the sounds of tubas and trumpets belting out a military march. 'Follow me if you want to save Susan!'

Somehow they fought their way through the crowds of people who were waving Union Jacks and cheering as the first of the carnival floats trundled past. Miss Quint blessed the fact that she had chosen to wear culottes, performing a scissor jump to convey herself over the barriers and into the road.

Arthur happened upon his father and sister in the melee and thrust his bicycle at them with only the briefest of explanations. Then he followed Miss Quint, vaulting the barrier to land in the path of the town's brass band.

He dashed after Miss Quint, who had caught up with the leading float and was running alongside it. The float was a monstrous lorry with a platform mounted on its trailer. Just as Miss Quint had said, it was carrying the members of the Women's Institute. Made to resemble an island paradise in the Pacific, the float had been covered with sand and planted with artificial palm trees fashioned from cardboard, chicken wire, felt and crêpe paper. In the centre of the float was a papier mâché volcano, and around it, dressed in grass skirts and garlands of tissue-paper flowers, were the ladies of the Women's Institute.

In the manner of someone with a death wish, Miss Quint hurled herself in front of the lorry and waved her hands to halt it, causing the crowd to gasp in fear. The driver was forced to come to a stop and once he had applied his handbrake, Miss Quint hammered on the door of the cab until he opened it to ask her what the devil she thought she was doing.

'Out!' said Miss Quint, grabbing the startled lorry driver by the lapels of his shirt as he leaned towards her to tell her that she was unhinged. He fell unceremoniously out of the cab and, without wasting a second, Miss Quint picked up Scallywag and sprang into the driver's seat. Arthur raced round the front of the lorry to the passenger door, which Miss Quint duly opened for him, and climbed in next to her.

The driver tried to jump in front of his vehicle, but Miss Quint was not so compassionate as he had been and almost mowed him down.

'Idiot!' said Miss Quint as she wound down the window and shouted to the ladies on the trailer to hold on. Then she put the lorry into a higher gear and roared off up the street.

So many roads were cordoned off that Miss Quint had a fair idea of the route that Jimmy and the gang would have to take to get out of Plumford. Shooting past bemused spectators who had lined the streets to see the parade, Arthur glanced in the wing mirror and saw the hula-hula girls (most of whom were of pensionable age) clinging on to the palm trees with their mouths hanging open in shock.

'I think we'll go down here,' said Miss Quint, grappling with the oversized steering wheel and guiding the lorry through a row of bollards, crushing them under the lorry's massive wheels.

'Oops, I think we just lost Mrs Tidwell,' said Miss Quint, glancing in her mirror and biting her lip guiltily.

Arthur double-checked that he had put his seatbelt on.

The narrow streets of Plumford's shopping district were not designed for seven-ton lorries to hurtle down them at forty miles an hour. Miss Quint attracted a lot of attention as she scuffed kerbs, whacked the roofs of bus shelters and dented the odd rubbish bin or two. The spectacle of twenty or more terrified members of the Women's Institute, wearing Hawaiian costumes and holding on to handcrafted palm trees, drew even more amazed stares from everyone they passed.

Arthur heard the sound of sirens gradually getting louder and was torn between telling Miss Quint to put her foot down so that they could outrun the police and asking her to reduce her speed so that he did not have to hold on to the door handle to avoid being thrown around in his seat.

At one point, they heard thumps on the roof of the cab, and in their mirrors, Arthur and Miss Quint saw that some of the more sprightly members of the Women's Institute were hurling coconuts at them.

'I think we should go a bit slower,' he said. 'Our passengers are getting quite cross.'

'Nonsense!' insisted Miss Quint, pressing the horn to let an old man on a zebra crossing know that she was approaching fast. 'If they've got the energy to chuck armfuls of coconuts, they'll have the strength to hang on for hours yet!'

Eventually, having blundered through the heart of Plumford, they chanced upon Mr Hardbattle's van. Miss Quint attempted a war cry when she saw it and pressed the accelerator to the floor. In her excitement, she lost concentration and the seven-ton lorry weaved all over the road. There were screams from the ladies of the Women's Institute and a queue of people waiting by a hot dog stand found themselves buried in a heap of sand.

Miss Quint moved up a gear and steamed towards the van, and for the next five minutes, the two vehicles played a game of cat and mouse.

Finally, it seemed as if the gang of kidnappers had managed to get away when they took a turning down a narrow alley that the lorry could not get through without bringing down the buildings on either side. However, it was in this alleyway that the gang's luck ran out. Swerving to avoid a cat, which had darted into its path, the van ploughed into some dustbins, and its engine stalled. Miss Quint and Arthur heard a throbbing, whining noise as the van's engine struggled to restart.

'It won't fire up!' said Arthur.

'We've got 'em!' Miss Quint cried and switched off the lorry's engine.

Fearing that the stop was only temporary and that Miss Quint would start up the lorry again and continue the nightmarish journey, the ladies of the Women's Institute who had managed to remain on board deserted the lorry post-haste. Most of them scuttled to a nearby cafe for a much-needed cup of tea, but one or two preferred to nip to the pub next door for a glass of something stronger.

Once the lorry's engine had died, Scallywag emerged from the footwell where she had spent the entire journey skulking beside Arthur's feet. When Miss Quint and Arthur jumped down from the cab, Scallywag leaped after them and together they ran up the alleyway, determined to mete out some justice to the gang.

The doors at the front of the van opened before they got to it and Jimmy and his accomplices attempted to flee. Scallywag had got the measure of Mrs Voysey-Brown and, barking crazily, she pinned the woman against a wall. Arthur, who had started to learn rugby at school, performed a well-timed tackle and brought Jimmy to the ground. Then he sat on him so that he could not get away. It was left to Miss Quint to take on Mr Claggitt, but enlivened by the thrill of driving a lorry, she was not daunted one bit. Charging at him with a plastic lemonade bottle in her hand, she battered his broad back with it, then opened its top and sprayed him with its fizzy contents. Mr Claggitt coughed and spluttered and rubbed his stinging eyes, and while he was occupied with that, Miss Quint scooped up the keys of the van, which he had dropped on the cobbles.

When Miss Quint opened the rear doors of the van, Susan was the first to tumble out, shading her eyes against the dazzling sunlight. Before Arthur and Miss Quint could throw their arms around her, Susan held out a hand to the van's other passenger, who was slim and blonde, and dressed in a pink silk suit, a pearl choker and a fancy hat.

'Thank you, treasure,' said Lady Smythe-Hughes, taking Susan's hand. She alighted from the back of the van with the utmost grace as if such a skill had been taught to her at finishing school.

'Are you hurt, Your Ladyship?' enquired Miss Quint. She was unsure whether to curtsy, not having met a lady before.

'Oh, no, we're quite all right,' said Lady Smythe-Hughes. 'We're made of stern stuff, aren't we, Susan, hmm?'

For a member of the aristocracy, Lady Smythe-Hughes did not seem at all stuck up. She insisted that they should address her as Felicity, and when Scallywag ran over to her and was so keen to say hello that she put her paws on Lady Smythe-Hughes's skirt, she laughed and gave the dog a friendly pat.

Despite Lady Smythe-Hughes's down-to-earth ways, Arthur was embarrassed to be in her presence with smudges of dirt on his clothes, which he had acquired when he had rolled on the ground to apprehend Jimmy. Leaving Scallywag to guard the gang, Arthur hurriedly brushed himself down and approached Lady Smythe-Hughes and Susan with a beaming grin.

'You're quite safe now,' he told them.

'Thanks to you!' said Lady Smythe-Hughes. She reached out to shake Arthur's hand and made the same grateful gesture to Miss Quint.

As the sounds of police sirens drew closer, Miss Quint took Arthur to one side and they hastily discussed what should be done next. It was decided that Arthur should stay with Susan and Lady Smythe-Hughes to answer any questions the police might have while Miss Quint rounded up Jimmy's gang and spirited them away. As much as they deserved to be punished for committing a double kidnap, it was better all round if they avoided being caught.

While Arthur and Susan engaged Lady Smythe-Hughes in conversation, Miss Quint slipped away and ordered the gang to get into the back of Mr Hardbattle's van. Then she opened the bonnet and took a peek inside to try to work out why the engine had stalled. Diagnosing an overheated engine, which Mr Hardbattle had warned her might happen, she cooled it down using water from a bottle kept underneath the driver's seat. Once this had been done, the engine started up first time and Miss Quint drove up the alleyway, turning the corner with a squeal of tyres.

She was only just in time. Seconds later, a string of police cars screeched to a halt in front of the lorry, their blue lights flashing and flickering. The police were almost beaten to the scene by members of the local press, who swarmed around Lady Smythe-Hughes with their cameras, notepads and microphones.

'Smile, Suze!' said Arthur as a newspaper photographer took their picture. 'I think this might make the front page!'

Chapter Twenty-four

Trunk's find

Arthur and Susan basked in all the media attention, spelling out their names to journalists and hearing the click of cameras no matter which way they turned. After a few minutes, the police broke up the scrum and Susan and Arthur were whisked away in a police car, to be questioned at the local station about the whole kidnapping affair. The police were desperate to find out the identities of the kidnappers, but Arthur and Susan played dumb, providing vague descriptions that had the constable in charge of photofits scratching his head. When Arthur was asked who had been with him in the lorry, he was even more evasive and insisted that he could not think of her name.

'Come on, young fellow-me-lad!' prompted a chief inspector. 'You were sitting next to the woman! You must have known what she was called!'

'It's on the tip of my tongue,' Arthur said unhelpfully.

Arthur had heard the police officers talking and knew

that Miss Quint was in serious trouble, having broken several laws in her efforts to catch up with Mr Hardbattle's van. She had hijacked a lorry, exceeded the speed limit of thirty miles an hour, and driven like a lunatic or as the police preferred to put it, 'without due care and attention'. Neither Arthur nor Susan gave Miss Quint away, but because there had been several hundred witnesses (including twenty-seven irate hula-hula girls), Miss Quint's name was soon discovered by the police.

Miss Quint had foreseen that the police would come for her. She had parked the van outside Hardbattle Books, leaving Jimmy, Mr Claggitt and Mrs Voysey-Brown with their hands tied behind their backs, locked inside. Then Miss Quint had changed out of her vest top and culottes into a sensible blouse and skirt and a pair of court shoes, which she felt was a more appropriate outfit to wear inside an interview room. She had also been organised enough to pack a bag with a change of under-clothes should she be kept in a cell overnight. When PC Chubb showed up in his police car, Miss Quint was ready and waiting for him.

The telling-off she got was fierce and went on for a long time. Barely allowing her a chance to speak, a grumpy detective sergeant made Miss Quint admit that she had acted recklessly and foolishly, and that she had endangered the lives of some of Plumford's finest townswomen, not to mention Lionel Sayer, the driver of the lorry, and a Mr Wilfred Tottle, who had barely survived crossing the road.

Eventually, Miss Quint's severe reprimand came to an end when the station's chief inspector entered the room. He said that although she had broken quite a lot of laws, she had more than made up for her misdemeanours by rescuing Lady Smythe-Hughes and a child not fully identified, but claiming to be called Susan. Lady Smythe-Hughes, so the chief inspector said, was as pleased as punch with Miss Quint and her young helpers and had asked that they should receive the highest praise for displaying such courage and quick thinking.

The result was that Miss Quint got off scot-free.

Arthur, Susan and Miss Quint were driven in a police car to Hardbattle Books, and at the end of the journey, PC Chubb asked all three for their autographs. Arthur and Susan were happy to scribble their signatures in his pocketbook, but Miss Quint turned down PC Chubb's request with the words 'Don't be so ridiculous!'

'Get used to it. We're famous now,' said Arthur, handing the constable his pocketbook and pen.

'Better open up,' said PC Chubb, gesturing to the doorway of the bookshop, where the sign had been turned so that it said *Closed*. 'I think you'll find you've got a customer waiting.'

They looked to where the constable was pointing and saw a hunched old man standing patiently beside the door. He was wearing his hat and raincoat despite the sunny weather, and had a suitcase at his feet.

'It's Mr Hardbattle!' Miss Quint cried. 'Whatever is he thinking of? The daft old sausage! Why would he close the shop on a Saturday? What could have happened to make him do that?'

Arthur flung open the door of the police car and rushed to Mr Hardbattle's side. 'Have you got your oomph back?' he asked the old man. 'Are you going on another expedition round the country to find the You Know What a new home?'

Gazing at Arthur with dull, lifeless eyes, Mr Hardbattle patted Arthur's shoulder. 'It's time to face facts,' he uttered in a feeble voice. 'My bookselling days are behind me. I've been on the phone to an old people's home in Ivychurch. They said that if I didn't mind sharing a room I could move in right away.'

The others had piled out of the car and joined Arthur and Mr Hardbattle on the pavement. PC Chubb gave a cheerful wave as he drove away, but nobody waved back. They were far too busy digesting Mr Hardbattle's shocker of an announcement. Their elation at foiling the kidnap plot was replaced with a feeling of dismay.

Mr Hardbattle picked up his suitcase with a weary grunt. 'There's just one thing, Arthur, before I catch my bus: could I depend on you to look after old Scallywag? They don't allow dogs at Sunset Lodge.'

'But, Mr Hardbattle, you *can't* –' began Arthur.

'You're worried about your aunt and uncles, I know,' Mr Hardbattle said. 'They're welcome to stay until the lease runs out, but then they'll have to move on, I'm afraid. The same goes for you and your niece, Miss Quint,' he said, giving them all a watery smile. 'I'm glad that I waited until you got back. Didn't want to leave without saying goodbye.' He handed the shop keys to Miss Quint, and lifted his hat in farewell.

There was a moment of dreadful silence, during which Scallywag whimpered, and Arthur, Susan and Miss Quint each tried to think of what they might say to change Mr Hardbattle's mind.

'But there's still a week to go!' said Arthur as Mr Hardbattle turned to leave. 'All sorts of things might've happened by then. We could find a new place for the magic tomorrow! You mustn't quit! Not yet!'

'I'll miss you!' said Susan, close to tears.

'Well, I won't!' said Miss Quint, the harshness of her words making Susan and Arthur gape. 'Nor will Trunk, I shouldn't think,' continued Miss Quint heartlessly, 'and as for Scallywag – she'll forget you in a trice! She's bound to prefer to have a nice, *young* master. I'm really looking forward to driving your van. I might even take it up to Scotland on holiday. Five hundred miles all in one go shouldn't put too much of a strain on the engine, and once we've got to Scotland I think it would enjoy zooming up and down all those *enormous* hills . . .'

She hesitated, worried that she might have gone too far. Miss Quint knew that she was taking a huge gamble by pretending that Mr Hardbattle's imminent departure did not bother her.

Mr Hardbattle failed to take a single step in the direction of the bus stop. He wavered, as if he were a fern whose fronds had been caught in a gentle breeze.

Sensing that his nerve was weakening, Miss Quint prepared to deliver her killer blow. 'It's a shame you couldn't have delayed for an hour or two,' she said. 'I'd made up my mind to come clean at last! There are a few things that I should have told you. You see . . . I didn't follow your instructions to the letter. Still, if you're sure you have to go *right this minute*, you better had. So long!'

Mr Hardbattle put down his suitcase. A touch of his old spirit flickered in his eyes. 'You've called my bluff!' he said to Miss Quint, not seeming to be too displeased about it. 'The wiles of women are a wonder to behold!'

Miss Quint seized Mr Hardbattle's elbow with one hand and unlocked the door of the bookshop with the other. The bell jingle-jangled as she led him inside. Trunk, who had been sitting on his shelf, feeling lonely, clambered to his feet and did a little jig.

'So, you didn't mean all those things you said?' said Susan to Miss Quint. 'Phew! I'm glad about that!'

Once they had all trooped into the shop, Miss Quint

sent Susan upstairs to put a kettle on the stove. In the meantime, she and Arthur made short work of revealing to Mr Hardbattle all that had happened in the week that he had not been in Plumford. To their surprise, he took it all in his stride. When he found out about the lies he had been told, he was hurt and a little cross, but quickly decided to forgive them. His mood had improved considerably since Miss Quint had persuaded him to stay.

'Good gracious me!' Mr Hardbattle murmured as he stroked a bookend, which had jumped into his lap. 'What goings-on! All those wishes! A tea party, a winged girl and stolen goods, you say!' He was not outraged so much as astounded. Grateful to both Miss Quint and Arthur for helping to rescue him from the doldrums, he gazed at them with affection.

Susan arrived with a tray of teacups and a plate of pink wafer biscuits, which Miss Quint did not like and, for that reason, were the only ones left in the tin.

'Ah, here's the winged wonder!' Mr Hardbattle said, eyeing Susan with interest as she lifted the teapot and prepared to pour out.

Revitalised by their refreshments, they began to discuss what should be done about the three kidnapping burglars who were locked inside the van. Mr Hardbattle argued in favour of letting them out, but the others were less willing to give them their freedom, knowing how cunning they could be.

'What we really need to do is return them to their books!' pronounced Mr Hardbattle, putting his teacup aside and rising from his chair. 'If we all have a good snoop, I'm sure we'll turn them up!'

Arthur and Miss Quint, who had searched every inch of the bookshop more than once, without success, did not share his optimism. Nevertheless, they humoured the old man and joined in the hunt.

Searching on his knees under the desk that held the cash register, Arthur paused to say hello to the origami sheep before straightening up and going through the objects on top of the desk. When he heard a soft thumping noise above his head, he looked up and saw that Trunk had gone doolally again. The elephant was charging up and down his shelf, coiling and unfurling his trunk by turns. He had behaved in such a way before, when Arthur had been searching for the missing books on his own and again when Miss Quint had turned the bookshop upside down for the identical purpose.

'Trunk!' called Arthur. 'Whatever is the matter with you?'

As soon as the elephant realised that he had got someone's attention, he stood stock-still and extended his trunk, almost as if he were trying to point something out. Arthur followed the direction in which the elephant's trunk was aiming and his eyes settled on the fireplace.

'You want us to light the fire? Is that it?' asked Arthur, extremely bewildered. 'But it's the beginning of June! The temperature's warm enough, don't you think?'

Arthur turned away and sought out another area of the shop in which to ferret. He did not see Trunk watching him sadly with his black felt eyes or notice the great shuddering sigh that the elephant gave. No one witnessed what happened next, apart from the black cat bookends and one of the ducks from the painting that was flying past Trunk's shelf at the time and almost crashed into the hatstand in confusion.

It was a sight that had never been seen before in Hardbattle Books. Trunk shuffled forward to the edge of his shelf, where he had spent every single day since his little girl had left him behind, and let himself fall.

He landed with a thump on his bean-filled backside and sat still for a moment, in shock. Then he got to his feet and walked across the wooden floor, past the origami sheep, which bleated with surprise, and the wastepaper basket, which toppled over in alarm, emptying its rubbish all over the floor. Trunk continued across the room and came to a stop in front of the fireplace. His ears crinkled when it occurred to him how dirty he was going to get, but with a do-or-die kind of shrug, he scrambled into the grate. Instantly, he sank up to his bottom in ash. Reminding himself that he could be sponged clean (it said so on his label), Trunk ignored his predicament and looked up the chimney. He knew what he was searching for and spotted it in less than a minute: a little cubbyhole above the chimney breast, which had something tucked inside.

Trunk waded through the slough of ash and jumped on to the hearthrug. Then he studied the fire irons and selected a tool. Grasping the poker between his soft front feet, he plunged back into the grate, and gave the things in the cubbyhole a good hard prod. *FLUMP* . . . *FLUMP* . . . *FLUMP* went the books as they landed in the ash heap, covering Trunk from head to toe in pale grey powder. He flapped his large ears and blinked.

The sound of the books falling in the fireplace alerted all the others to the elephant's discovery. When they had got over the shock of seeing Trunk in another place than on his shelf, they reached into the grate and seized the books.

'Well I never!' Mr Hardbattle said, blowing ash from the book that he held so that he could read the title. Miss Quint and Susan did the same with theirs. Feeling ashamed that he had not realised what Trunk had been trying to communicate, Arthur chose to lift out Trunk and told him that he was a superstar.

'These are the books we've been looking for!' confirmed Miss Quint, flicking through the soot-covered book in her hands, entitled *Tinseltown Ticket*. 'But how did Trunk know where they were?'

'He must have seen the culprit put them there!' suggested Arthur.

Mr Hardbattle frowned. 'Aren't we expecting to find one more? Perhaps I should have a feel around.' He stooped to pick up the poker, but Arthur stopped him.

'No!' he said quickly. 'That's all of them! I mean . . . Trunk's the sort of elephant to have done a thorough job. If there was another book up there I'm sure he would have found it.'

Arthur felt himself blushing. He tried to avoid Mr Hardbattle's searching gaze.

'Um . . .' said Arthur. 'What shall we do now?'

'I think it's high time we let those scoundrels out of my van,' Mr Hardbattle said, 'don't you?'

272

Chapter Twenty-five
Brought to Book

Having had their hands untied, the three gang members crawled out of the back of the van with scowls on their faces and stood in sullen silence. As well as being peeved that their plan to kidnap Lady Smythe-Hughes had come to nothing, they were also sore about being imprisoned in a van for hours on end. While Mr Hardbattle locked the van doors, Miss Quint and Scallywag made sure that the wily trio did not make a run for it.

'Into the bookshop, if you please,' Mr Hardbattle said, leading the gang over the threshold. Miss Quint and Scallywag brought up the rear.

Standing next to each other behind a table, they looked like the accused in the dock of a courtroom. From their perch on Mr Hardbattle's desk, Arthur and Susan watched the three ne'er-do-wells, feeling only faintly afraid. The gang's appearance was dishevelled. All of them were sweating after their long stint in the van. Mrs

Voysey-Brown's mascara had melted in the heat and there were black smudges all around her eyes. However, she was not as damp as Jimmy, whose bellhop's suit was mostly polyester, or Mr Claggitt, whose hair was sticking up in spikes, having had a litre of lemonade sprayed over it.

'Nice nephew, you are!' Jimmy growled at Arthur, raising his arm to shake his fist. His sleeve was torn and muddied. 'I could get the cops to arrest you for assault!'

'That fib has been confessed to,' Mr Hardbattle said. 'You're not Arthur's uncle. I'm aware of who you really are. No more lies, please, and no more threatening language either! It surprises me that you'd want to involve the police. I should think they'd be more interested in your gang than in young Arthur here.'

'If we go down, we'll take you with us!' vowed Mr Claggitt angrily. 'One mountaineer goes over the edge, all the rest follow. That's how it is. We're like a climbing party that's attached to the same length of rope!'

'What he means,' said Mrs Voysey-Brown, casting her eyes to the ceiling in a long-suffering way, 'is that we'll tell the police that you helped us.'

'They wouldn't believe you!' said Arthur.

'You seriously think they'd take your word over ours?' Mr Hardbattle said, getting quite hot under the collar. 'The testimony of well-brought-up children, a respected member of the Women's Institute, and a chap who works in a bookshop?'

'You're the proprietor,' murmured Miss Quint. 'Don't do yourself down.'

'That *we* would be thought more unreliable than a scurrilous bunch of sponging layabouts?' Mr Hardbattle shook his head.

Despite being warned that if they were not careful they would find themselves in a police cell, Jimmy, Mr Claggitt and Mrs Voysey-Brown persisted in being sulky and insolent. Only when Mr Hardbattle drew their attention to the three books which Trunk had discovered in the chimney – *Tinseltown Ticket*, *Rockfall!* and *Champagne for Geraldine* – did their attitudes improve.

'We're sorry, ain't we, mates? We were wrong to do what we did!' said Jimmy, falling over himself to apologise. 'Let us make it up to you, eh? Tell you what, guv'nor . . . how's about we give you a hand in the shop? I'll shelve these books for you, shall I?'

He moved to pick up the books that Mr Hardbattle had slid on to a nearby shelf, but Miss Quint was too quick for him. She snatched up a newspaper, rolled it into a tube and rapped Jimmy smartly on his knuckles.

'I'll thank you to leave those books where they are!' Miss Quint told him sternly.

In an attempt to improve relations between the two camps, Mr Claggitt spoke up next. 'You're a reasonable chap, Hardbattle, I can see that,' he said, giving the old man a forthright nod. 'Can't we let bygones be bygones?

We've broken the law, I won't deny that, but thanks to your good self and your fine team of helpers, we've seen the error of our ways. We shan't be tempted back into a life of crime so keep your head, sir, I beg you, and don't do anything hasty.' When Mr Claggitt had finished his speech, he smiled in a weak, affected way that made Arthur feel quite ill.

The word 'sorry' was not in Mrs Voysey-Brown's vocabulary. Instead of taking her cue from her colleagues' attempts to appear repentant, she placed the blame squarely on their shoulders, insisting that she had been a pawn in the whole affair.

'This wretched venture was Jimmy's idea,' she grumbled in her husky voice, 'and Claggitt urged him on. I wanted nothing to do with it! It's those two who you should punish, not me!'

Mrs Voysey-Brown's flagrant attack on her two companions heralded a free-for-all during which the three gang members turned on one another.

'What nonsense!' exclaimed Mr Claggitt, his eyebrows shooting towards his hairline. 'How could you tell such barefaced lies? You're as much to blame as the rest of us.'

'I'm not as grasping though,' retorted Mrs Voysey-Brown, distancing herself from the burly mountaineer. 'I would have been content with a suite at the Savoy, but *you* had to set your sights on *Switzerland*!'

'Deny me the Eiger, would you?' Mr Claggitt roared. 'You're a heartless woman, Dolores! It's been hell this past week without a summit to conquer!'

'Shut your cakeholes, the pair of you!' Jimmy said, losing his temper. 'If I hadn't been so quick off the mark and worked out that Miss Quint wasn't kidding when she said that we'd been sprung from books, you wouldn't be here at all, you thankless nerks!'

When their differences of opinion looked like developing into a brawl, Miss Quint stepped in and told them to pipe down and pull themselves together. She glanced at Mr Hardbattle, and then at Arthur and Susan, and finally at the three books on the shelf.

'Let's do it, shall we?' Miss Quint said.

While her friends flicked through each book to find a suitable page so that they could begin the unwishing, Susan sat down quietly on a chair by the hearth. She held Trunk in her lap and patted his plump body to get rid of all the ash that still coated his velour hide. She had no idea why, but the recent dramas and disclosures had given her a sinking feeling in her stomach. Susan did not understand what Arthur and the others were about to do. All she knew was that she did not want to play any part in it. Sensing her anxiety, Scallywag did what she could to alleviate Susan's feelings of distress, and licked her ankles.

Overjoyed to be on the verge of getting rid of the three troublemakers, Miss Quint and Arthur forgot to think of an errand on which to send Susan so that she would leave the room. As a result, Susan was there on the shop floor, watching, when the last three party guests were unwished.

Having traded insults and fallen out with each other, none of the gang members seemed upset to learn that they were being sent back to their books. Their dream of living in the lap of luxury in Switzerland was in tatters and, having come close to getting caught by the police, it no longer seemed such a terrible thing to be returned to their stories.

Before the unwishing got under way, the thieves were made to hand over the money that they had made from selling their haul of stolen goods, and Arthur unpinned the diamond brooch worn by Mrs Voysey-Brown. He also remembered to ask them to write down all the names and addresses of the dealers to whom they had sold purloined items. Miss Quint said that she would arrange for the details of the dealers to be left with the bag of money and the unsold antiques (currently in the cupboard under the stairs) on the doorstep of Plumford Police Station.

Mr Claggitt and Mrs Voysey-Brown were dealt with first. The magic disposed of them swiftly, snuffing them out like feeble flames. When it came to Jimmy's turn, Mr Hardbattle chose to impart some words of wisdom before the deed was done.

'It's clear that you possess brains, young man,' Mr Hardbattle said, eyeing Jimmy earnestly. 'It's a great pity, however, that you could not think of better ways to make use of them. I trust you will endeavour to do so in future.'

'Don't bank on it!' Jimmy said, and flashed his cock-sure grin.

Mr Hardbattle sighed.

Glancing down at *Champagne for Geraldine*, Arthur found Jimmy's name in the text. He put his finger on it and started to say the words that would send Jimmy home. At the critical moment, the arrogant sneer on Jimmy's face faded and, for a brief second, he looked downcast.

When the bookshop had been emptied of the three undesirables, there followed several minutes of celebration. Miss Quint seized Mr Hardbattle's hand and waltzed him around the shop; Arthur whooped for joy and Scallywag chased her tail. Over by the fireplace, Susan gave Trunk a kiss, which caused the plump little elephant to turn a backwards somersault. Susan was pleased that the robbers had been sent packing, but she did not feel as cock-a-hoop about it as the others. The method of the gang's removal had shocked her to the core and she suddenly felt an urge to be by herself. Deciding to take a walk in the park, she got up from her seat and replaced Trunk gently on the cushion of the chair. Before she could reach the door, however, it opened and the bell above it jangled as a customer entered the shop.

All the joy in Arthur's heart evaporated when he saw that the customer was Mr Beaglehole. Scallywag was similarly horrified, and Arthur's reactions had to be quick to grab hold of her collar before she launched herself at the man and punctured his skin with her teeth.

'Come about my book!' Mr Beaglehole said in his usual abrasive manner. He marched up to Mr Hardbattle's desk and planted his fat, pink hands on it. Then he began to examine the pile of books that he found there. It being a hot summer's day, Mr Beaglehole was wearing shorts, and the sight of his bulging, fleshy calves was too much for Scallywag to bear. Arthur clung to her manfully as she bared her teeth and scrabbled at the floor, straining to get close enough to give him a nip.

'The name's Beaglehole,' said Arthur's teacher, his eyes settling on Mr Hardbattle, whom he decided was the person in charge. 'I ordered the damn thing days ago. What kind of shambolic outfit are you running here?'

When Mr Beaglehole revealed who he was, Mr Hardbattle's back stiffened and he carefully adjusted his spectacles.

'I am the manager of this bookshop,' Mr Hardbattle said. He removed his hand from Miss Quint's waist and dipped his head politely, thanking her for their impromptu dance. Then he walked behind his desk.

'Is that your teacher?' whispered Miss Quint, stooping to speak to Arthur.

He nodded, unable to stop a look of intense dislike from creeping on to his face.

Miss Quint glared too, and so did Susan. Even Trunk made an effort to fill his eyes with loathing, but as they were very small and made from felt, it was quite a challenge to get the emotion across.

Mr Hardbattle turned to rummage through some books in a box behind him and drew out a slim blue volume with a triumphant 'Aha!'

'That mine?' Mr Beaglehole asked.

'Yes, by good fortune it seems that your book has arrived,' Mr Hardbattle told him. He glanced at the book's title and a nervous tic jiggled his eye. '*The Future Is Nuclear*, hmm?' he said. 'I hope very much that that *won't* be the case. There are preferable, less toxic alternatives.'

'Yeah? What would you know about it?' Mr Beaglehole said.

'Bits and bobs,' Mr Hardbattle answered.

Mr Beaglehole made a disparaging noise. 'Well, I happen to teach that boy over there geography so I think we can both assume that I'm more of an expert than you!'

Mr Beaglehole may have majored in geography, but he was woefully uninformed about the subject of magic. He did not know, for example, that if a bookshop filled with magic is exposed to a glut of negative energy emitted by several persons and directed at one point of focus at the same time, it can cause palms to tremble in their pots and stairs to turn to custard.

In the bookshop, there was a kind of a lull. The only sound was the blaring, monotonous voice of Mr Beaglehole, making one complaint after another. Arthur glanced about him. The air seemed to be pulsing. It felt like a storm was brewing.

'Sixteen pounds ninety-nine?' raged Mr Beaglehole. 'For that teeny-weeny paperback?' He snatched the book from Mr Hardbattle's grip – and that was the moment that all hell broke loose.

Books flew off the shelves, flapping their board covers as if they were wings, and dropped like rocks on to Mr Beaglehole's head.

'*Ouch! Yow! Ooh!*' cried Mr Beaglehole, too surprised to comprehend what was going on. He tossed *The Future Is Nuclear* on to the desk and folded his arms over his head to protect it. 'Goodenough, is that you?' he bellowed. 'You'd better stop throwing those books at once!'

Arthur could not help laughing. 'It's nothing to do with me, sir,' he said.

Next, the staples and drawing pins combined their forces to launch an offensive on Mr Beaglehole's toes. (His feet were clad in sandals, which made them vulnerable to attack.) Breaking out of their corral of coloured pencils, the origami sheep joined in the onslaught, tickling his ankles with their paper hooves as the staples and drawing pins did their worst.

Mr Beaglehole lifted his knees and danced on the spot, wailing with pain.

'Watch out!' warned Miss Quint. 'The rubber bands want their share of glory!'

Mr Hardbattle ducked down behind his desk as the entire box of rubber bands lined up on a rug and pinged themselves at the teacher's bare legs. That final assault proved to be the last straw and, dodging the black cat bookends, which were attempting to trip him up, Mr Beaglehole stumbled out of the doorway and ran off down the street.

Chapter Twenty-Six
Pastures New

'You were awesome!' cried Arthur, applauding the magic. He had enjoyed the spectacle of his bullying form teacher reduced to a cowering wreck.

Mr Hardbattle frowned and shook his head. 'You mustn't show such appreciation, Arthur. That sort of behaviour oughtn't to be encouraged.'

Reluctantly, Arthur stopped clapping. He tidied up the shop instead, helping the others to pick up the books which had bombarded Mr Beaglehole. After that chore was done, he crouched on the floor to collect all the staples, drawing pins and rubber bands. He sorted them into piles and replaced them in their containers.

'Well done, everyone!' Arthur whispered when he thought that Mr Hardbattle was out of earshot.

Arthur jumped when he felt a tap on the shoulder. 'Now then, Arthur!' Mr Hardbattle scolded. 'That teacher fellow needed bringing down a peg or two, I'd agree with you on that, but you must accept that the magic overstepped the mark. It's totally out of control.'

Proving, once more, that he was a thorough sort of chap, Mr Hardbattle broached another subject. 'Before we resume our search for somewhere else to put my magic,' he said to Arthur, 'I think there's another matter that we should attend to, don't you?'

Arthur felt a horrible prickling sensation creep up his spine. The uncomfortable feeling had almost reached the nape of his neck when the shop bell jingle-jangled and his dad peered round the door.

'Arthur, there you are!' said his dad with relief. 'I wasn't sure if this was the place. I've brought your bicycle, just as you asked. What were you thinking of earlier, charging off in that great big lorry? You wait till your mother hears what you did!'

Trying not to sound too conceited, Arthur informed him that he had been on a rescue mission to secure the safe return of Lady Smythe-Hughes. 'You must have heard that she'd been kidnapped,' said Arthur. 'You wait and see: my picture will be in the paper and my friend's will too.' He beckoned to Susan so that he could introduce her.

'Gracious heavens!' Arthur's father said. 'What a heroic thing to do!' He held out a hand to Susan. 'Pleased to meet you, pet.'

'And this is Mr Hardbattle and this is Miss Quint,' said Arthur, completing the introductions. 'Oh! Where's

Tilly?' he asked his father.

'Right here,' his father said, tugging on a small hand. Tilly's arm and sleeve were visible, but the rest of her remained out of sight, loitering just beyond the doorway. 'She's the reason we didn't get here sooner,' Arthur's dad explained. 'Your sister said she wanted to see the whole parade. She's been rabbiting to all and sundry for the entire day, but, bless her, she's suddenly decided to be shy!'

It was Susan who persuaded Tilly to come into the shop, by telling the little girl that there was magic inside. Wrinkling her nose and declaring that the shop smelt pooey, Tilly stepped through the doorway and began to look around.

On the cushion of the chair where Susan had left him, Trunk sat bolt upright and his ears unfolded and raised themselves high. Keeping his black felt eyes trained on Tilly, he pushed himself off the seat cushion and landed on his bottom on the floor. Once he had jumped up, he approached the girl in stops and starts, until he shook off his hesitance and ran to her with his front feet out-stretched.

'Look, Daddy!' Tilly said, cupping her hands around her knees and bending over to look at him. 'A walking hippopotamus!'

Trunk did not appear to mind that he had been misidentified. He took the last few centimetres in one bound, then jumped into her arms.

'He's all squishy-squashy!' said Tilly delightedly, hugging the elephant to her chest.

Everyone in the bookshop stared. Arthur, Mr Hardbattle, Susan and Miss Quint could not believe their eyes. Before today, it had not been known for Trunk to stray from his shelf and now, here he was, in the embrace of a little girl. Not having come across a soft toy that could move of its own accord, Arthur's father was more mystified than anyone.

'But that's not . . .' began Arthur. He knew that Trunk had been left behind in the bookshop, and since that day had been waiting for his little girl to return to claim him, but Arthur was sure that Tilly had never owned an elephant and was just as certain that she had not set foot in the bookshop before. 'Mr Hardbattle,' he whispered, 'Trunk's made a mistake. I think I'd better tell him –'

'Don't you dare,' Mr Hardbattle breathed. He gave Arthur a steely look before addressing Arthur's dad. 'My elephant seems to have taken a shine to your daughter, sir. I wonder if she'd like to keep him?'

Arthur gasped. 'Mr Hardbattle! But . . . you can't . . . what about the other girl?'

'A word, Arthur,' Mr Hardbattle said. He steered Arthur across the shop to a more secluded area. 'Now listen,' he said to Arthur on reaching a suitably quiet corner. 'Trunk has been sitting on that shelf above my desk, mooning over his owner, for the past ten years. She's never going to walk back through that door – at least, not as the little girl that Trunk remembers.'

'Oh,' said Arthur, swallowing, 'I see.'

When their little tête-à-tête was over, they rejoined the others. Miss Quint had been explaining to Arthur's dad about the magic in the shop and although he had voiced disbelief at first, he had started to realise that Miss Quint must be telling the truth.

'There's magic all around me now? Fancy that!' he said.

His aged knees protesting as he did so, Mr Hardbattle crouched down to speak to Arthur's five-year-old sister. 'Why don't you choose a book, my dear, and read the little fellow a story? I'm sure that would go down a treat.'

Tilly nodded and ran to a rack of picture books. She selected one, sat down and crossed her legs, then settled the elephant in her lap.

Although no one could have guessed it from the euphoric angle of his tusks, Trunk knew that Tilly Goodenough was not his owner. A few hours ago, this knowledge would have bothered him, but since leaving his shelf he had felt like a different elephant. It was as if he had leaped from the past into the present when he jumped those few metres on to the floor.

The little girl who was reading to him had brown eyes instead of blue, but otherwise she was very like his little girl. She had the same rosy cheeks and clear-cut voice and the identical way of squeezing him gently round his middle. Trunk had come to feel at home in the bookshop, but what he wanted most of all was to be loved and cuddled and read stories to, and if this little girl was Arthur's sister there was a good chance that she was a nice, caring child and a fair possibility that he was destined to be a very happy elephant.

'Time to go, Tilly!' said her father. 'The animals have got to be fed, and I'm cooking supper tonight. Arthur, you'll be home by six, won't you?'

Tilly closed the picture book and scooped up Trunk. As she and her father left the shop, the elephant peeped over Tilly's arms and waved his trunk at them all to say farewell.

A tear slithered down Mr Hardbattle's cheek.

'I'm a sentimental old fool, that's what I am,' he said, dabbing his eyes with his handkerchief.

Susan stood at the door and waved at Trunk and his new mistress until they were out of sight. 'I'm jolly glad he's found a new home,' she said. 'He looked awfully happy, didn't he?'

'He did,' agreed Mr Hardbattle. 'Everyone has a place where they feel that they should be. Mine is this bookshop, and yours . . .'

Susan wondered why Mr Hardbattle had stopped in mid-sentence. He had been about to tell her where it was that she belonged. Feeling puzzled and bewildered, she thought about asking him to continue with what he had been going to say. Then she saw that Mr Hardbattle was staring intently at Arthur, and that Arthur had his eyes fixed on the floor.

'I'll come straight out with it,' Mr Hardbattle said. 'I think you know where this young lady's book is, Arthur.'

'I . . .' Arthur began and got no further.

Mr Hardbattle nodded. 'I thought so,' he said. 'I think you'd better fetch it, don't you?'

Arthur's eyes flicked up guiltily and met Mr Hardbattle's unflinching gaze. He knew that there was no denying it. Mr Hardbattle was far too shrewd, and lying was not Arthur's strong point. Without a word, even to Miss Quint, who was staring at him, open-mouthed, Arthur went outside, got on his bike and rode home.

The book was under his mattress, where he had shoved it a week ago, realising that he did not want Susan to be unwished. He had told himself that he was merely *borrowing* the book, and hoped that Mr Hardbattle would not imagine that his furtive deed had been the same as stealing. As he cycled back to the book-shop with *High Jinks* in his saddlebag, Arthur thought of a hundred reasons to convince Mr Hardbattle that Susan should stay in Plumford and not be returned to her book.

When he re-entered Hardbattle Books, Arthur discovered that Miss Quint had been thinking along the same lines as him. She and Mr Hardbattle were embroiled in an argument.

'She could live with me. I could adopt her,' said Miss Quint, holding on tightly to Susan's hand.

Mr Hardbattle's mouth contracted. Clearly he did not agree. 'That wouldn't work! Susan isn't a real child. There's no certificate recording her birth. You'd get into hot water with the authorities –'

'Paperwork can be faked!' Miss Quint insisted stubbornly. 'If Jimmy's gang can get hold of dodgy dealers, I can find a forger.'

'You're missing the point,' Mr Hardbattle said, frustrated that Miss Quint would not see reason. 'Susan isn't like other children. She's a character from a book. She won't get any older. Don't you think people will find that odd? How will you cope in a few years' time when she's still eleven and you're an old lady?'

Miss Quint looked ready to thump him. 'I'm only forty-four!' she shrieked. 'I'm in my prime! You make me sound as if I'm already drawing my pension!'

Despite listing all the reasons that they had thought up, neither Arthur nor Miss Quint could persuade Mr Hardbattle that Susan should remain with them. He was sympathetic, but firm.

'This is what comes of being careless and not sticking to my instructions,' he said, wagging a finger at Miss

Quint. Not letting Arthur off the hook either, Mr Hardbattle aimed his next rebuke at him. 'If you hadn't hidden her book, and had sent Susan back earlier –'

'I couldn't!' said Arthur, the words sticking in his throat. 'I'd got to like her. She'd become my friend.'

Mr Hardbattle was not unmoved by Arthur's admission, but he still would not let it influence his judgement. He handed Miss Quint the copy of *High Jinks* and asked her to find the appropriate page. Miss Quint could barely see through the films of unshed tears in her eyes. She took some time about it.

While Miss Quint was leafing blindly through the book and Arthur was frowning, lost in thought, Susan stood quietly between them, taking everything in. She had known somewhere, lost down, that she did not belong in this world, but she had desperately yearned to be a part of it and that desire had confused her memory. She had grown very fond of Miss Quint and Arthur and dear old Scallywag the dog, and to be parted from them was a dreadful blow. If she had not felt so hollow inside she might have kicked up a fuss, but making a scene was not in her nature, and besides, she knew that it would do no good. Her fate was sealed and she would have to grin and bear it.

Arthur, however, had not finished protesting. 'This isn't fair!' he railed. 'It's cruel, that's what it is! Susan's happy here with us. If you send her back to the book, what kind of a life will she have? She'll have to stand by those dumb old railings, waiting for a go on those stupid swings today and every day afterwards . . . FOR EVER!' Arthur's throat felt tight and hurt so much that he could not utter another word.

When they had said goodbye to Trunk, they had known that he had a wonderful future ahead of him. Susan's departure was not like that at all.

After five whole minutes of looking, Miss Quint came across the right page and felt her heart plummet.

'Found it,' she told Mr Hardbattle.

Susan put her arms around Arthur and hugged him. Then she stood on tiptoes to kiss Miss Quint and bent down to say goodbye to Scallywag. Finally, after straightening her shoulders, she nodded at Mr Hardbattle to show that she was ready to leave.

At the moment of unwishing, Arthur turned away. He missed seeing Susan grow fainter and fainter until she was a mere ghost and eventually disappeared.

Miss Quint started. She had felt a tingling in her fingers and, wiping away her tears, she looked down at the copy of *High Jinks* that she held in her hand. The book was growing. Its spine was stretching and its pages were multiplying. It carried on getting larger and larger and heavier and heavier until it had doubled in size.

'Ooh!' she exclaimed. 'Well I never! Arthur, look!'

Despondently, Arthur lifted his head.

On the front cover, which had been plain green, the face of a girl was slowly forming. She had a lively smile and long brown hair and was wearing a T-shirt with sequins on it.

Another change was taking place on the cover of the book. Little by little, the title was fading and new words were appearing in its place. Arthur cried out when he realised what it said. The book had renamed itself *The Adventures of Susan*.

Arthur felt a sudden wave of happiness wash over him. 'How did that happen?' he asked Miss Quint.

She was as astounded as Arthur, but between them, it did not take them long to work it out.

'Remember *A Tale of Derring-do*?' Miss Quint said. 'When we sent the knight back without his sword? It altered the whole story.'

'Susan changed a lot while she was with us,' said Arthur, thinking of the strange, clueless girl she had been and the plucky, fun friend she had turned into.

'Yes!' said Miss Quint, remembering only too well the dreary child without a name whom she had longed to get rid of. 'And think of all the thrilling things we've done together! When we sent Susan back, the book would hardly have recognised her. It couldn't make such an interesting girl stand by the swings for all eternity!'

'It had to give her more exciting things to do,' said Arthur, smiling at the picture of Susan on the book's front cover. 'Good old Suze! I bet she's having a whale of a time. I can't wait to read what she gets up to!'

'May I?' Mr Hardbattle said, taking the book from Miss Quint's hands. He had not enjoyed making Miss Quint and Arthur do something which caused them so much grief, and was as pleased about the outcome as they were. 'How about that!' he said, and passed the book to Arthur. 'Something to put on your bookshelf, Arthur, I think.'

Arthur was required to say a double thank you because, at that moment, the paper boy arrived with the evening edition of the *Plumford Gazette*. On its front page, just below the headline, *COURAGEOUS KIDS OUTWIT CROOKS*, there was a photograph of Susan, Lady Smythe-Hughes and himself. Mr Hardbattle insisted that Arthur should keep it as a souvenir.

'There's this as well,' said the paper boy, crouching on the floor to pick up an envelope that someone had dropped through the letter box and on to the doormat. It had a gold coat of arms on the front and was addressed to Arthur, Susan and Miss Quint. The envelope was passed to Arthur, and he turned it over, broke the wax seal on the back and opened it up.

'It's an invitation!' he said, glancing at Miss Quint and grinning. 'Lady Smythe-Hughes has asked us to tea!'

'When?' said Miss Quint, clapping a hand to her mouth.

'This Tuesday coming, at four o'clock.'

Miss Quint gave a squeak of excitement, and rushed to the telephone to make an appointment at the hairdresser's.

When Tuesday came round, Miss Quint and Arthur were picked up from Hardbattle Books by a chauffeur-driven Mercedes. They sat on the red leather seats, pulling faces at each other and pressing the intercom button to talk to the driver, whose name was Phil. When they neared Thiselton House, the home of Lord and Lady Smythe-Hughes, Miss Quint grew fidgety and insisted that Arthur should tell her if her hair could do with one more brush or if her lipstick needed touching up. She had bought a new hat for the occasion and kept adjusting its angle, until Arthur pleaded with her to leave it alone. Arthur loosened the knot of the tie that his mother had made him wear. He felt as if he were being strangled.

The driveway was so long that Arthur mistook it for a road. It passed through fields, a wood and miles of rhododendrons. Finally, the driveway came to an end, sweeping in a grandiose curve in front of a large, pearl grey mansion with more windows than Arthur could count. They did not have to yank the bell pull to announce that they had arrived. A butler was already waiting for them with a door held open. As they walked down a hall with a marble floor, they saw three or four people (who they learned were only a small fraction of the staff) and were taken to a huge, high-ceilinged drawing room where tea had been laid out on a linen tablecloth. Opposite the drawing room was the library, and Arthur took the opportunity of taking a peek inside.

'Look! They like books!' he said. 'Perhaps Lord and Lady Smythe-Hughes would like to visit Mr Hardbattle's shop, and buy up some of his!'

'It might be an idea,' said Miss Quint, crossing the hall to join him. 'Mr Hardbattle needs to find money from somewhere. He said that if he had the funds he'd take me on as assistant manager, but we're no nearer finding a place for the magic, and there are only three days left!'

Lady Smythe-Hughes arrived soon afterwards and they all assembled in the drawing room for tea, which was beautifully displayed on delicate plates with a rose and chrysanthemum design. Lady Smythe-Hughes was extremely pleased to see them, but disappointed to hear that Susan had not been able to come. They exchanged pleasantries at first, but soon progressed to the juicier topic of the kidnap. Lady Smythe-Hughes explained that the gang had swooped on her when she had left the judging booth and popped into the public library to use the lavatory.

Miss Quint almost choked on her smoked salmon sandwich to hear a woman of such good breeding mentioning the toilet.

'Oh, I nearly forgot!' said Arthur, reaching into his blazer pocket. 'I think this might belong to you.' He brought out the bow-shaped diamond brooch and offered it to Lady Smythe-Hughes, who pounced on it in delight.

'Arthur! You darling boy!' she said. 'I lost this when we were burgled! Wherever did you find it?'

Arthur thought very carefully before he gave her an answer. 'In the road,' he said at last. 'The robbers must have dropped it there.'

'I'm really so terribly grateful for what you did,' gushed Lady Smythe-Hughes. 'If there's a favour that I could do for you in return, you only have to ask!'

After they had eaten their fill of exquisite sandwiches and cakes, Lady Smythe-Hughes volunteered to show them her fine collection of antique perfume bottles. They walked into the hall and there they met her husband, Lord Smythe-Hughes, who was taking off a pair of muddy green wellingtons.

Lady Smythe-Hughes introduced her husband to Arthur and Miss Quint. He had heard of their role in the rescue of his wife and said that he was honoured to make their acquaintance. Lady Smythe-Hughes explained that they had just had tea, and that she was taking her guests to view her perfume bottle collection.

Seeing the unimpressed look on Arthur's face and guessing that Arthur felt the same way about perfume bottles as he did, Lord Smythe-Hughes clapped Arthur on the shoulder and made a suggestion: 'Like to take a walk around my poultry farm, young chap?'

'I heard someone say you were a paltry millionaire,' said Arthur, waiting while Lord Smythe-Hughes put on his boots again.

'*Poultry* millionaire!' corrected Lord Smythe-Hughes, finding Arthur's error most amusing.

While Miss Quint and Lady Smythe-Hughes disappeared to the East Wing to coo over odd-shaped pieces of glass, Arthur strolled around several acres at the rear of the house, which had been given over to Lord Smythe-Hughes's poultry business. It was a free-range poultry farm and the birds wandered wherever they pleased, only popping into their huts at night-time or to lay an egg. There were huts and sheds dotted all over the plot, and even a lake the size of a playing field, with an island for ducks and geese.

In one rather overgrown corner, Arthur and Lord Smythe-Hughes passed by a tall, cylindrical tower with battlements at the top. The building was old, with only a handful of windows, and its bricks were overrun with ivy.

Chickens were wandering in and out through its open doorway, and Arthur heard clucking coming from inside.

'That's the funniest chicken house I've ever seen!' he said, peering through the entrance and seeing nests scattered about with brown, speckled eggs in one or two of them. As Arthur turned to leave, his hand snagged on a cobweb, and he paused and took another, more deliberate look inside.

'It's not really supposed to be a chicken house,' said Lord Smythe-Hughes. He went on to explain that the building was a folly, which was an ornamental building erected on a whim. Lord Smythe-Hughes said that he was loath to pull it down as it was part of the history of the estate, but he had no real use for it.

'Couldn't somebody live here?' asked Arthur.

'Good heavens, no!' Lord Smythe-Hughes chuckled. 'Who'd want to live in a tumbledown tower without gas or water, right in the middle of a chicken compound?'

Arthur said nothing, but grinned to himself.

As they continued with their walk, Lord Smythe-Hughes pointed out dozens of different breeds of chickens and ducks, some of which were rather rare, but Arthur found it difficult to concentrate. He was itching for the tour to be over so that he could go back to the house and relate what he had seen to Miss Quint.

Eventually, they reached the rear of Thiselton House, and Arthur ran up some steps and dashed inside, but before he could locate Miss Quint, he bumped into Lady Smythe-Hughes, who was tending to a magnificent flower arrangement in the hall.

'Hello, Arthur!' she said, smiling. 'Did you enjoy your walk amongst all those feathered creatures? They're my husband's pride and joy!'

'Yes,' said Arthur, swiftly moving on to the thing that was at the forefront of his mind. 'Lady Smythe-Hughes, could I ask you something? It's about that *favour* . . .'